WHEN HE KISSED HER

He bent to add more coals to the fire. The small blaze that flared up sent no warmth to Charlotte. She wanted to move closer to the hearth, but would not while he stood there.

His coat clung as he bent over the fire, revealing the graceful curves and musculature of his back. A warmth in her face not attributable to the temperature in the room, she looked away, trying not to remember the kiss he had pressed on her a short while ago. She should be shaking from dread of what was to come, but she could not summon up any fear at all. The most amazing surge of pure energy had shot through her when Rayfield kissed her, like liquid fire . . .

BOOK YOUR PLACE ON OUR WEBSITE AND MAKE THE READING CONNECTION!

We've created a customized website just for our very special readers, where you can get the inside scoop on everything that's going on with Zebra, Pinnacle and Kensington books.

When you come online, you'll have the exciting opportunity to:

- View covers of upcoming books
- Read sample chapters
- Learn about our future publishing schedule (listed by publication month *and author*)
- Find out when your favorite authors will be visiting a city near you
- Search for and order backlist books from our online catalog
- Check out author bios and background information
- Send e-mail to your favorite authors
- Meet the Kensington staff online
- Join us in weekly chats with authors, readers and other guests
- Get writing guidelines
- AND MUCH MORE!

**Visit our website at
http://www.kensingtonbooks.com**

THE
LADY IN
QUESTION

JUDITH LAIK

ZEBRA BOOKS
Kensington Publishing Corp.
www.kensingtonbooks.com

ZEBRA BOOKS are published by

Kensington Publishing Corp.
850 Third Avenue
New York, NY 10022

·All Kensington titles, imprints, and distributed lines are available at special quantity discounts for bulk purchases for sales promotion, premiums, fund-raising, educational, or institutional use.

Special book excerpts or customized printings can also be created to fit specific needs. For details, write or phone the office of the Kensington Special Sales Manager: Attn. Special Sales Department. Kensington Publishing Corp., 850 Third Avenue, New York, NY 10022. Phone: 1-800-221-2647.

Zebra and the Z logo Reg. U.S. Pat. & TM Off.

ISBN 0-8217-7828-5

First Printing: August 2005
10 9 8 7 6 5 4 3 2 1

Printed in the United States of America

To my wonderful critique partners:
Heather L, Joleen, Gina, Heather H,
Michele, Gerri, and Jacquie.

Thanks for the laughter, the learning,
and the sharing—of goals, heartaches,
triumphs, and disappointments.

I could never have made it
without all of you.

CHAPTER ONE

From the case notebook of Hugh Broderick Brooks, the Earl of Rayfield, premier spy hunter during the Napoleonic Wars. Case of M. Mansson, an anagram of Sans Nom (Mr. Nameless), British traitor seeking to incite revolution in Britain:

Suspects:
1—Francis, Viscount Treadwell. Gamester, deeply in debt. Only son killed in the act of bringing French spy and incriminating papers over from France.

Entry dated 27ᵗʰ of January, 1812:
Tonight I encountered Treadwell at Lady Bristow's. Late in the evening, he invited me to Treadwell House for additional gaming. I almost laughed at the perfect opportunity he had handed me to investigate him further.

(Decoded by Alphonsius McMasters, PhD, LLC, AKC, OBE, BMW, historian and author of The Secret Wars of Napoleon, *2005.)*

London, Winter, 1812

Viscount Treadwell fussed about, breaking open a deck of cards, moving the branch of candles about on the game table in an attempt to cast more light on the surface.

The Earl of Rayfield casually leaned against a pillar, arms crossed. *Don't gamble with Rayfield,* Treadwell had been told. *He will accept any bet and he never loses. At least, so seldom it's as good as never.* That's what Treadwell was counting on. He would be a gracious loser.

Rubbing his hands, he looked up at Rayfield. The man's blasé air gave him pause. Had he chosen wrongly? *It's too late for second thoughts.* All he had heard about Rayfield testified to his aptness. A gamester and a rake, but a man of honor. He'd do the right thing. "Shall we make ourselves comfortable?"

Rayfield raised an eyebrow, his expression seeming to deny the possibility of comfort in the drafty room.

Spencer came in and stirred to life the coals in the massive fireplace, raising the temperature in the hall by a barely perceptible amount. That blaze and the glow from the candles on the game table provided the room's only illumination. *Added to the atmosphere. Down at the heels, like its owner.*

"Brandy, Spencer!" Treadwell took his place on one of the heavy mahogany armchairs by the table and shuffled the cards. "Yes, my lord," Spencer said and bowed before leaving.

Treadwell gestured to Rayfield to sit. "Piquet?" he queried, and at his guest's abrupt nod, dealt.

The elderly butler brought in a half-full decanter of brandy and two glasses, poured generous measures and left again.

Over the next hours, as they played, Treadwell reined in his impatience. Showing his hand too soon would send Rayfield running. Charley's future rested upon tonight's events. He would be gone and no help to her. It was all he could do to control the tremor that ran through him and out his fingertips. For a man who was a noted expert in the art of losing at games of chance, he was finding this night surprisingly hard work.

To counteract the heat that burned his face, he took off his coat and loosened his cravat.

Rayfield said, "I cannot recall seeing you at Parliament."

Treadwell poured more brandy to steady his nerves. "Never go there. Made a mull of m'own properties. Cannot imagine my interference would improve the country." He cast a glance at Rayfield's snifter, which was untouched. *Not a promising sign.*

Rayfield seemed to have some aim that he was reluctant to abandon. "What think you of these Luddites stirring things up?"

"What? Oh, I don't think of them at all. Nothing to do with me." Treadwell tipped the decanter at his elbow into his glass, as he had already done several times. Despite the heavy imbibing, his mind was extraordinarily clear. Was he overdoing the drunken act? He had to appear sufficiently castaway to make plausible the outrageous wager he was about to propose, but not so much that Rayfield could doubt he meant to honor it.

Rayfield rubbed his chin, his blue eyes scouring Treadwell.

From time to time Spencer replenished the fire. The room remained chillingly cold, a draft blowing through as if the two tall windows at the end of the vast room had no panes, a proposition confounded by their rattling to each gust of wind.

At last Treadwell flung down his cards. "Routed again! I swear, Rayfield, you have the most uncanny luck!"

The earl folded his cards slowly, and stood. "I think it is time I took my leave." Tucking Treadwell's vowels into his coat pocket, he picked up his evening cloak, hat and gloves.

"Stay!" Treadwell rose. His hands moved into a gesture of supplication. "What say you to another wager?" He scarcely breathed, his voice vibrating inside his taut chest.

Rayfield settled himself again and reached for his snifter, lowering his lids.

Treadwell had not missed the quick spark of interest in Rayfield's expression before he concealed it. He had played the man just like a fish on his line. Now was the moment to set the hook. He hesitated, gripping the edge of the table. "I will wager my daughter on the outcome of the next game."

Hugh sputtered, nearly spewing his brandy. "You're mad!"

"P'raps. Then again, p'raps not."

"I must decline your offer." Heat coursed through him and he clenched his fists. Drawing the shards of his customary *sangfroid* around him, Hugh stood and edged toward the door.

"Hear me out, Rayfield." Treadwell stood, reaching out as if to stop him, a desperate pleading in his voice.

Hugh halted, caught despite himself by Treadwell's anguished tones.

"Know people say . . . deliberately tried to ruin myself." Lord Treadwell spoke in a rush, his words slurring from the brandy. "Always been a gamester—nothing I could do. After losing m'wife and son, it was worse. Nothing mattered. Six years now since Jamie died." A shadow crossed Treadwell's face: grief at his son's death? Or remorse over leading the young man into the treachery that caused his death?

Why would he mention his son's death to Hugh? The young man's betrayal of his country had been hushed up. Did Treadwell realize Hugh knew the story?

No one in the *ton* knew of Hugh's secret activities, not even his closest friends. But his identity was known in French intelligence circles. He had disrupted too many of their plots to remain anonymous. If Treadwell had knowledge of Hugh's assignment, it marked him unquestionably as the man he sought.

Treadwell said, "I'm at a standstill, barely outrunning the constable." Hugh gestured to check him, but Treadwell swept on. "All's up with me. Don't mind for m'self, but must provide for Charlotte. Nothing left after the creditors take their due— they won't even get that much! You're a rake, but fair . . . won't leave her destitute. Nothing else I can do."

Was it all an act? "What would your daughter say to such a wager?" Did Miss Treadwell know about her father's activities? Could the two Treadwells be planning to set her to spy on Hugh's investigation, to prevent his uncovering their plot?

"She'll obey me."

Hugh frowned at the flat certainty in the viscount's voice. "I must see for myself that she agrees." Likely she was part of the plan. If so, he would turn the pact to his own advantage. Or was she merely some milk-and-water miss, too cowed to protest such cavalier treatment? He intended to watch closely, and if such appeared to be the case, he would put a stop to this outlandish wager. "I won't take an unwilling woman to mistress."

Treadwell's eyes widened, but he said, "Very well." What had the man expected? That he would marry the chit? He'd not be tied to a traitor. Not that he would take her in keeping, either, but he wouldn't reveal his own plans unnecessarily.

The elderly butler came in just then, and Treadwell said, "Ah, Spencer, fetch Miss Treadwell."

"I believe she retired some time ago, my lord."

"Then get her up! I want her here immediately."

"Very good, sir." Spencer left.

As they waited, tattered tapestries fluttered against stone walls. Fire hissed and leapt in the massive, blackened fireplace, dancing in tune to the wind that gusted down the chimney. Hugh, standing by the gaming table, covered his impatience with a calm face.

The door opened and Miss Treadwell ran toward her father. "Papa, what is the matter?" Her voice had a mature timbre that revealed she was probably in her early twenties, despite the youthful appearance given by dark brown hair tumbling over her shoulders and sleepy eyes, the pupils huge to accommodate the dim light. Sighting Hugh, she drew back. "Oh, I thought . . . I didn't know you had company. Spencer said I was urgently needed." She drew the thin wrapper more tightly around herself and stood uncertainly, deep pink color staining her cheeks.

Hugh suspected that had they met in more conventional circumstances, he might have dismissed any interest in her. Her face was too strong for the current ideal of beauty, with high cheekbones, square jaw, an aquiline nose, and nearly straight brows over large green eyes. Her full lips provided a contrast and gave a surprising hint of sensuality.

At the moment embarrassment and hasty awakening heightened the girl's color, while her dishabille softened and emphasized her femininity, quickening his breath.

* * *

Charlotte tightened the sash that cinched her wrapper. She was decently covered, although the garments were not those in which one should appear before strangers.

What was it this time? Some foolish wager again. She swallowed her disappointment that her father never really looked at *her,* never needed her for anything other than to facilitate another bet. Again, she would have to hold a playing card in the air while her father proved he could shoot it out of her hand, or act as arbiter for some other contest of skill. She fixed a too-bright smile on her face and flicked a quick glance at Papa's guest. Her heart sank. This man was dangerous. *Oh, Papa, when will you learn?*

The stranger looked ordinary enough. Brown hair, average height, regular but unmemorable features. Clothing that marked him as a gentleman but without any particular distinction. It was the eyes that gave him away. A light blue that pierced, seemingly straight through to the soul. She shivered, momentarily unable to look away, fascinated despite herself.

"I've made a little bet with Rayfield, Charley," Papa said. "He insists on knowing that you give your permission." He gave the little finger waggle that was their secret signal. She was expected to cooperate with her father's scheme.

All her instincts screamed that something was different about this wager. She tried to read clues in Papa's eyes, but his gaze shifted away. "I told him you are a game one. You'll go along with a wager, won't you?" He chuckled unconvincingly.

"What your father is trying to say, Miss Treadwell, is that *you* are the subject of the wager." Lord Rayfield's smooth baritone voice cut through Papa's evasions.

She frowned, abandoning her attempt to appear at ease. "What—what am I expected to do?"

"If Lord Treadwell loses the wager, you will be mine."

She gasped, whirling to face her father. "Is this true?"

He chuckled weakly again. More intense finger waggling. "Heh, heh. Yes, that's right."

She glared at him, for once speechless. Everything inside her, from her brain to her feet, seemed to have emptied, leaving a vast pit. Silence hung ominously in the room but for the snap of the fire and an occasional gust of wind rattling the windows.

Rayfield said, "Miss Treadwell, if you do not agree to the terms, you need only say so and the bet is off."

About to assert that indeed the bet was off, Charlotte caught the desperate plea in Papa's eyes. *What had he done this time?* He must have a plan. He would not allow her to end up in Rayfield's hands. She had heard of the man's reputation: an adventurer, known for seeking out risks and frequenting the stews and rookeries of London—for what aberrant pleasures? For all Papa's faults, he would not wish such a fate on her. He often landed them in some *imbroglio,* but always managed to extricate them again. She had to trust him.

"Indeed, Lord Rayfield, why should you suppose me to be unwilling? I expect it is you who wished to see me before you agreed to the wager. Am I so complete an antidote that you decline to put yourself at risk of winning me?"

"Not at all." Rayfield's lids dropped, half obscuring his eyes, and Charlotte had the feeling her words had confirmed some speculation in his mind.

Papa audibly exhaled. "What say you to hazard? Put us on equal footing, eh?"

"If you like." Rayfield's tone was mild, almost bored.

"A wager of five thousand pounds plus the vowels I paid you tonight against my daughter? If I win, it's enough to pay the most pressing of my debts and buy a little time."

"Agreed."

What kind of man could afford a wager like that? Either he was even more foolish than Papa, or he was exceedingly rich. Charlotte closed her eyes in a silent prayer that her father would win this bet. That he would win and this time declare he had finally gotten his fill of the thrill of risking the last of his security on the turn of a card or throw of dice.

Papa reached into a drawer and lifted out his dice box. He didn't speak but for comments on the game. "Four, my lord.

Throw again . . . Eight's your main. Eight again—you've nicked it. It looks as if you've bested me again." Papa's voice still sounded cheerful. "Will you join me in a brandy before you take her away with you?"

"No!" Her voice came out in a squeak. She had held her breath through the game of hazard. The room seemed to spin for a moment. Her stomach threatened to rebel, and the bitter taste of bile rose in her throat. The two men stared at her.

Papa's eyes pled with her to cease protesting. Rayfield's expression was unreadable, a slight lifting of his brow as if amused or curious. Her years of acting a part steadied her. "That is, you don't mean for me to go tonight, Papa?"

"Of course I do. Always pay your gambling debts promptly, that's my motto," he said heartily.

He had a plan. He would rescue her. Whatever crazy scheme he had, he couldn't mean for her to end up in Rayfield's power.

"All right, Papa. I'll go pack."

"No, you will not. You'll go with Rayfield now."

"I can't take her tonight! I've no place for her." Rayfield's eyes glared wildly. He did not seem all that eager to gain possession of her, and Charlotte relaxed a little.

"She goes tonight." Papa's tone was harsh. "You'll take her or she'll spend the rest of the night in the street."

"Look here, Treadwell. You can't really mean to turn your daughter out without a stitch," Rayfield protested.

"If you knew me better, you'd not say such a thing. I always mean what I say. Charlotte?" Treadwell directed a questioning look at her.

"He means it." She looked steadily at her father. What she saw did not reassure her. He would not meet her gaze. But that must be because Papa did not want Rayfield to guess he planned to stop what seemed to be happening.

"Too bad you wouldn't join me in a toast, Rayfield." Papa poured the last of the brandy into the snifter. "Ah, there isn't enough left, anyway." He lifted the glass. "To your success with the fair sex." He set down the glass and made a shooing motion with his hand. "Be off with you now. Spencer!" he called in a louder voice.

The servant opened the door. "Show these people out."

Spencer hesitated, looking to Charlotte. She gave a short nod, and he turned and walked down the hall, his back rigid with the disapproval only a long-time family retainer could show.

Hugh suddenly felt out of his depth, unsure what he had stumbled into. Was Treadwell's daughter a part of his plot? She looked angry and frightened. It could be an act. He had seen too many moods flit across her face to be sure what role she played in this farce.

He had no doubt Treadwell meant him to be forced to marry his daughter. Any place he brought her, clad only in her night rail, would ensure the girl's ruin and leave him no choice but to offer for her. He grasped the girl's arm, trying not to be aware of the feel of bare smooth flesh under his gloved fingers. A fragrance of roses drifted to him.

"Come with me." She went along, moving slowly. At the front door, he took off his cloak and offered it to her.

She stepped back, glaring at him. "I don't understand you. Why are you lending yourself to this . . . this disgrace? I know Papa's purpose. He's a gamester. He cannot help but wager on whatever anyone proposes. But what of you? You cannot be so desperate for a woman's attentions."

"Oddly enough, Miss Treadwell, your father proposed this. I would never have suggested such an imprudent wager." He held the cloak out to her.

She glanced at her father, sighed and accepted the wrap.

Spencer opened the front door and followed them out into the dark. Hugh raised his eyebrows. The butler shrugged. "I cannot let her go alone, my lord."

"Thank you, Spencer," Miss Treadwell said, touching his sleeve, her voice sounding delighted.

Hugh laughed, a short, fierce burst, reflecting anything but amusement. He had acquired two dependents this night. *Was*

Spencer's presence part of a conspiracy? "No, I suppose you cannot. In that case, please try to procure a hackney."

The butler hurried down the street, hopping stiffly over several large puddles. The storm had ended, and the air was almost still, with a thin mist curling about them like scarves.

Treadwell House ranged along the Thames, no doubt built as a courtier's principal residence some two centuries ago. At one time other great houses had sat along the river around Treadwell House, but the area had undergone a sad comedown and the house now was in a less than respectable quarter. Could Spencer find a hackney so late and so far from the more prosperous areas?

Hugh looked down at Miss Treadwell, who huddled into his mantle. The thin slippers on her feet offered no protection from the elements. Though she was but a few inches shorter than he, the cloak dragged the ground, becoming sopped with water and mud. She did not speak.

He wrapped the cloak more tightly around her. What role did she play in the game just past? *Time to find out.* "I think I should have a little sample of what I've just won," he said, bending closer to her.

She scrambled backward, fetching up against the stone wall of Treadwell House. "What are you doing?"

"As I said, sweeting. Finding out what sort of bargain I've made." He held her shoulders firmly and touched her lips with his own. She twisted her head aside, but he followed, capturing her again. She resisted for a long moment and then her lips softened and pressed back. He pulled her against his body, and tentatively flicked his tongue over her lips. She started but didn't draw back. Desire flaring in him, he teased at the opening with his tongue. She gasped and pulled away from him, the mantle falling open, allowing a glimpse of her pale garments and paler skin.

Breathing harshly, Hugh stepped back. He watched her closely, damning himself for trying the experiment when it was too dark to see her features clearly. What was going on? Why had she seemed so cooperative inside, played the role of a woman who was sexually experienced when she clearly was an innocent? Fear of her father? He had not sensed fear in her before, and did not now. A desperate willingness to defend herself was more like it. He laughed. "This round's to you, my sweet. But the contest isn't over."

"Y-you don't want to . . . to do anything tonight. It's so late." Her voice trembled.

Her tone took on more assurance as she went on, "We're both tired. It would be better to wait until tomorrow." He could feel her shaking under his hands still clasping her shoulders.

Spencer came back. "I could not find a hackney, my lord."

"Then we'll walk." Whether or not Miss Treadwell was a traitor, he would not marry her and could not ruin her. That left him with only one choice of place to take her: Flash Annie's. A foolish choice if she and her father were the spies he sought. With no alternative, he had to take the risk. He would take a circuitous route to prevent her from finding her way back there at some future time. The mist was an ally, at least. Tomorrow, after he procured her some decent clothing, he would take her to his sister. Surely Sylvia would help him with this pressing problem. Yes, that was an excellent solution.

Perhaps Lord Adair, Sylvia's husband, was the one Hugh should appeal to. No, he would ask Lord Wescott, his superior, to approach Adair. Although Miss Treadwell would ostensibly stay with Sylvia to be sponsored for the upcoming Season, in reality her every move would be watched. If she was involved in her father's treachery, the truth would be uncovered.

He frowned. Despite the briefness of his acquaintance with Miss Treadwell, an unpleasant clutch in his gut accompanied thoughts of her as a traitor. He must guard against allowing sentiment to interfere with his duty.

Almost stumbling from fatigue, Charlotte walked beside Rayfield. Spencer trailed behind, his footsteps echoing in the mist that had settled about them, obscuring their surroundings. Moist air cooled her face and prickled in her hair. No lights illuminated the streets, and she tripped on the rough pavement, causing pain to shoot through her numbed feet.

Rayfield murmured something and took her arm. Even through the fabric of the cloak, the warmth of his arm dissipated some of her chilliness. She suddenly felt safe—a foolish notion indeed. She was anything but safe with this stranger.

Occasional insubstantial forms passed them in the dark. Footsteps, theirs and the others', echoed hollowly. The odor of rotting vegetation drifted through the heavy air, along with more noisome smells. They were near Covent Garden, she thought. Rayfield led them on a route that twisted and turned. Charlotte wondered how he knew his way in the fog. As they proceeded, the alley narrowed and buildings closed around them, almost touching them and revealing dilapidation and decay. The ugliness was beyond her worst experiences, which intensified her feeling of menace. She was falling deeper into a nightmare, that worst of phantasms in which she possessed no power of speech or resistance, but only proceeded will-she, nill-she.

From out of the darkness, pounding footsteps approached.

CHAPTER TWO

Rayfield propelled Charlotte toward Spencer. She stumbled against the butler, who pushed her to the wall behind them and stepped in front of her. Unable to see what followed, Charlotte heard grunts and thuds and the scraping of shoes on pavement. Her own heart thudded, her gut tightening at the violence she could sense. With a louder grunt a body fell heavily to the pavement and lay still. The noises of men grappling continued, the rasp of labored breathing and blows. Then there was a cry of pain and pounding footsteps, fading away into the mist.

"Are you all right, Miss Treadwell?" Rayfield hovered over her, his voice registering concern.

"Yes. What was that?"

He shrugged. "Footpads who thought us an easy target." Taking her arm again, he started forward.

Spencer suddenly said in a belligerent tone, "'Ere now, where are you taking Miss Treadwell? This ain't no place for a gentle-born lady like 'er." The dropped aitches revealed his agitation; she'd never heard him forget to employ proper speech.

Rayfield's grip on her arm tightened as he whirled to face the old servant. "Where would you have me take her?" he asked.

"Why . . ." Even in the dark Charlotte sensed Spencer's confused face. "There must be some place," he finished feebly.

"I'm doing as I think best. I have a friend nearby who'll keep Miss Treadwell safe until I acquire more seemly attire."

"Whatever you will, my lord." Spencer caved in to the other's authority.

His easy capitulation sprang something loose in Charlotte. Whatever her father had in mind, it did not seem that his plan would prevent her spending the night in Rayfield's bed. Spencer could not protect her, so she had to take a stand herself. Setting her feet, she resisted the tug on her arm as Rayfield started forward again. "It is not 'whatever you will' with me. What sort of friend do you find in an area like this?"

Rayfield stopped, turning to face her. "As you wish, Miss Treadwell, I'll tell you the sort of friend she is. The sort of friend who won't trumpet this night's business to the known world. The sort of friend who lives where no one in the *ton* will see you out in your night rail at this hour of the night and draw the worst conclusion."

As he spoke, he leaned closer, his face very near to hers. "The sort of friend who will help you stave off ruin. Unless I miss my guess, you would prefer such an outcome. If I am wrong and being ruined was your aim, then you picked the wrong man. I won't be responsible for it." He stepped back and waited.

Tears pricked her eyes. No, of course he wasn't wrong. However, she had practically told him otherwise when her father proposed the wager. And whatever rig her father was running depended somehow on her appearing to agree. How had Rayfield guessed it wasn't true? And why would he care? In any case, she was suddenly hopeful that he did not intend to share a bed with her when they arrived wherever they were going.

It could not hurt to pretend a little longer that she found no problem in being the object of a wager and might give her and Papa an advantage when he came to rescue her. "Forgive me. I'm cold and tired, that is all. Do we have much farther to go?"

"Not far," he said in a gentler tone. He took her arm again and adjusted his pace so that she could more easily adapt.

Indeed, but a few minutes later they turned into a narrow passage, and he knocked on a door. He repeated the knock several times before the door cracked open the minutest bit. "What d'you want?" A woman's surly voice, thick with sleep.

"I need to see Annie."

The aperture widened. "'Tis Broddie, i'nt it?"

"Yes. Let us in, Pearl."

The door swung open, revealing a young woman dressed in a tattered robe. The stub of a candle in her hand burned fitfully. Pushing Charlotte inside, Rayfield quickly followed and beckoned to Spencer to enter, then shoved the door closed.

Pearl said, "Annie's gorn to bed."

"Awaken her, please. These people need a place to stay the night. I'll make it worth Annie's while."

The girl looked at him and his companions doubtfully before she said, "You can wait there if you like." Pointing at a closed door partway down the narrow hallway, she exited through another door at the far end, taking the light.

He seemed to know the way, guiding Charlotte to the door. Inside the room, embers of an earlier fire still glowed in the fireplace. From its coals, he lit a candle taken from a table.

Given the feeble light cast by the candle, Charlotte looked around the tiny room, with its dingy, peeling paper of an indeterminate pattern and its bare wood floors that appeared not to have seen a mop in some time. A low settle and the table on which the candle stood comprised the only furniture.

Rayfield strode to the fireplace and placed a booted foot on the fender, looking down into the dying coals. Spencer stood in the doorway, his lean, elderly form stiffly erect and formal.

The open door admitted a frosty draft from the hallway, and Charlotte drew the cloak about herself. The man's scent wafted up from the cloth, masculine and spicy.

Pearl came in with a bucket half-filled with coal and dropped it in front of the fireplace. "Annie'll be down in a bit." She directed the words to Rayfield, then left again.

He bent to add more coals to the fire. The small blaze that flared up sent no warmth to Charlotte. She wanted to move closer to the hearth, but would not while he stood there.

His coat clung as he bent over the fire, revealing the

graceful curves and musculature of his back. A warmth in her face not attributable to the temperature in the room, she looked away, trying not to remember the kiss he had pressed on her a short while ago. She should be shaking from dread of what was to come, but she could not summon up any fear at all. The most amazing surge of pure energy had shot through her when Rayfield kissed her, like liquid fire, and pooled low in her belly.

That was what she really feared—that if he claimed her, she would slide easily into his arms.

For the first time she understood what Sukey Twitchell, her abdomen swelling with the baby inside her, had meant when she said, "But I couldn't tell him no, Miss Charlotte." The baby's father, one of Jamie's men, had been transported to Botany Bay by then. Charlotte thrust aside that thought.

A kiss was far different than the intimacies Rayfield would expect from her. She had to keep him from claiming his prize tonight, until her father could rescue her—tomorrow? Yes, surely tomorrow. She had almost laughed with joy when Spencer followed them. Papa would have told him the plan.

In a few minutes, the door opened and a woman, presumably Annie, came in. She was small of stature with improbably bright, tousled yellow hair. Her flamboyant wrapper ended at her ankles, showing bare feet. In a rough voice she said, "Broddie, y'er late. I'd give up seeing you tonight."

Rayfield went quickly to her, and taking her arm, led her to the hall, shutting the door behind them. Charlotte wished to listen at the door, but this was her opportunity to speak with Spencer. "Quick, before he comes back, what does Papa have planned to rescue me?"

"He has a plan? I didn't hear that. What did he say to you, Miss Charley?"

"You mean he never said anything to you? Oh, Spencer, I was sure when you came along with us that you were supposed to help me get away, to meet Papa somewhere." The ground beneath her seemed to disappear, leaving her with a falling sensation. She held out her hands, to regain her balance, to hold on to something solid in a world that spun crazily awry.

"Miss, this will be all right. Your papa trusted Lord Rayfield—he's the kind of man who'll see you through."

"No," she breathed. "Papa wouldn't . . . he couldn't have meant for this to end like this." Her eyes stung and she sniffed against the moisture that gathered in her nose. "I am sure he meant to rescue me. But he would not foresee Rayfield would bring us to this . . . this awful place. He'd expect we were at his town house, or bachelor quarters, wherever he lives during the Season. Or even at some . . . some nest he has set up for his mistress—if he doesn't already have someone living there."

Yes, he would have a mistress. Probably a temperamental opera dancer. If she learned of this night's business she would no doubt treat him to a royal display of jealousy. The poor woman. Having met the man just tonight, Charlotte already knew any woman who expected fidelity from him was doomed to disappointment. A man who would wager for a woman was a reprobate of the first order.

"Papa intended to rescue me," she insisted, "but he won't know how to find us. I shall have to get away without his help. You'll help me, won't you, Spencer?"

"I wouldn't know how to get you away from here. You must wait and see what Lord Rayfield has planned." Spencer looked down at the floor, his shoulders hunched.

He's exhausted, poor man. She could expect no help from him.

"Miss Charlotte, I am sure he picked out Lord Rayfield because he knew the man would behave in an honorable way and marry you."

"I can't marry him!" A man just like her father. Nothing and no one would ever be as important as the next wager. But she couldn't say that to Spencer. As close as she was to him, and to Mrs. Whislehurst, their housekeeper, there were still some bounds one couldn't cross. And criticism of her father was one of them.

She must get away. And she would have to do it on her own.

* * *

"I apologize for the intrusion, Annie. I didn't know where else to bring her." Hugh raked his fingers through his hair.

Annie looked at him, her head cocked at an angle, her deep-set golden eyes bright. "You gonna marry the girl, Broddie?"

He shuddered. "Good Lord, no! Her father is one of my suspects. For all I know she is up to her ears in the plot to start a revolution."

"Broddie! You shouldn't have brought 'er 'ere!"

"I'll make sure she doesn't know how to find her way back when I take her away. I don't have any proof that either she or her father is the person for whom I'm searching. If she's innocent, I just want to get her out of this with both our reputations intact, which they won't be if any of the *ton* catch wind of it. Tomorrow, or I should say, later today, after I set it up and get her some decent clothes, I'll take her to my sister's."

"I can give 'er the Heaper's room. 'E hasn't showed up yet. There's a little room off it that I use for storage. 'Er servant can stay there."

Hugh frowned. "What happened to the Heaper?"

"Nothing to get het up about. He probably found another trail to sniff after. It 'appens often enough."

Accepting this explanation, he grabbed her hand and held it fervently. "I'm grateful for this, Annie."

With a stiff smile, Annie pulled her hand free. "I'll hold you to that, your lordship. It will take a while to get the rooms ready. I'll send Pearl in with some hot toddies—that should take the chill off her, and you as well."

"Not for me, Annie. I must deal not only with Scott, but with my sister today. Of the two, my sister will be the toughest. If I look haggard and dissipated, I'll never convince her to take the girl in. I'll leave Miss Treadwell in your capable hands." With a feeling of relief tantamount to deliverance, Hugh made his escape.

* * *

The servant, Pearl, brought hot toddies into the room where Charlotte waited. Spencer refused the drink. "It isn't proper for me to partake with you, Miss Charlotte." She also refused, determined not to accept any of the meager hospitality offered by this prison she planned to escape as soon as possible. Her butler shook his finger at her. "You take that drink, Miss Charlotte. You need something to restore you after such a disturbance as you've had."

"Only if you do, Spencer. You are equally in need of restoration." Indeed, the elderly servant looked far from well. Charlotte had slept for a few hours before her shocking awakening, but Spencer had not. He must feel as upset and uncertain about his future, and be as damp and chilled as she.

He agreed, and they took the steaming mugs. Charlotte anxiously asked, "Does Lord Rayfield intend to join us?" She didn't want him to suppose she desired his company, but if she had any hope of escape, she needed to know his whereabouts.

The maid replied, " 'E's gorn, miss. 'E'll be back later this mornin'."

Thank God, she would not be ravished soon. Some of the knots inside Charlotte untangled. She sipped her toddy, feeling the drink both burn and soothe her throat, and the rest of her tension dissipated.

Still, her problem remained. She could not stay here, but how could she leave without Spencer to protect her?

Pearl showed them to their rooms. She obviously believed Charlotte would sleep, but she paced, waiting until enough time had passed for the household to settle.

The risks of staying until Rayfield returned were simply too great. She must attempt to sneak out, hoping to avoid Pearl and Annie, and anyone else who might occupy the place. As soon as it became light enough outside to see her way, she would go. The area would surely be less dangerous in daylight, and she would soon find her way.

She would have to leave Spencer behind. She would send for him as soon as she might, however.

As Charlotte left the room, she came face to face with Pearl. "Oh," she exclaimed, feeling the blood drain from her face.

The streets around Annie's place appeared even more sinister in the pale shimmer of dawn than Charlotte had realized the night before. She pulled Rayfield's cloak more tightly around her, hurrying to keep up with Flea, the escort Pearl arranged. Beneath the cloak she wore the other girl's second-best dress.

The maid had expressed delight with the exchange of Charlotte's nightgown and wrapper of fine lawn for the bright yellow calico gown. "Coo, won't the 'Eaper just about fancy me in this," she exulted. Charlotte pushed aside thoughts of their relationship, grateful for something other than a nightgown to wear for her return home. As well, she shut her mind to the picture of just how snugly her night rail would fit Pearl's more generous proportions. The calico flopped loosely at Charlotte's bust.

Pearl had also unearthed a pair of much-worn but sturdy shoes, as Charlotte's slippers were ruined. The shoes fit her ill, too wide and short, pinching her toes. Still, they were better than thin slippers for what promised to be a long walk.

The servant additionally provided her younger brother to show Charlotte the way out of the slums.

"Stay close to me now," Flea ordered in a hushed voice as they passed a couple of men swaying drunkenly. She needed no such command. Averting her gaze as the men looked her up and down insolently, she pressed close to the small boy.

Flea's astonishingly scrawny, dirty form was enwrapped in a collection of rags bearing little resemblance to clothing. A shapeless, battered beaver hat crowned a mop of curly red hair. Underneath the dirt, freckles spattered his sharp, cunning face. His jaunty walk conferred an air of confidence far beyond his years, giving Charlotte a surprising sense of safety.

"How old are you?" Charlotte asked her protector.

"Coo, I don't know. I guess I'd be about twelve. Anyways, that's what Pearl says."

"You and your sister do not look much alike." Charlotte hid her surprise at his age. He looked undersized for twelve.

The boy laughed. "She ain't my sister for real. My da and 'er ma was married-like for a while." His green eyes took on a dreamy, reminiscing expression. "Them were the best times I ever knew. My da didn't drink so much Blue Ruin when 'e were with Pearl's ma, and even when 'e were cup-shot, she didn't let 'im beat me too often."

Flea's matter-of-fact account of his early years shocked Charlotte. "Your father and Pearl's mother are not, er, married any more?"

"Nah. She died, and then Pearl got took in by Flash Annie, so it was just me and my da again. I couldn't take it no more, so I 'opped the twig."

" 'Hopped the twig?' "

"Loped off, er, scarpered." The boy frowned at Charlotte's slowness.

"Do you mean you ran away?"

"That's wot I said, din't I?"

"Who takes care of you now? Do you live at Annie's with Pearl?" They crossed a street, avoiding huge, muddy puddles in the gutters at both sides, and turned into another narrow, garbage-infested alley.

"I takes care of myself!" A dirty thumb poked vigorously at his chest punctuated these words.

"You don't live with Pearl, then?"

"Nah. Flash Annie'd make me work fer 'er if I did."

"You live all by yourself?"

Flea grinned at her. "Not by myself. Me and my mates 'ave a bob ken. We does very well for ourselves."

As the day slowly brightened, they progressed out of the slum into an area of prosperous shops, still shuttered and dark. The streets were occupied only by shopgirls and clerks making their way to work. Charlotte looked around, but saw no hackneys waiting for custom at this early hour. She would have to walk still farther to reach home. She welcomed Flea's company, despite deeming his life to be most disturbing.

"How do you live?"

"I does lots of things. Run errands for swells, 'old their horses fer 'em. I even 'elps Lord Broddie sometimes."

"Lord Broddie? Do you mean Lord Rayfield?"

"We ain't s'posed to know 'is real name," Flea said.

"What do you mean? Is he up to something nefarious?"

"Ain't s'posed to talk about it. Don't know no Ferryus, anyways."

Ever more glad of her escape from Rayfield's villainous clutches, Charlotte had little wish to question Flea further about the man's actions, especially since Flea showed signs of becoming truculent in defense of "Lord Broddie." Still, she was concerned about the boy's involvement in the presumably criminal enterprise. In her short time with the boy, she had taken a liking to his high-spirited and sanguine outlook on life. She could not help speculating what illicit career occupied Lord Rayfield. No wonder the man knew characters with names such as Flash Annie and the Heaper, who dwelled in that sordid slum.

Silence fell between the two. Charlotte finally recognized landmarks that showed they neared Treadwell House. "It isn't much farther," she told the boy. "I will give you your reward for showing me the way after we get home."

When Charlotte and Flea arrived at the servants' entrance, Mrs. Whislehurst expressed her indignation. "Here now, miss, this won't do! What are you doing coming to this door?" A tiny woman of middle years, with gray-streaked black hair and a sprightly manner, she wore an immaculate white apron over her black bombazine gown cut in the style of a dozen years ago.

"I had to know what's happening ˈ re Papa found out I had come home," Charlotte explaineᵈ. Have you spoken to him? Did he say anything about me? He planned to rescue me, didn't he?"

"As to his plans, I couldn't say. Right after you left last night, he ordered Horn to pack his valise and went out himself. Told Horn to find another position. Fine goings-on—Mr.

Spencer came and told me about the shameful bet your father made. Woke me out of a sound sleep. I'd have gone with you too, except I couldn't get dressed in time."

"Papa left? And he hasn't come back?" Charlotte walked past the housekeeper into the kitchen.

"By the looks of his valise, he doesn't mean to come back soon. Packed as much as it would hold, Horn said."

"Whatever is going on? I've never known him to wish to travel." A yawning black hole gaped inside Charlotte. From Papa's gambling her away and ordering her to leave in her nightclothes to this new action of his . . . none of it made sense. Finally, completely, she knew that her world had forever changed. And, as well, that he might have intended her to remain with Rayfield. She collapsed into Mrs. Whislehurst's chair, so lightheaded for a moment that she couldn't stand.

Flea came to the servant's notice. "Miss Charlotte, what are you doing with the likes of him? Get away, you filthy ragamuffin." She shooed at him with her apron.

"No, Whizzie, he has done me a service." Straightening up and taking several deep breaths, Charlotte forced herself to think. She removed her shoes and rubbed her sore toes. "Where do you think Papa went?"

"Lit out for the continent to avoid the bailiffs, is what I would say," the housekeeper huffed.

"The bailiffs! Has it come to that?"

"If not yet, they'll be here soon enough, I vow." For some time, Charlotte had been the recipient of the older woman's opinions about Lord Treadwell. She had not scrupled to show her contempt for her employer before his daughter.

Charlotte's fear sharpened, bringing urgency to her plans. Would the bailiffs imprison her if they came and could not find her father? "If Papa believed he was in danger of his assets being seized, it must be true. We shall have to take as many of our belongings as we can and leave. Perhaps I might sell a piece of my mother's jewelry and stay at a hotel while I look for a position as a governess or companion."

"There's no need for that. Rosella will let us both stay with her." Mrs. Whislehurst's sister and her innkeeper husband owned a comfortable inn across the Thames in Lambeth.

"I could not like to be a burden to her," Charlotte said.

"Nonsense. There's plenty of room. She'll be glad enough of a chance to coddle somebody, and we've scarce had a chance to have a comfortable coze since we were children."

"Very well, Whizzie. We shall go there." Charlotte was nearly overcome by fatigue. She wished she could lie down right in the kitchen and sleep for days. She noticed Flea still waiting for his money, shifting his weight from one foot to the next. "Could you pay this young gentleman what I owe him out of your household money?"

With a snort, the diminutive woman went to fetch the purse with which she paid tradesmen.

Flea stowed his money and tipped his disreputable chapeau to them. "Pearl'll know 'ow to find me if you needs any further assistance," he reassured Charlotte, starting out the door.

"Wait," Charlotte hastily called him back. "Flea, would you take some more money to Spencer so he may come back home?"

"You aren't going to trust this rapscallion! He'll take the money for himself and Spencer will never see a groat."

"I am sure I can trust him. He has been most helpful. Flea, will you please see that this money is used for Mr. Spencer to take a hackney back here?"

The boy sniffed indignantly. "I told you that I do honest work. I wouldn't diddle you."

"See, I told you, Whizzie. I am going to go to my room to rest. It has been a most exhausting night."

Hugh arose from a restless sleep and prepared to face his new responsibilities. He sent his valet, Bracegirdle, to go in disguise to a shop that dealt in used clothing. The valet had grown accustomed to carrying out confidential tasks, and scarcely raised an eyebrow over this one, even given the sketchy description of the young lady's proportions.

Later, he called on Lord Wescott, and recounted the events of the previous evening.

"It seems you mishandled matters with Treadwell, Rayfield." His superior frowned at him.

"With respect, sir, I don't believe I have. It's by no means certain that Treadwell suspects I am investigating him, or even that he is the spy. If he is, it is unclear whether his daughter is involved. I believe that my plan will best enable us to watch their activities while at the same time minimizing the damage to Miss Treadwell if she is merely an innocent victim of her father's machinations."

By the time his preparations were completed and Hugh made his way to Flash Annie's, the afternoon was advanced. No doubt Miss Treadwell would be in considerable anxiety about his plans for her. The unexpected outcome to his evening with Treadwell had left him scrambling to make decisions. Last night he had no idea what to tell her, and even now the development of his plan depended upon enlisting Sylvia's support.

He hoped Miss Treadwell would agree to cooperate with the effort to win Sylvia to her cause. Surely, whether or not she was a part of a scheme by Treadwell to start a revolution in England, she would not openly argue to stay with Hugh.

All his plans withstood a check when he arrived at Flash Annie's. "Gone! But where . . . when . . . Good God!"

"She went back to Treadwell 'Ouse. She got Pearl to 'elp her. I never thought to tell Pearl to keep 'er 'ere."

"No, though it never occurred to me to leave such instructions—I didn't think she would do such a thing—but she certainly was not to be held prisoner, either. What did they hope to gain by this whole maneuver? I confess I am totally puzzled." He shook his head. "What about the old servant?"

"She sent for 'im after she got 'ome. 'E's gorn, too. Did you want to talk to Pearl?"

"I must, I suppose. Though it's hardly likely that she has any enlightenment to offer. Whatever Miss Treadwell told her would not necessarily be the truth."

He stepped in and waited in the small parlor that Miss Treadwell and her servant had waited in the night before.

In a few minutes, Pearl came in, her usually saucy manner subdued. "You ain't angry at me?" she asked.

"No, Pearl, this start of Miss Treadwell's has taken us all by surprise. Tell me what you know."

"She said as she needed to get back 'ome. And she said as she feared you would make free o' 'er."

"She feared I would demand, er, sexual congress with her?"

"That's wot she said."

Who was the real Miss Treadwell? When she had agreed to the wager, she had acted as if the possibility of his physically claiming her caused her no trepidation. But the later kiss, and now her words to Pearl, told a different story.

"You are certain she made it safely home?"

"Flea 'companied 'er. She were safe as 'ouses with 'im."

"I must talk with Flea, I suppose."

"I'll send for 'im."

Flea was fiercely protective of his secrecy regarding his place of residence. No doubt Hugh could have pushed the issue, either with Flea himself or Pearl, but despite his usefulness, the boy was hardly an essential part of his organization.

While he waited at Flash Annie's, he talked to the Heaper. The big man didn't sugarcoat his news, his rough face carrying an unaccustomed seriousness. "I made the rounds of our informers up north. They all say the trouble is growing. And no one 'as any more information to offer about 'oo's stirring it up. Oates, Wood, & Smithson's Mill outside Leeds was attacked and fired. There've been reports from several areas of men with blacked face going about in bands late at night."

"Damnation! This has to be stopped before people are killed. We must have men to keep an eye on the Treadwells and report on whomever they meet. We need to step up our efforts in the north as well, get more men to gain access to the Luddites and find out who's inciting them."

"It will take awhile to get men to Treadwell 'Ouse."

"Flea will go in the interim. Get your men there as soon as you can."

CHAPTER THREE

It was, perhaps, the most dangerous period in English history. Numerous disturbances occurred in Nottingham among the stocking-frame knitters in late 1811 and early 1812. The disturbances quickly spread to other counties, principally Yorkshire, Lancashire and Cheshire. In the midst of all this unrest, late in 1811 a British intelligence agent intercepted an encoded message addressed to an 'M. Mansson.' When the missive was decoded, the name was revealed as an alias for an English aristocrat in the pay of the French. M. Mansson was an anagram of sans nom, *or 'Mr. Nameless.' The memorandum instructed M. Mansson to use the frame-workers' insurrection to incite a general revolution, beginning in the textile manufacturing districts. It was a diabolically clever plan, most likely conceived by Talleyrand, that most Machiavellian of Napoleon's advisors.*

(From The Secret Wars of Napoleon, *by Alphonsius McMasters, PhD, LLC, AKC, OBE, BMW, 2005.)*

Charlotte could not sleep. How could she relax, given her uncertain future and the momentous events of the past six hours? The happenings that had followed her abrupt awakening by Spencer kept replaying in her mind, jerkily, like a magic lantern show.

Among a mélange of bizarre events, those with Rayfield in them figured most. Various images arose. The intensity in his blue eyes. The leashed power she sensed in him. His strong, muscled back as he bent over the fire. His looming presence as he brought her to Flash Annie's, like an umbra that eclipsed all light. The misleading sense of safety with him beside her. But, he *had* protected her, had vanquished the footpads.

The kiss. She groaned and flung her arm across her eyes, wishing away the sensations that stroked through her at the remembrance of the passion in his lips. Even his casual touches had conveyed a sensory thrill, were she honest with herself.

She had to set such thoughts aside.

Her future. All Charlotte had ever wanted was to be safe and secure. Last night's events had pushed the attainment of her ambition further into the future, if ever. It looked as if Papa would not come back soon, and she must provide for herself. She pushed aside the apprehension such thoughts aroused.

Her life had changed irrevocably before—at her mother's death, when Jamie was killed, and when Papa sold Queen's Treat and brought her to London. For the first time, however, she was completely on her own. She would manage; she always had.

Giving up on rest, she arose and packed what she thought she would need for a career as a governess or companion. Mrs. Whislehurst insisted she also bring away those few remaining items of value that had belonged to her mother. "No point in giving 'em to your father's creditors. You can sell 'em yourself and get a bit of blunt to lay by."

When Spencer returned from Flash Annie's, he asserted he would stay at Treadwell House to look after things. He would not leave the house unguarded.

In vain Charlotte argued with her butler. What if Rayfield came looking for her? And what would happen when the bailiffs came? She could make no dent in his devotion to duty. However, she would not listen to his claim that she had an obligation to inform Rayfield where she had gone, and made him promise he would not give that information to the man if he came asking.

Whizzie had sent a message to the Owl and Crown, the inn owned by Orwin and Rosella Parrsley.

Orwin came to bring them to the inn. Charlotte tried to convince herself as they drove away that she would return someday to Treadwell House. Her old life could not have vanished so completely. First Queen's Treat, and now this. She straightened her spine and refused to give in to tears.

At the inn, Rosella greeted her and Whizzie warmly, assuring them they were welcome to stay as long as they liked. The Parrsleys would not hear of a viscount's daughter helping out in an inn. Charlotte had always had some purpose to her days. She had nursed her ailing mother for several years until her death when Charlotte was twelve.

After that, she turned her efforts to her father's tenants. His lifelong neglect of Queen's Treat, his country property, meant great hardship for his dependents. Charlotte did what she could to lessen their misery, sharing food from her home garden and creating herbal concoctions for their ailments from her mother's book of country remedies.

The plight of the families was even more desperate after Jamie died, when several of the menfolk were transported or sent to the prison hulks. Until her father sold Queen's Treat and brought her to London, she had never lacked for some task to do.

In London, she earned some money making fair copies of documents for lawyers and others. Her earnings had kept Treadwell House afloat for the past two years, and she managed to set aside a little money to send to Mr. Mitchell, the vicar at her old country parish, for the relief of the families. Such work could not support her now that she would have to pay for lodgings. She must take a position that included her board.

Resolved to relieve the Parrsleys of the burden she represented as soon as possible, Charlotte immediately set about finding a post, and wrote to all the advertisements for employment that seemed suitable.

* * *

Flea approached Treadwell House for the second time in a day. Clouds had covered the sky again as the day advanced, and twilight arrived early. But he had light enough to see the dusty cart waiting in the street outside, with an aged, sway-backed horse in the traces.

He found a place from which he could see the house without being noticed, across the road in an alcove between buildings. He had scarcely tucked himself into the space when Miss Treadwell and the woman she had called Whizzie came out of the servants' door, accompanied by the cart's driver and followed by Spencer. All four carried burdens, Miss Treadwell a large portmanteau and the others boxes. They loaded them in the cart. Miss Treadwell hugged Spencer, then the driver assisted the women in climbing onto the seat. The elderly butler stood watching them. The driver joined the ladies on the wagon seat, clucked to the horse and they started out.

"Keep an eye on her and her father until I get my men into place to watch their movements," Lord Broddie'd said. That was going to be too late, wasn't it? Flea didn't think she was planning to come back.

"Where are you runnin' to, Miss French-traitor?" he muttered. She wasn't getting away, not from him. A lady had no business acting so nice and making him think she really liked him when she was just using him to keep Lord Broddie from catching on to her evil.

The memory crowded in, of Broddie saying, "That lady you helped go from Flash Annie's to her home, her father is one of the men who could be the French traitor. She might be helping him." Flea's eyes had even prickled like he was going to cry. He never cried and sure wasn't going to over no traitor. A raw burning started in his gut.

The streets were crowded with traffic, slowing the cart. Flea had no difficulty in following at first. It made for Westminster Bridge. Nobody in that cart would notice a small boy following behind, but he kept back and to the shadows just the same. He joined a throng of homebound workers crossing the bridge. On the other side, it took an effort to break free of them and look for the cart.

For a moment he thought it had disappeared. The increasing darkness made it difficult to distinguish one vehicle from another. Then he saw it turning a corner and raced to catch up. The cart made several turns into increasingly narrow streets, slowing each time and making it easy for Flea to keep it in sight. Finally, it turned into the yard of a small inn and stopped. Lanterns hung from building wall illuminated the yard.

A very plump woman bustled out of the inn as the occupants of the cart climbed down. The woman enfolded Whizzie in an embrace that threatened to smother the tiny woman, and then she fussed over Miss Treadwell. Several other people also came out of the inn and unloaded the boxes and portmanteau, and then everybody went inside.

Flea waited. Was Miss Treadwell going to leave again? The inn looked too small, and was probably too far off the main roads, to be a coaching inn. That did not mean that she wasn't going to head for the coast, though. Who knew what she had planned? If he left to report to Broddie and Miss Treadwell took it into her head to lope off, Broddie probably wouldn't know where to look for her next.

He had not paid much attention to the plans Miss Treadwell discussed with Whizzie. He'd been thinking he'd never see those people again once he got the ten bob he'd been promised for leading her out of Flash Annie's neighborhood. But they had mentioned a Rosella. Maybe that was the plump woman. He had to find out from somebody.

Just then the driver of the cart came out of the inn and led the horse, still hitched to the cart, into the stable, yelling at somebody named Jemmie. A boy about his own age came around the corner and followed the man inside the building. Shortly, the man came back out and went into the inn.

Flea hated horses. He'd just as soon stay a long way away from the stable, but that boy could be his chance to find out what was going on. Flea quickly glanced around the innyard to be sure nobody was watching. If Miss Treadwell came back out, she would likely recognize him. Nobody was in sight, and he made a dash into the doorway of the stable.

By the light of a lantern hung from a crossbeam, the boy rubbed down the spavined horse that had brought Miss Treadwell.

Flea backed up a step, sweat forming on his upper lip. His foot clanged against a tin pail, making the boy look up. "Hey! You there! Whatcher doin' in here?"

Caught out, Flea moved forward. Not too close to the blasted beast. "Nothin'. I weren't doin' nothin'—jus' thought I'd see about work."

"Work?" Jemmie looked Flea up and down, his lip curling like he could see Flea's fear. "We don't got no work. Got enough helpers." The boy gave a pat to the horse's neck and led him toward a stall within touch of where Flea stood.

Flea flattened himself against the wall. "Oh. No 'arm in asking, is there?"

The other boy opened the stall door, slipped the halter off the horse and gave it a slap on the rear. As the horse moved slowly inside, Jemmie forked some hay into an open box on the inside wall, then closed the door. "You'd better go now."

"Who were those people who just got 'ere?" Flea blurted.

"Why you wanna know?"

"Thought that older lady looked like somebody my ma worked with, is all. That's what give me the idea to ask about work 'ere. They just calling on your mistress?"

"Nah, that's Mrs. Parrsley's sister and her 'ployer. They'll be staying for awhile. Mrs. Whislehurst din't live in Lunnon 'til a year or so ago, so I doesn't think she were the one your ma worked with."

Flea grinned. He had the information he needed. "Guess I'll be goin' then."

Hugh placed men to watch the Parrsleys' inn, and also at Treadwell House. Lord Treadwell had not departed with Miss

Treadwell and her housekeeper. And, unless Spencer had gone between the time Flea followed the cart carrying Miss Treadwell away and when his men arrived to cover the place, he was still there. Perhaps the butler would give him information.

Spencer answered the door. "There's no one here except myself, my lord," the old servant said. "When I woke up at Flash Annie's, Miss Treadwell was already gone, so I came here. Lord Treadwell had left as well. Someone needs to look after the place, so I stayed." And at Hugh's further questioning, he denied all knowledge of either Treadwell's present location.

This last was not said with the firmness of his other declarations. Hugh, who knew much of what Spencer said was false, was equally certain the man knew where Miss Treadwell had gone. But Hugh already knew where she was. What he had hoped to obtain from the butler was something of more substance that revealed her purpose. He could think of no way to force the issue with Miss Treadwell's loyal servant.

He called on his sister, who knew all there was to know about members of the *ton,* to find out what she knew about the Treadwells. Sylvia had nothing to add to the rumors and gossip he had already gained from other sources.

In the days that followed, his men reported that Treadwell had made no appearance at his house. Unless there was a secret way in, it appeared Spencer resided there alone. He had no callers except, on a couple of occasions, tradesmen, and once Miss Treadwell stopped by. She did not remain long, however.

The men following her reported that her other excursions away from the inn, usually accompanied by the middle-aged former housekeeper, were to employment agencies, jewelers known to buy heirlooms from insolvent aristocrats, and dealers in used goods.

Where had Treadwell gone, and what was Miss Treadwell about? Their behavior matched no pattern he had ever seen. Treadwell's flight could be an indication of guilt, or it could be merely the sign of a man fleeing from his debts.

He made arrangements with his secretary, Hamnet Williams, to get access to Treadwell House in whatever way he could, even if it meant purchasing it, and conducting a thorough search for any incriminating evidence.

The most likely explanation for Miss Treadwell's actions was that she had been abandoned without resources and was trying to make it alone. It seemed Treadwell's purpose in wagering over her was to provide for her, as he had said.

Hugh appeased the guilt this thought engendered by the reminder that he could not have forced Miss Treadwell to remain with him, and he could not rush in now to carry her away, even though his intentions were not the lascivious ones she apparently imputed to him. He doubted she would trust his claim he only wished to place her with his sister, who could help her find a husband, a man more to her taste than Hugh.

Unbidden, the memory of Miss Treadwell's response to his kiss laid waste to this thought, and to his peace of mind. He could bring back all too easily how she had stirred his senses, the enticing rose scent of her, the feel of her in his arms.

He brushed the thoughts aside. The lady gave evidence of a physical attraction to him, but in every other way had made it plain she wanted nothing to do with him. It was too soon to draw any conclusion, but Miss Treadwell seemed to be innocent. And England's danger required all his attention.

In a few days, Charlotte obtained an interview with a woman who had traveled to London looking for a governess for her two young daughters.

Mrs. Goddings had taken rooms at the Pulteney Hotel, and Charlotte was ushered into her presence by a uniformed maid. Her prospective employer, with silver hair that crowned a dignified figure, and clothing in the latest fashion, sat writing some letters at a lady's secretaire. The elegant surroundings and Mrs. Goddings' refined appearance reassured Charlotte that she would be comfortable in the position.

Until the woman opened her mouth. "My 'usban' owns a mill in Garwick, near Leeds," she said. "My son is away a' school, and I want my daughters ter 'ave a gran' education."

As the interview progressed, Charlotte discovered that Mrs. Goddings was a dedicated and relentless seeker after an advanced position in society for her daughters, and what she wanted was not so much an education for them as a veneer of gentility that would permit them to move up in the world.

When Mrs. Goddings learned Charlotte was the daughter of a viscount, she made it clear she must have Miss Treadwell for her girls. Charlotte accepted the position despite her unease over being hired for her perceived social position rather than the knowledge she could impart. Indeed, she felt faintly dishonest since she had not had a Season, nor did she have any contacts in the world she might have been supposed to have inhabited.

She kept her feelings at bay with frenzied activity to prepare for her remove to Yorkshire. She wrote enthusiastic references for Spencer and Mrs. Whislehurst, gave them as much as she could spare of the profits from the sale of her mother's jewelry and small knick-knacks she had brought from Treadwell House. She set aside money for her coach fare and for postage for the letters she promised to write to her old servants. The rest she reserved for some future need.

" 'Tisn't right," Whizzie said as Charlotte was nearly ready to go.

"What do you mean, Whizzie?" she asked, kneeling by her trunk and debating which of two dated, drab gowns to pack.

"You taking this position. 'Tisn't dignified for you to be working for some Cit." The housekeeper clutched a pile of Charlotte's shifts, which she had washed and pressed.

"I have no choice." Charlotte closed her eyes against the stab of sorrow at loss of her old life and fear of setting out into the unknown. "Don't make it harder for me, please?"

"You should have stayed with Rayfield."

"Whizzie! I cannot believe you would advise me to choose so ruinous a course. I could not be mistress to such a man."

"Of course not. He would have married you, Miss Charlotte. He could hardly do else."

Charlotte jumped up. "You have no evidence on which to

base that conclusion. In any case, I have no wish to be trapped in such a marriage, forced onto both parties with no love on either side. He is not the man for me. I—if there had ever been a chance for me to wed—I wanted someone steady and honest, who would be by my side and not always in London pursuing his own pleasures. That's not Rayfield." As well as being a gamester, he was almost certainly a criminal, with a friend such as Flash Annie, whose house was clearly a thieves' den.

Whizzie closed her mouth, but tears appeared in her eyes. "I'm sorry, Miss Charlotte. I only wish what's best for you."

"I know." Charlotte hugged the older woman, sparing a little wish for herself. Perhaps she would find fulfillment teaching the Goddings girls.

As she set out for Yorkshire, she declared firmly to herself that she was pleased the remote location made it highly unlikely she would ever encounter Lord Rayfield again.

CHAPTER FOUR

From the case notebook of Hugh Broderick Brooks, the Earl of Rayfield:

Suspects:
2—*Lord Leyland: Lives at a level of elegancy beyond his means; his deceased wife was from France and he has relatives still there who are Bonapartists; he has property in areas of Luddite activity.*
3—*Reginald Thorne, heir to Lord Sinclair: His father has been in financial distress for some time and is dying of syphilis; he is reputed to be looking for an heiress to wed to repair fortunes, but seems to follow his father's course; he spent time on the continent and has property in one of the Luddite counties.*

Entry dated 3rd of February, 1812. Went to Lady Bristow's. My other primary suspects were both there.

(Decoded by Alphonsius McMasters, PhD, LLC, AKC, OBE, BMW, historian and author of The Secret Wars of Napoleon, *2005.)*

A few days after Hugh's abortive encounter with the Tread-wells, Wescott's informant forwarded another message that had fallen into his hands.

The message, as before, was addressed to M. Mansson and instructed the traitor to organize disaffected workers into more efficient, militant cadres. This information escalated the urgency of Hugh's mission. He worked off his mystification and fury toward Miss Treadwell in renewed zeal over his inquiry.

One cold evening early in February, he dropped into Lady Bristow's gaming hell. The proprietress herself came to welcome him. "Good evening, Drusilla," Hugh greeted the middle-aged woman, glancing around the crowded main drawing room. "You've gathered the cream of London here, as usual."

Lady Bristow gave a self-satisfied glance around the room. "It's nice to see so many people enjoying my little at-home evenings. Of course, I offer only the best food and wine, and I insist upon an easy atmosphere, with everyone encouraged to enjoy themselves just as they please." She smiled at him. "Please help yourself to refreshments and enjoy yourself. There are no seats open, but I believe Lord Wescott mentioned another engagement later this evening, so you could take his place."

Hugh nodded, smiling in confederacy at Lady Bristow, who was one of the few people who knew his secret role. Many of the *ton* came to her exclusive and discreet gaming establishment, which made it the perfect meeting place for the upper echelon of Wescott's organization. Few of the mostly male clientele who frequented Lady Bristow's gaming house had any notion of its dual role, or that of the lady herself as Lord Wescott's long-time mistress and partner.

"I have hired some new musicians." She pointed to a corner of her large salon, where two young, attractive women in low-cut evening gowns were providing entertainment. "I am most eager to hear your opinion of their playing."

The blonde woman in blue played a cello. Her accompanist, on the pianoforte and with a haunting soprano voice, was a dark-haired woman. Her superficial resemblance to Charlotte Treadwell gave him an unpleasant wrench. Drawn despite himself, Hugh drifted in that direction. Several other patrons sat upon settees or upholstered chairs in the area, listening to the music or conversing, Hugh's friend Hollesley among them.

"Sings like an angel, doesn't she?" The Honorable Philip Hollesley was a few years younger than Hugh, heir to a viscountcy, and a noted connoisseur of women.

"You intend to pursue her?"

"Regrettably not. Lady B. made it clear they are ladies fallen upon hard times and for listening only, not touching."

"Rotten luck, old boy." Hugh clapped a hand on Hollesley's shoulder and moved on, uncomfortably reminded of another young lady fallen upon hard times.

He wandered casually into the room where Wescott played whist with three other gentlemen, and noted one of his suspects at the same table. In his forties, lean and hardened, Leyland appeared indolent, but his keen eyes belied the pose.

The players focused on the game, but Lord Wescott looked up briefly and greeted Hugh, adding, "As soon as we've finished this rubber, I must leave. You may sit in if you like."

Hugh agreed and strolled into one of the other rooms, catching sight of another of his suspects, Reginald Thorne, son and heir of Lord Sinclair. Sinclair played at hazard with a group of rowdy young men. Hugh had no wish to join their play, settling his decision to concentrate for the evening on Leyland.

Returning to the whist game, he found Wescott on the point of departing and sat at his place. For the next few hours, he covertly observed Leyland, partnering him through several rubbers. In the main the cards ran against them, but their combined skill minimized their losses. When the game finally broke up, Leyland gave him a wry smile and said, "I prefer to have you on my side, Rayfield."

"It's only a game," Hugh said. "Now, in a more serious matter, I hope we would always be on the same side." He watched the older man closely, but Leyland only laughed as he walked away.

What did Leyland's words mean? Could he refer to Hugh's investigation? The hint that the man knew of his secret role brought him to the forefront of Hugh's suspects. Still, he had so far received no evidence that the man harbored a guilty secret.

Guilty secrets seemed to be the province of Miss Charlotte Treadwell.

At Flash Annie's the morning after his visit to Lady Bristow's, Hugh stared at the Heaper. "Good God, you say she interviewed for a position as governess to the children of a textile mill owner?" Heat rose into his face, and his hands clenched. He should have been able to prevent this development.

"Took the position, too, is what the 'otel maid told me." The Heaper stood holding his cap, looking vaguely guilty, as though he believed he should have been able to avert such action by Miss Treadwell. "'Cording to my men who've been watching 'er, she's packing to leave almost immediately for Yorkshire—outside o' Leeds, it is."

One of his major suspects had found a way to credibly place herself in easy reach of the disaffected population that the English traitor was instructed to incite to revolution. What were the odds of this being merely coincidence?

No, mere chance did not seem likely. His agents had been unable to find any trace of Lord Treadwell, and he had probably fled to France, to direct his daughter from there. Such a course seemed impractical, but now the logic was clear. Who would be less suspicious than an insignificant governess? Her freedom of movement would be somewhat limited, but a clever woman could get around that restriction.

The men watching her had not discovered any sign of communication with her father. But she must be in contact with him. It only remained to catch her in the act, and to obtain proof her father attempted to whip up the stockingers to riot.

He must go himself.

The matter was too important for underlings to handle. Elation fizzed through his blood at the prospect of taking action. He threw off the lethargy that had gripped him since Miss Treadwell entered and left his life so abruptly.

* * *

"I know a great deal about disguises." Hugh paced about Sir Guy Chase's study. "In the ordinary way of things, I would not need advice. But this assignment requires me to befriend someone who has met me in my true identity, and my disguise must be impenetrable." The room was almost jewel-like, with two walls of books in colorful leather bindings, and Oriental carpets in bright shades of red, blue, and gold spilled in profusion over the floor.

Sir Guy said, "The key is to fully imagine your role and then step into it—*become* that person. You do not ever allow yourself to think it is only a role. If you believe you are the person whose disguise you adopt, anyone who meets you will also believe." Sir Guy sat behind his oak desk, light spilling onto him through the French doors and windows flanking them, nearly the entire wall made of glass.

The former actor was a highly placed operative in Wescott's organization. His experience in disappearing into a role on stage made him a sought-after expert on disguise.

"How do I maintain my own powers of observing and reasoning if I become someone else?" Hugh stopped, frowning at the actor.

The white-maned, craggy-faced man stared out at the gardens, spare and nearly colorless in their winter garb. The windows were equally plainly dressed, with linen curtains.

At Wescott's advice, Hugh had revealed no details of his case. Not because Wescott didn't trust Sir Guy, but his policy was to uphold secrecy except for those who needed to know.

Sir Guy glanced briefly at Hugh before turning his attention to his garden again. "It's simple enough. Become a man with your same faculties."

A little girl ran by, accompanied by a nursery maid. She stopped at the doors and waved to him. He returned her wave and the child ran out of sight around the corner of the house.

This must have been what Sir Guy was waiting for, because he then turned all his attention to Hugh. "You build your false character from the inside out. Decide what qualities he must have and how he must look, and then you practice to make him so. It is in your speech, your mannerisms, the way you move your body, everything. You must never fall out of character until the assignment is over. And scents. Make a substantial change in your diet. The foods you eat have a great effect on the basic odor of your body. Use a different soap for shaving and washing. Don't bring any clothing you have worn."

"Surely it isn't necessary to go so far."

"You did say you must fool someone who knows you. Has this person been close enough to touch?"

Hugh pictured his arm around Miss Treadwell, escorting her to the door of Treadwell House, walking to Flash Annie's with her arm in his. Kissing her. "We've been that close."

"You never know what triggers a memory. If your case is important, you mustn't overlook any detail." He pulled several sheets of foolscap in front of him. "Who do you want to be?"

Hugh told him.

They spent the rest of the afternoon going over every detail of accent and facial expressions. Sir Guy rehearsed him in holding and moving his body differently than his usual studied nonchalance, the pose of the indolent, pleasure-seeking aristocrat, which was as false as the new identity he was adopting. They discussed what physical alterations could be made to add to the illusion. Hugh practiced, over and over, until he knew what his character would say and do in every conceivable circumstance.

At last Sir Guy said, "You are as ready as you can be."

Hugh said, "Thank you, sir," and reached to shake his hand, eager to be on his way.

"In character!" the actor said sharply. "You *are* your character from now on."

"We need 'is pay." Mrs. Tait shrugged, her eyes half shamed, half defiant, raised to Charlotte's. "I can't 'elp it."

They both looked out the doorway at the small boy playing in the dirt with his sisters.

"But Petey is so bright, Mrs. Tait. He deserves to be schooled." Charlotte kept her impatience and disappointment well controlled. She would gain nothing by setting Mrs. Tait against her.

Mr. Arnold, a retired schoolteacher who lived in the town of Garwick, had agreed to give lessons to a few of the stockingers' children. But the hours at the mill were too long and the work too tiring to expect the children to be able to attend to lessons after a day's work. Charlotte needed to persuade a few families to allow one of their children to leave the job to accept this bounteous windfall.

Seven-year-old Petey Tait was one of the children singled out as a likely candidate for schooling, if she could but persuade his parents. Defeat and poverty were evident in Mrs. Tait's bowed posture. The other children, a girl of perhaps twelve, another girl a little younger than Petey, played at a game that appeared to use stones and a great deal of ingenuity. The baby in Mrs. Tait's arms stared solemnly up at Charlotte. All the Taits were ragged and grimy, the girls' hair hanging in tangled hanks. The filthy, ill-lit hut seemed too cramped to hold them all and smelled of wool and unwashed bodies.

"Your husband still has not found a job?" Charlotte asked.

"Nay, 'e ain't," Mrs. Tait spoke low and tight. "Lately 'e ain't been lookin'. He's tooken up with them meetin's."

"Has he joined the Luddites, Mrs. Tait?"

The woman's glance slid away. "I dunno."

But Charlotte had caught the fear in the other woman's eyes just before she turned aside. Her heart sank. "You have to persuade him to stop."

Mrs. Tait remained silent, her face shuttered against Charlotte. What could she tell her to enlist her trust? The task of helping those poorer than she had never felt so urgent, nor so hopeless.

She had her half-day off each week, during which she visited the homes of the mill workers to give what aid she could.

She used outdoor excursions with the girls to gather herbs to make remedies for the sick. And she had surreptitious outings late at night or in the pre-dawn, to visit those she had been unable to call on during her free afternoon.

Now she must sneak out from Mill House on another occasion, to find Ben Tait and plead with him to give up his illegal activities, and to let Petey attend school.

A couple of nights later, she at last found Mr. Tait, in the back room at Clegg's Tavern, deep in conversation with several other men. Charlotte recognized some of them from her attempts to help the families of the workers in Goddings' Mill, but there were a couple of strangers among them. Charlotte ignored the other men, focused on reaching Ben Tait with her pleas to give up his Luddite activities. She went straight up to him. "I need to speak to you, Mr. Tait."

He brushed her off. "I'm busy now."

"It's about Petey."

He jumped up. "My boy? 'As something 'appened to 'im?"

"He is fine. Let us speak in private, just for a moment."

They went to a corner of the room, away from the fire and where no other customers sat. The inn seemed all to be drawn in sepia hues: the browns of the wood benches and tables and the earthy tones of the men's clothing, the muted glow of the fire and lanterns hanging from low rafters. Charlotte stood against one rough-hewn wall.

Mr. Tait stood uncomfortably close, giving off odors of musk and ale. Charlotte fought the urge to slide away, to give up the argument before she even began. There was a kind of power in the man, a quiet menace, which made her suddenly fearful. "Mr. Tait, I came to ask you to give up the Luddites, for your family's sake."

"What d'ye know about t'Luddites?" The threat emanating from the man intensified as he bent forward and thrust his face repellingly close.

She felt sweat prickle her neck, and swallowed against the

bile that rose in her throat. "Just what everyone around here knows—that many men have been twisted in, there's marching and threats. I know the anger is justified, but I've seen the results to the families of men who take the law into their own hands. It isn't worth the risk you're taking."

"You'd best stay owt o' things that ain't your business," he grunted, glaring at her.

"This is my business. I've been trying to set up a school for boys like Petey, to give them a better future. You must let him go. I know how angry you must feel, but this doesn't help." Charlotte forced herself to stand as tall as she could and look him in the eye.

"Nothin' 'elps. Last month I went with a bunch o' t'other men to ask Goddings not to put in gig mills and shearing frames, not to take jobs away from t'men. He said they'd already been ordered and nothin' would stop progress. He fired me just because of asking. It's nowt right to take food owt o' people's mouths. Summat 'as to be done." He wiped the back of his neck with a dirty hand. Defeat and pride shone forth in his sad-angry eyes.

A man with nothing left to lose—the most dangerous kind. She understood his anger, but she needed to convince him there was another way before he destroyed his last hope of improvement. "You could find another job."

"Bloody lot you know. Nobody'll 'ire me. Word got out that I'm an 'agitator.' It's gone beyond stoppin', and ye best not carry tales to your boss."

"I'd never do that. But the time will come when you'll be arrested all the same. What will your family do when you're transported or hung?"

"I've said all I'm goin' to say." He turned away and went back to the table.

He spoke a few words to the men sitting with him, and they looked suspiciously at Charlotte. She had had no chance to speak of educating Petey but could do nothing more tonight.

CHAPTER FIVE

Letter from Prudence Whislehurst, Gaylers House, Essex, to Lucius Spencer, London, 25th of February, 1812:

I have to agree with your assessment. I think it must be you, Mr. Spencer. If accident or illness befell me, my situation so far removed from London would make our plan untenable. If I were able to travel to London, Miss Charlotte would rightly expect my sister Rosella to take me in, and would therefore expect I have no need of her. Your nephew's circumstances would make it quite impossible for him to come to your aid. I shall leave it to you to devise the calamity that makes it necessary for her to rush to the rescue. I am certain we shall see her suitably settled yet.

A sharp tap on the schoolroom door preceded the entrance of the servant, Minnie. "Missus Goddings says ye're to come right away," the girl said in a breathless tone.

"Mrs. Goddings knows this is class time with the girls!" Glancing at the girls' smirking faces, Charlotte sighed. Their schooling followed many other concerns in importance to their mother, and the girls knew it.

Furthermore, Charlotte knew from experience that she would have to chase them down after she gave her advice about the colors of the new draperies, or endured an endless tea with Mrs.

Goddings' callers. Charlotte had quickly become the arbiter of taste and indispensable prop to Mrs. Goddings.

"Very well, Minnie, tell her I'll be down as soon as I may." As the door banged shut, Charlotte said, "Adela, continue with your conjugation of French irregular verbs. Enid, you keep writing the alphabet until I return."

"Yes, Miss Treadwell," the girls echoed, but she caught them grinning at each other, and knew they would abandon these occupations the moment she left. *Why do I bother?* At the top of the staircase, she smoothed her hands over the sides of her head, checking for stray tendrils that might have escaped her chignon, and shook out the skirts of her old black bombazine gown before she went down.

When Mrs. Goddings finally released Charlotte, she returned to the schoolroom. As she had expected, the girls had vanished.

Hit by a wave of weariness, Charlotte contemplated leaving the girls to their own devices. Certainly their education was not a high priority with Mrs. Goddings, despite her claim at the first interview. And she could use a rest after her late night excursions in aid of the workers' families, whom Mr. Goddings' dismissal left destitute.

However, Charlotte could not in good conscience give her job anything less than her best effort. She must try to give the girls a good understanding of the world they would inhabit. They would become wives, perhaps not as highly placed in society as their mother hoped, but undoubtedly they would marry men of substance and influence.

She donned her cloak and a stout pair of boots. Outdoors, an icy drizzle greeted her. She pulled the hood of her cloak more closely about her head and trudged to the stables.

To her relief, both girls were there. Seven-year-old Enid played with the litter of kittens born three weeks earlier.

Thirteen-year-old Adela was standing by a groom who curried one of Mr. Goddings' grays. She was standing rather close, in fact. Too close. Charlotte had not seen the man before.

The man was most likely in his late twenties, powerfully built, nearly barrel-chested, with sideburns and curly black hair, a trifle long and shaggy looking. He was not handsome, but there was some magnetism in him that Charlotte felt across the distance between them.

He spoke to Adela, and, as Charlotte watched, took one of the girl's hands, placing the curry in it and, still holding her hand, stroked it over the horse's flank. Adela leaned toward the groom. It appeared that he subtly pulled back, not encouraging her, although Charlotte could not be certain.

A little tension left her. Perhaps she need not fear this man might take advantage of Adela's preternatural coquetry. She dared not count on it, however. At that moment, he looked up and his eyes met Charlotte's. He grinned. As though he had aimed some invisible arrow at her, she felt a punch in her abdomen and her legs went weak.

Danvers, the head coachman, hovered nearby, and Charlotte gave him a questioning glance. "That's Sam, miss. 'E's my sister's nephew."

"Your sister's nephew?"

"That's right. Her 'usband's sister's son. Been a sojer in the Peninsula, wounded and invalided out."

"I see."

"No need to fret, miss, I'll keep my eye on 'im. Never knew any o' Sukey's 'usband's family. Sukey vouches for 'im, but I like to decide for m'self."

"Thank you, Danvers." There was no telling what mischief the headstrong Adela might get up to. What was more disturbing, however, was Charlotte's own reaction to the man. Where did her recent vulnerability come from? She had never had a physical reaction to any man. Now, within a few weeks, two very different men had evoked a similar response in her. First Rayfield, and now this groom, Sam. Both of them wildly inappropriate men for her.

The next morning, the girls seemed out of sorts. The

continuing dreary weather kept them confined to the nursery. Enid had too much energy to submit easily to being thus cooped up, and Adela sulked because the rain thwarted her wish to go riding. Charlotte did not inform the girl she intended to ensure the groom, Sam, would not accompany her on her rides.

Would Charlotte be able to handle Adela as time passed? The girl threatened to become quite a trial. This was the capricious, willful girl's second unsuitable infatuation since Charlotte arrived.

Shortly after Charlotte's arrival, she had caught Adela in an embrace with an under footman. This time, her infatuation posed a greater danger. The footman had been nearly as young as Adela, and no real hazard to her virtue. This groom was a man, frighteningly male in fact, and undoubtedly experienced with women. He had soldiered on the Peninsula, Danvers said. Yes, undoubtedly a man with expertise in seducing a young girl—or even one not so young.

Charlotte wondered if she could arrange for Sam's dismissal from his position.

He had been wounded, Danvers said. Trying to have him dismissed seemed a poor repayment for his service to his country, especially as she had no evidence he imperiled Adela.

She would have to talk with Sam, decide for herself whether he could be trusted. As soon as the day's lessons were over, she intended to seek him out.

Charlotte's plan to speak to Sam was thwarted when Mrs. Goddings called for her after luncheon.

"Miss Treadwell, I desire you to take the girls to Mrs. Roper's this afternoon and buy new frocks for them. I want you to make up a list of t'fabrics to purchase."

"But madam, the girls have lessons this afternoon. And the weather is not conducive to an outing." Irritation at Mrs. God-

dings' caprice and indifference to the girls' education sharpened
her tone.

"I've seen they've grown of late and are comin' owt o' their
clothes. As to t'weather, it is scarce rainin' at all. 'Ave the
girls dress warmly."

Mrs. Goddings could be very stubborn once she took an
idea into her head. Charlotte gave in and sat at the little desk,
pulling a sheet of paper from the drawer. Her employer re-
cited what she wished the girls to have. "And buy a new dress
for yerself, Miss Treadwell."

"I regret I cannot do that."

"You think to shame me before my guests?"

"I have told you that it is not proper for you to include me
when you have callers." She stared Mrs. Goddings down, and
the other woman gave a little chuckle. "I can't win an argument wi'you, can I?"

"You win most of them." Charlotte smiled back.

The Goddingses' extravagant mansion sat on the edge of
Garwick, but the town was small enough that the trek to its
center was quite short.

"It looks like your mother was correct about the weather,"
Charlotte said as she and the girls started out. She turned her
face up to the thin mist that refreshed her skin.

Enid raced ahead.

"I hope Mrs. Roper has the latest fashion plates from London," Adela said. "Last time everything she had was from last
year. I have told Mama over and over that she must take me to
Leeds, but she says I am too young to worry about fashion."

Uneven footsteps sounded behind Charlotte and she
turned. The very man who had been on her mind walked toward them with a lurching gait. His left leg did not bend at
the knee, forcing him to swing the leg out to the side and
around in a half circle at every other step.

"Why are you following us?" she demanded.

"Escorting you and your charges where you're going." His
voice was raspy, his Yorkshire accent muted, probably by his
time away in the army.

She should be glad for the opportunity that meant she would not have to seek him out, but instead she was irritated. She could not warn him off Adela when she was present, and the moment he appeared the girl gravitated to his other side. "Have you no duties you should be about? Sam, is it?"

He nodded acknowledgment of the name. "My duty is the safety of you and the girls." His scent drifted toward her on the wind, horses and leather and sweat, clean and earthy at the same time.

"Oh, for heaven's sake. It's only a step to the dressmaker's. There is no danger."

"Ye must be blind if ye don't see what's goin' on around ye." His voice roughened and his accent became stronger.

Charlotte looked around.

The streets bore more people than one would expect in daytime in an industrial town. The crowd was mostly men, testimony to Mr. Goddings' dismissals when he had installed his new machines. They huddled in doorways or gathered in groups, speaking low-voiced and looking about guardedly. Their faces were lean and sullen. The few women, wrapped in shawls, walked briskly, some with small children held by the hand.

Charlotte called Enid back to her side. She understood the hunger and despair the townspeople felt. But they knew her, knew she was working to help them. No one would lay a hand on her or the girls.

"I know far more than you imagine!" She slowed her pace and turned to look at Sam.

Under his billed cap, his hair was a flat black that gave off no lights even in this mist. It curled wildly against the collar of his jacket, faded navy blue, probably the uniform from his army service. His sideburns and eyebrows were a lighter shade, dark brown. His eyes were narrow, and he had a large scar on his forehead. He shouldn't be the least attractive to her, but her heart was thumping out a staccato beat.

He seemed to notice her gaze, for he reached up and tugged a lock of hair to cover the scar. "What do you mean?"

He gave her a squinty-eyed look that made her back a step warily.

"I mean I am well acquainted with most of these families. I have been bringing them medicines and food almost since I first took this position."

He grunted, still looking hard-eyed at her, as if he could see into her very being. She shivered. "Then you know that a good many of the men are Luddites?" he said softly.

Adela watched intently, and Enid was close enough to hear. Charlotte wished not to alarm them. "We cannot discuss this now." They were at the dressmaker's. Charlotte lifted the knocker. "Thank you for your escort. We are safe enough now."

"I'll wait."

"That's not necessary."

"Nonetheless."

She tightened her lips and pushed the girls ahead of her as Mrs. Roper's maid opened the door. As the maid shut the door behind them, she caught a glimpse of Sam's mocking smile.

The man was too insolent to be a mere groom. Charlotte caught her breath as she suddenly wondered, could Mr. Goddings have hired him as a guard for his daughters, despite his slighting of Charlotte's concerns?

While Mrs. Roper measured the girls, Charlotte's mind flew with speculations. A mere groom, hired as a guard? The man *had* been a soldier. But he was a cripple—how much good would he be if the need arose? Unbidden, the memory came to her of an attack in the mist and Rayfield's speedy dispatch of the footpads. This man was sturdy enough, but surely his ruined leg would impede his ability to fight.

And Mr. Goddings had been so brusque, so overconfident. She had sought him in his office at the mill one afternoon when his wife had taken the girls to call on a friend who had children of the same ages. He suffered the interruption with ill grace. "If you've got complaints about your job, take 'em to Mrs. Goddings. The girls are her affair."

"That isn't why I came. I wished to ask you to hire back the men you laid off when you bought the new machinery."

"Why would I do that? Those machines cost a pretty penny, and I bought them to save on wages. I can't afford to keep on those men. As 'tis, I'll be hurtin' 'til the machinery 'as made up in savings over its cost."

"But there's such poverty and misery in the village. Haven't you seen how your people are suffering?"

"They'll 'ave to look for other jobs, or go on parish relief. If I gave a handout to everyone who asked, I'd be bankrupt. I hire as many as I can afford to pay now, and no more. Stay out of matters that don't concern you. You're hired to teach my girls to be ladies and nothing more."

Charlotte stiffened. "Your family will be affected if the conflict spreads from Nottinghamshire. I understand a mill not far from here was fired last month."

Mr. Goddings asked, "What do you know about this? Are you aware of Luddites in the area?"

"Of course not."

It was not much of a lie. Most of her knowledge of Luddites was mere suspicion and speculation. And she would not betray men whose only concern was feeding their families. She had seen first-hand how those left behind suffered when their men were taken up for breaking the law.

Jamie had done what he did as a lark, but his men had seen only a chance to help out families who had suffered through years of mismanagement of their lands by Charlotte's father.

Mr. Goddings had said, "I've no fear of Luddites here in Garwick. And I canna' hire back any men now." Clearly, he had closed the subject, and she had had no choice but to leave.

The measurements taken, Mrs. Roper looked to Charlotte. She brought forth the list, and she and the dressmaker discussed what to have made for the girls.

By the time they had completed the errand, it was late afternoon and darkness impended. After her gloomy thoughts, she was almost glad that Sam had waited for them. As the girls chattered among themselves on the way, or mostly Adela prattled to Enid about her new clothes, Charlotte took the opportunity to say low-voiced to him, "I must talk to you."

"By all means!" He grinned, his voice matching hers for quietness.

"No, I must see you alone—without the girls, that is."

His grin widened. "Why, miss, I thought you didn't like me!"

"Oh, will you be serious! This is important." A flush climbed up her neck and face, offsetting the twilight winter air.

He sobered. "What did you have in mind?"

"I have Wednesday afternoons off. Will you meet me?"

"I am at your disposal, miss."

Where could they meet? The weather was not conducive to meeting out of doors, but any building, on the mansion grounds or in town, could not provide the privacy she needed, both for the nature of the discussion and for the very fact of the governess meeting with a mere groom. If it were discovered, her reputation would be in shreds. Her need to protect Adela overcame any vacillation about the wisdom of her course.

"It would raise no questions if I accompanied you riding," he suggested, perhaps guessing her dilemma.

"No! That is, the Goddingses have not given me leave to use any of their horses." Charlotte had not ridden since her brother's death and had no intention of ever doing so again.

"There is an abandoned tower on the road to Nethercot. Just off the road, far enough not to be observed." Her heart pounded—fear of the cost of discovery, she told herself.

"Very well." His lips tilted up in a very knowing manner that made her fear he expected a far different purpose for this tryst.

Almost, she changed her mind, but the girls were giving her speculative looks and she said only, "At two o'clock. You can arrange to get away?"

"I'll be there."

CHAPTER SIX

Letter from Lucius Spencer, London, to Prudence Whisle-hurst, Gaylers House, Essex, 16ᵗʰ of March, 1812:

I have written to Miss Charlotte. She is on her way, even as I write this letter. I have already written to Lord Rayfield. Our plan is in motion.

I shall never set out to deceive anyone again, even in a good cause. I am quite persuaded that by usurping God's right to dispose the fates of us all, I have called down His retribution upon my person. I slipped and fell on the marble floor of the entry hall in Lord Scapthurst's townhouse. My ankle broken, I shall be incapacitated for several weeks. I have lost my excellent position with Lord Scapthurst. What is to become of me, my friend, I have no idea, for you know I have no savings. I can only pray that Miss Charlotte will yet become established as we hoped and plotted, for I know she would forgive my scheming and pension me generously, although equally certain she would be most upset to learn how we contrived to arrange her life. Never mind the scold I can hear you already forming. I shall never tell her of our manipulations, and I pray most humbly to the God in whose bad Graces I presently am that she will never learn.

We shall see if our scheme has the results for which we hoped.

* * *

What was Charlotte Treadwell about? Hugh had feared for a moment that she had penetrated his disguise. Although he could not be sure, her behavior toward him revealed no hint she guessed who he was.

Was it possible that she sought an assignation with a groom? He could see her with her hair pulled severely into a knot and her drab, prim gown, and he felt strangely captivated at the thought of unloosing her passion. She must be one of a handful of women in the whole of England who could still look desirable in such a guise. The strong, beautiful bones of her face were accentuated with no finery to soften the lines.

However, seduction seemed contrary to what he knew of her character. Perhaps she believed him a likely recruit to her traitorous cause. He snorted. That would be a fine wrap-up to a business that was taking too long and becoming too desperate.

That night, the Heaper showed up at their set meeting place. " 'Ow's your investigation of Miss Treadwell?" he asked.

"I've learned a great deal. She sneaks out of Goddings' House at times no respectable governess would, meets with the Luddites' families. The other night she met Tait, one of the leaders here, right in Clegg's Tavern, where the Luddites meet almost nightly. Two of the traveling agitators were there."

"You've got 'er!"

"Not yet. I still have no proof. A skilled barrister could make a case that her visits were merely those of a Good Samaritan. She brings the families food and her little herbal concoctions to treat their various complaints. When she met Tait, I saw no sign that any communication passed between her and the agitators. She might have given a message to them through Tait, however. I stayed to watch what the men did after Miss Treadwell left rather than following her, so I cannot rule out the possibility she met with someone else after leaving."

"You still want that meeting you asked me to set up?"

"Yes, I have to know what else is going on. In case she's innocent, I can't afford to let any other leads drop."

"I arranged for tomorrow night at an inn I know. 'Tisn't a pretty place, but it's quiet-like. No one will take note of us, and I'll take an oath the landlord'll keep 'is clapper shut."

The Heaper had not exaggerated the charms of the Cock and Stag. Located in the slums, the building was in dilapidated condition, and upon first entering, Hugh saw at once the place was a thieves' den. Wearing clothing a few steps down in quality from his groom's attire, a disreputable snuff-colored coat he'd obtained from a rag-picker, much-mended breeches and a shapeless cap, he attracted no notice.

He gave the landlord the Heaper's name and was shown to the room his associate bespoke. Symms was already there, and within a few minutes the Heaper and two others arrived.

"Ever'thin's been quiet," the Heaper glumly announced, seconded by nods from the others. "We 'aven't 'eard so much as a peep of any organizing or drilling going on."

"Damnation! There must be something!" Hugh twisted his cap about. "The agent in France sent the message on through channels once he'd copied it for us." He turned to Cropper Kennet. "There's no secret meetings among your co-workers?"

Kennet was a cropper, one of an elite group among the cloth workers, a balding, bandy-legged man in his fifties. The chance to meet Kennet face to face was a benefit of the sojourn in the north. Kennet took a greater risk by working for Hugh than most of his other agents, and could not travel as far as London.

The older man coughed and spat. "Aye, there's always meetings. What there isn't, is anything out o' t'usual." His eyes narrowed. "Why d'you care what the workers is doing? You said you was looking for a French spy."

"I am. If we are to track down the spy, we must work from both ends." Hugh paced about the room. "He—or she—is operating much like I am: not meeting personally with the workers, but sending agents out to agitate and stir them up." If it were Miss Treadwell, she did meet with workers. She still needed agents to carry her activities on in the other areas. "I'm trying to find that connection—the go-betweens—and trace them back to find whom they report to. I need you to let me know when outsiders show up at the meetings and who they are."

"You ain't tryin' to put any o' t'workers' necks in a noose?" Kennet coughed again and glared at Hugh.

"I've told you—my investigation has nothing to do with Luddites themselves. I may need the go-betweens' testimony to convict the traitor, but my investigations will make no difference to your friends. I can't give them immunity from the authorities if they are arrested in the midst of their activities, however, no matter how sympathetic I may be."

"Let him be," said Norris. "Lord Broddie's a man of his word; you can count on that." Norris, the son of the gamekeeper at Rayfield Hall, had served with the army in the Peninsula. Having lost an eye in that service, he had been discharged.

When Hugh happened upon him, he worked for a cent-per-center, helping to persuade reluctant clients to pay back their loans. The muscular young man gladly gave up this employment for a job with Hugh and the promise of help to establish himself respectably when the investigation was over.

The moment of tension passed. "That's that," Hugh said. "Continue as you have. If you discover anything, report to me."

Hugh arrived early at the old tower. He wanted time to set the scene. He spread the old blanket over the dirt floor and placed the jug of cheap wine and two mugs next to it. Even with these efforts, the romantic effect was somewhat lacking. He should have brought candles. Even on a bright day the tower would have been dim. On this afternoon it was murky.

He had done what he could, however. If Miss Treadwell had seduction in mind, he would be ready. The groom, Sam, would have no hesitation in making this a true tryst.

Not that Hugh would actually take advantage of her lapse in good taste. Although thoughts of her in his arms set his heart thumping and heat to spread through his body. However, if such was her purpose, he would find some way to put a damper on things before they progressed too far. He thrust aside the niggling thought that Charlotte—Miss Treadwell— might not be easy for him to resist.

For all he knew, she had decided to make Sam her new charitable project. Now there was a thought to splash cold water on a man's ardor.

Having arranged the scene, Hugh paced the confines of the round room. The wooden door had long ago rotted away, and the windows had never been glazed, but were mere slits, high up, through which the tower's occupants could view others' approach. Remains of the framework for a wooden staircase wound up the inside walls, but not enough remained, even if one wished to risk a climb. There were no floors above him to step onto, in any case. The rock walls were rough, the mortar crumbling between them, leaving still more apertures through which the cold wind of a stormy March day blew. The gusts made a nearly constant, and disturbingly eerie, moaning sound.

Perhaps he should have brought materials to make a fire, although, glancing at the debris-strewn fireplace against one wall, he doubted the condition of the chimney.

He had to remember this wasn't really a seduction scene. They might be chilled just sitting here, but they were not going to shed their clothing. The thought brought an image of Charlotte in her thin night rail, absorbing the news of her father's outrageous wager. The image was disturbingly erotic and, at the same time, a reminder that she was made of very sturdy stuff. She would not be easily overcome if she were the traitor. He smiled in reluctant admiration.

Footsteps crunched through the crushed stone scattered on the ground outside the tower, and then Miss Treadwell's voice called, "Hallooo? Anybody there?"

Hugh strode eagerly to the doorway to greet her.

She was windblown, hatless under the upturned hood of her serviceable gray wool cloak. Her dark brown hair glistened with moisture and tendrils had pulled free from their knot and curled about her face; her cheeks were pink and her eyes bright. On impulse he pulled her into his arms. He was in trouble already.

Her arms came up between them, pushing against his chest. "That's not why I asked you to meet me."

"All right," he said agreeably, backing away. "Then tell me why you did ask me." His breathing came a little hard and fast, and he could still feel her imprint against his body.

"I must talk to you about Adela." She pushed back her hood.

He was caught by the sight of her hair, longing to reach out and stroke it. "Adela?" he said blankly.

"Miss Goddings. I must ask you not to . . . to encourage her . . . her flirtation with you."

"You cannot call her innocent attentions a 'flirtation.' She is but a child."

"I caught that 'innocent child' kissing a footman shortly after I came to work here."

"Ah, no innocent then. However, I assure you she is still safe from me." He put a slight emphasis on "she," and Miss Treadwell's eyes widened. He grinned. "I'm no despoiler of children." *Under any of my guises.*

She sprang back. "Since that is settled, I must go."

He caught her arm. "Don't leave yet." She shook her head, and he added quickly, "It's nasty weather outside. Take a few minutes to get warmed up." Indeed, she was shivering, and he was instantly carried back to another time with her beside him. The images, then and now, overlapped in his mind with doubled force that almost took him to his knees.

Everything about that night seemed real again—Miss Treadwell wearing a different cloak, the rose scent that he could swear he smelled again, her shivering in his arms, *the kiss* . . . Aroused almost beyond bearing, not thinking of who she was, who he needed to be, he drew her into the tower.

When she saw the blanket, she pulled her arm against the

grip of his. "It's all right," he soothed. "I just want you to sit for a few minutes, have a cup of wine to warm you up." He blinked, forcing himself to remember he wasn't the Earl of Rayfield to her, to remember the part he had to play. Forcing himself to cool the desire that pounded in his blood, to remember who she was, or might be.

She folded herself down onto the blanket, but said, "I can't drink wine. I couldn't go back to the girls with it on my breath." She pulled the cloak more tightly around her, another gesture that reminded him of the first night.

"All right, we'll talk for a bit." He lowered himself, remembering to keep his "stiff" leg out straight. He kept the left knee wrapped with a strip of cloth to remind himself not to bend it. He sat, not close enough to touch her, wishing to still her suspicions, needing to keep his mind on his purpose.

"What do you wish to talk about?"

"Anything. Why don't you tell me what you know about Luddites in Garwick?" He turned slightly to face her, bracing an arm against the rough stone wall.

She paled. "Why would you suppose I know anything about Luddites?" A slight tremor in her voice gave away her fear. She was concealing something.

"You claimed you know what is going on in the town."

"I never mentioned Luddites. That was you. I work for Mr. Goddings; people would not tell me of anybody involved in illegal activities. I know much about the hardships people are going through. And I know that there have been no incidents of riot or machine breaking such as have happened other places in the country." She stared defiantly at him, her hands fisted in her lap, and tension evident in the set of her shoulders.

"So you do know about Luddism." He leaned slightly closer. Her chin lifted. "Only what anyone may hear."

"Men usually protect women from knowing about such things."

"I am not accustomed to being protected by a man." Color had come back into her face. "I will have a small bit of wine after all."

"Of course." He turned to pick up the jug, poured a generous amount of the deep red liquid into a cup and handed it to her, and then poured a smaller measure for himself. He bent his right leg, balancing the mug against his bent knee while he rested his weight on his right hand, facing her.

She took a sip, made a face, leaned back against the stone wall. "And you, Sam, you are much too commanding to be a mere soldier. I cannot conceive of your taking orders."

"I took orders all right," he said grimly. "I gave 'em, too. I was made sergeant before I was wounded. I would rather take orders than give them. Too often when I had to give an order, men died. 'Tis a much easier business to be a groom." He drank the bitter wine in one gulp. "And I suppose," he leaned toward her, close enough to make her wonder if he would attempt a kiss, "you think I have ideas above my station?"

He was amused despite his disappointment at how she had evaded his questions and turned the tables on him. And tempted. He desperately wanted to kiss her. Her lips were moist from the wine, her eyes wide with . . . anticipation? fear? He reached out and caressed her cheek with the back of his gloveless hand, knowing his fingers were rough and probably scratched her tender skin. He had deliberately roughened them before coming to Yorkshire. She didn't move. For a long moment. Then she edged away with a little laugh.

"If your ideas have anything to do with me, then yes, they are above your station." Her voice was slightly breathless. "I met you only to protect Adela."

"And your own position as governess. You would not keep your position if Miss Goddings was ruined."

"That, as well," she admitted, rising. "I must go."

He didn't try to hold her this time, but watched as she nearly flew out the door. What was Miss Treadwell hiding? And why did he still want her?

Charlotte dashed away from the tower toward home with almost indecent haste. Until this meeting, she had nearly convinced herself that she had imagined the attraction she felt for a groom. It was one thing for him to show himself so willing to indulge in an intrigue with her, but for her to reciprocate was unthinkable.

Even had she been a more typical governess of merely genteel background, the rigidly hierarchical structure of servants' society would forbid any romance between a governess and a groom. Such a liaison would be nearly as scandalous as one between her and Sam if they had met when she was Miss Treadwell of Queen's Treat.

And yet, she had to admit, she was shockingly vulnerable to his attentions. She still felt quivery, from her skin all the way into her core, from the simple touch to her cheek. The raspy feel of his fingers lingered. She reached up to rub her cheek. Had she stayed in the old tower another few moments, she would probably have been in his arms.

She would have to avoid him in the future. He had denied any intent to take advantage of Adela, his protests sounding sincere. And Danvers had said he would keep an eye on him. Yes, there would be no risk to Adela if she stayed away from the stable in the future, and all too much risk to her if she allowed herself to venture there.

She let herself into the kitchen of the Goddingses' house. Mrs. Lawliss spared a glance from beating her cake batter and said, "A letter come for you while you were gone, dearie."

Charlotte found the butler to collect her mail. She recognized Spencer's elegant script, but it looked as if his hand had been unsteady. A chill settled in her as she broke the seal and unfolded the page. "Oh, no!"

She rushed into Mrs. Goddings' sitting room. "Ma'am, I have to go to London immediately."

Mrs. Goddings gave her an eager glance over her tatting. "'Ave you news of your father?" She had been most interested in the viscount from the beginning.

"No, it's my old butler. He has broken his ankle and is in desperate circumstances."

"I trust ye will not give up such an excellent post as this for the sake of an old servant." A chill invaded her voice.

"I hope it won't be necessary for me to give up my position here. I will be absent but a few weeks." Charlotte smiled at her employer, but Mrs. Goddings' face remained stiff.

"I have my girls' education to think of. And it does not speak to their governess's dedication for her to desert them for so slight a cause."

Her daughters' education had never been a priority before. "This is hardly a slight cause. Mr. Spencer was more of a father to me than my own father. I cannot leave him to suffer this calamity alone. If it causes me to lose my post, I am extremely sorry."

"Then I suggest you pack your belongings, Miss Treadwell." Mrs. Goddings returned her interest to the work in her hands, dismissing any further interest in Charlotte.

Once again, seemingly in the blink of an eye, Charlotte had to face the total annihilation of her life and the uncertainty of the future. For a mad moment she thought of retracting her words, saying she would stay. But she could not. In all of her life so far, Spencer and Mrs. Whislehurst had provided her with the only stability she had known, and she could not let Spencer down in his time of desperate need.

She packed, holding back her tears. She refused to allow the despair that threatened to swallow her. She would face down this challenge, as she had all the others that came her way.

She wrote to Spencer, informing him she was on her way. With the speed of the mail coach, it would arrive before her.

Later that evening, she spoke to Mrs. Lawliss, choked with emotion. "I'll write. I want to hear about Mr. Arnold and his school for those few children who can be spared from work."

Mrs. Lawliss hugged her, then wiped her face on her apron. "Ye'll be missed. Ye've made a difference for many a soul."

"Sometime I'll be able to help the families here again. It may be a long while, I'm afraid." She gave a little laugh. "I'm not even certain how I may provide for myself."

"Indeed, miss, ye don't worry about a thing. Ye mus' take care of ye'rself."

"I must ask a great favor, I fear. May I leave my trunk here? This inn where Spencer is staying doesn't sound very salubrious. I believe I must wait until I am fixed in a better place and send for it. But I would not wish to cause you trouble with Mrs. Goddings."

"'Tis no worry. I'll keep it for ye until ye can send for it."

CHAPTER SEVEN

The riverside inn where Spencer had fetched up was far worse than Flash Annie's house. When she stepped inside, the filth and the rank smell stopped her cold for a moment. One could not see if the floor were made of dirt or wood for the spilled food and drink. The tables were in equally repulsive condition. The place was packed with unwashed bodies of both sexes, all in various stages of advanced drunkenness. The whole was overlaid with the odors of sweat, ale, gin, spoiled food, some rotting product of the river, and smoke from cheap tobacco.

She had no choice. This was the place Spencer had given as his residence in the letter. She made her way to the barkeep to ask about her servant. The eyes of the denizens following her as she fought her way through made her skin feel unclean. She controlled her tremors, expecting to be assaulted at any moment. She must get Spencer out of here.

"What d'ya want w' 'im? An old man and a cripple besides. You'd do much better w' me," the barkeep leered at her.

Thank God, Spencer was here at least. "No, I'm afraid no one else will serve," she said, hoping to strike the right note of firmness without giving insult.

"If you're sure, 'e's up the stairs in back, second door on the right. Be sure to get the right door or you may get a surprise, fine lady like you!"

"Thank you," Charlotte essayed a smile and moved toward

the stairway. A large body rose up and blocked her way. He made a grab for her, and she screamed.

"None o' that!" The barkeep raised a stout truncheon, threatening Charlotte's attacker. "Leave 'er alone, ya hear?"

Charlotte did not know how the barman progressed from a would-be seducer to a champion, but she shot him a grateful glance before continuing on her way.

The stairway was as dilapidated and choked with debris as the taproom. It swayed frighteningly as she trod the steps.

Finally at the door to Spencer's room, she knocked. A weak voice told her to enter.

Her first sight of Spencer brought tears to her eyes. He lay upon a bare mattress with only a thin blanket over him—filthy and no doubt lice-infested. His white hair stood out like a mad halo, his face was pale, and he looked ten years older than when she had left him.

"Miss Charlotte, you shouldn't have come." His voice was hoarse and whispery, difficult to hear. "When I wrote you I hadn't seen this place yet. I was staying at another lodging, one that was respectable, but I couldn't afford it for all the weeks I was going to be laid up. Someone suggested this place as being reasonable cost, so I wrote to you. If I had come here first, I would never have disturbed you."

"I would never have forgiven you if you had not," she said sternly. "Now that I am here we will see about finding a better place for you to rest and get well."

"I can't afford anything better."

"You must not worry, Spencer. I still have money put by."

"I won't take your money," he insisted stubbornly.

"Then we have a problem, do we not? I don't believe I'm safe here, but I won't leave you. You shall either come with me or we will both stay and risk whatever happens."

"Very well, you win." His voice sounded weak, and tears began to silently pour down his face, smiting her. Almost she recanted. But it was for his own good. He could not heal in such surroundings, and she did not think she could bear to stay.

Before she arranged to have him moved, however, he badly

needed strengthening. She doubted anyone had taken care of him, seeing that he ate, cleaning him or his room. He had a several-day growth of grizzled beard. And from the smell, the bedpan had not been emptied in some time.

Two hours later, Spencer had reluctantly swallowed a bowl of greasy soup and some bread, and, with the help of a slatternly maid, Charlotte had managed to get him relatively clean. She left him to nap while she sought better quarters. She wasted just a moment to wish she had help. Rayfield's image came to her—the efficient way he had bested the footpads, the sense of safety she had felt with him beside her.

Even Sam, with his air of rough confidence, would be welcome. But she had no one, and instead of being protected, she had Spencer to care for.

As soon as she got to the bottom of the stairs, she saw Flea. "What are you doing here?" she asked in shock.

"I could ask the same thing." He cast a look of supreme disgust at her. "This be no place for a lady like you."

Behind him, two hulking, menacing figures closed in on her.

Hugh arrived at his townhouse, mud-spattered and tired, after pushing himself and a series of rented horses in one long ride from Yorkshire. Miss Treadwell's flight had caught him by surprise. He had been gone two days from the Goddingses', checking with some of his agents, and returned to find her gone.

"She got a message, said it was from her old butler," Danvers told him.

Hugh tracked her south, seeing that she also had pressed hard on the journey, as much as one could traveling by public conveyance. He arrived in London only a few hours behind her. Finding her in the city would be a challenge, but he would put his men to the task and eventually turn her up.

Hamnet Williams met him with a letter. "I was about to send for you. Miss Treadwell's former butler wrote to you,

and I thought you might wish to tend to this matter yourself."
He handed Hugh a letter.

Hugh took it and as he began to read, Williams said, "The letter states that Spencer broke his ankle and asks your help."

"My help with what?" Hugh stared at the paper as if he could absorb Williams' words through it, the actual words on the page wavering as he listened.

"Due to his injury, he lost his post and is destitute. He is staying at a inn near the docks, called, er, your pardon, my lord—" He took back the letter. "Yes, here it is, 'The Blue Ruin.'" He handed the letter over again and smiled, his young, nearly beardless face as open as if he had never harbored a secret.

Hugh hastily scanned the letter. "Is his injury real?"

"As nearly as I can tell. He certainly lost his post, and has been immured in that inn for at least a week. Appalling place, by the way, shouldn't think anyone would stay by choice."

Hugh walked into his study and sat at his desk, where he stared again at the letter. "I see he doesn't specify what he wants from me. Have you any idea what it might be?"

"Rescue?" Williams stood at the other side of the desk and raised his eyebrows, conveying surprise at Hugh's denseness.

Hugh swiped a hand through his shaggy hair, getting a harsh reminder of the disguise he still wore. "Why me? I've seen him but once since the night Treadwell gambled for Miss Treadwell."

He still did not understand Miss Treadwell's puzzling behavior. Was this part of some new plot, as he had first suspected? Had Miss Treadwell even discovered the true identity of Sam, just as he once theorized Treadwell had caught on to Hugh's harboring suspicions of him and fled? It seemed a message *had* come from Spencer, however, and precipitated her sudden trip south. The question remained whether Spencer's accident was genuine. And, a second question: was Miss Treadwell's only purpose to help her former servant?

"I took the liberty of sending Flea to the inn to keep an eye on matters," Williams said.

"Good God, you sent the boy to some low den?"

"Flea is remarkably adept at surviving such places, my lord. I sent a couple of your sturdiest men there as well."

"Yes, of course. The main problem with the boy is that both Spencer and Miss Treadwell know him by sight."

"I supposed that since Spencer wrote to you, you would not find it necessary to conceal your interest in them."

"Very well," Hugh said, rising again. "I am tempted to leave Miss Treadwell to solve her own difficulties. But I shall have Bracegirdle bring back the Earl of Rayfield, in case I do decide to call upon them at the, er, Blue Ruin. Miss Treadwell might have never realized who Sam the groom really was. Becoming Rayfield will take a little time, and give me a chance to decide what to do about this new problem."

"Actually, sir," Williams' face was covered with a sheen of sweat, and he hesitated before completing his sentence, "they are already here."

"Who?" Hugh frowned.

"Miss Treadwell and Spencer, my lord."

"They are *here*? At Rayfield House. *Here*?" His voice rose as he spoke and he felt the blood rush to his head.

"It was beginning to appear impossible to keep them safe at the Blue Ruin," Williams placated. "You were not available to consult, and I acted as seemed best."

"Quite right, Williams. I concede the point. Did Miss Treadwell actually agree to this plan?"

"Not exactly, my lord." He pinched his lips shut.

"What 'exactly' did she say?"

"I believe your men never actually gave her a chance to say much. They just sort of scooped her up along with Mr. Spencer and brought them here."

"Good God, you mean they kidnapped her! I shall expect to have charges laid against me!" Hugh angrily strode around his study, his fatigue dissipated.

"I believe Flea explained that the men were yours, sir, and that she was in no danger. I also have spoken to her since she came. And Mr. Spencer was very willing to leave his current place of residence and come here."

"She can't stay here!"

"Yes, sir. I have taken the liberty to write Lady Adair."

"So, on top of all else, I shall have Sylvia descending upon me at any time?"

"That is most likely the case."

"You have taken a remarkable lot of liberties, it seems."

"I realize it, sir. I regret doing so."

"Rayfield will have to face everybody, not Sam. Help me get to my chambers without being discovered. Where is Miss Treadwell now?"

"She is resting in the chamber I assigned to her."

"And that is . . . ?"

"The blue room, sir."

In the other wing from his suite of rooms, at least. "Check that she is there and keep her in place until I am restored."

"I should also tell you, sir, that while you were gone, Treadwell House came up for auction and I purchased it. I and some of the men have gone over the whole pile and found nothing incriminating."

"That's of a piece with the rest of this mess. Now I'll have to find a way to dispose of it again. But that will have to wait until the inquiry is wrapped up."

By the time Bracegirdle had returned Hugh's hair to its normal color and trimmed it, shaved the sideburns and repaired most of the ravages of the harder life he had to live as Sam, his sister had arrived. She and Miss Treadwell had met in the gold drawing room, and by the appearance of their two faces set in dislike and distress when Hugh walked in, their encounter was not going well. He concealed the sinking feeling this gave him and said, cheerily, "I see you two have become acquainted."

Sylvia rushed to him. "Hugh, explain what is going on!"

"Has Miss Treadwell not put you in the picture?" he equivocated, hoping for a clue to what Sylvia had been told.

"She says she was forced to come here against her will."

"Sylvia, I believe you will find that, although Miss Treadwell is justifiably upset, the situation is by no means as dire as that."

"They picked me up and carried me to your carriage! I certainly never gave permission for that!" Miss Treadwell's voice rang with her sense of ill-usage, and she glared at him. She looked much like a spitting kitten. And he was far too tempted to stroke and soothe her. He must maintain his objectivity until he understood what would lead her to leave her position and rush to Town for an old servant.

"I believe your servant expressed a wish to be brought to Rayfield House? The way I heard it, you refused to be parted from him, and in the meanwhile the outlook at the, ah, Blue Ruin, was it? was becoming increasingly untenable. Perhaps my men should have left you there to be raped or worse?"

Sylvia gasped and Miss Treadwell flushed. Ignoring Sylvia, Hugh stared Miss Treadwell down, and she looked away, but he caught the tears glistening in her eyes and felt a measure of guilt for bullying her. God, he wanted to wrap her in his arms and promise nothing would ever hurt her again. What was wrong with him?

Sylvia ventured, "What is worse than being raped?"

"Being sold to a brothel, kept there against your will, drugged and forced to, er, 'service' any customer who happens along, until your will is destroyed and you believe you belong in such a place." He kept his gaze on Miss Treadwell, and she flinched at every word as if it were a blow.

"Is that—is that really what would have happened to her?"

"Very likely. The Blue Ruin is not the safest place for a gently born female."

"I was on the point of arranging for Spencer to be removed to better quarters." Miss Treadwell's voice was sulky and defiant.

"I beg pardon for correcting you, Miss Treadwell, but you would not have been allowed to leave."

"By your men?"

"No, by the denizens of the inn. One of them, a man who goes by the sobriquet of One-Eyed Bully, has quite a reputation for kidnapping young girls who come to Town to be servants and selling them to brothels. There were a number of similarly unsavory characters in the place. You looked like fair game to them, coming in unaccompanied, and with only a crippled old man as your companion."

"How do you know any of this? You weren't there, or at least that is what was told to me."

"I wasn't. I have talked to my men who were, however. I wanted to know exactly what had happened before I spoke to you."

"She cannot remain at your house unchaperoned. She must come to me," Sylvia said.

"That is why Mr. Williams asked for you, Sylvia. I would be most grateful if you could take Miss Treadwell in."

"I won't be a burden to anybody. I will find rooms someplace." Charlotte's thin supply of courage was evaporating. Her determination to stand on her own had suffered numerous blows, topped by the worst day she had ever experienced.

Hugh said, "You will have difficulty being admitted at any respectable hotel or other establishment, with no maid accompanying you."

"Why are you doing this to me?" She was on the verge of breaking down in tears and her voice quavered, sounding weak instead of resolute.

Lady Adair moved forward and took Charlotte's arm. "Come, Miss Treadwell. You need a good meal and a rest. Once you are restored to your usual spirits, we can discuss what is best for you to do." Her voice was soothing, gentle, and suddenly Charlotte had no will to fight any more.

"What about Spencer?"

"I will see that a surgeon examines him and that he has the care he needs, Miss Treadwell." Rayfield was all smooth and gracious also, now that it appeared he had won.

"Shall I be able to see Spencer tomorrow?"

"Certainly, you may come back, with a chaperone." Rayfield answered.

"I expect to see you as well, Hugh," Sylvia said. "I am not certain I understand what is happening here."

"I will call on you tomorrow," he said.

Lady Adair was right. Charlotte was too tired to fight any longer. Tomorrow, after she had rested and figured out what to do, she would talk to Spencer and persuade him to leave with her. It was her responsibility to care for him, and she could not allow herself to be beholden to the earl.

Charlotte waited in Lady Adair's drawing room the following afternoon for Rayfield to call and convey her to visit Spencer. Lady Adair had assigned a young chambermaid to chaperone, who waited with her.

Charlotte's more disagreeable companions were her thoughts of the conversation that morning with Lady Adair. Was she selfish to wish to remove Spencer from Rayfield's house and care for him herself? Lady Adair simply didn't understand Charlotte's need to escape from the dangerous attraction Rayfield posed.

He arrived promptly at four.

"How is Spencer?" she asked immediately upon his being shown into Lady Adair's drawing room.

"We can discuss him on the way there," he said.

"Is something wrong?"

"Indeed, no. We may sit and talk about Spencer all you like. I presumed you would prefer to see him as soon as possible. I left my horses standing upon the doorstep."

"Of course. I am most anxious to see him." Charlotte rose, subtly put in the wrong. She had her cloak ready, and the three of them went immediately to Rayfield's carriage. During the short drive to his townhouse, she asked, "What did the surgeon say about Spencer? How did he rest over the night? Will he be all right?"

"Miss Treadwell, I could answer, but you will wish to ask Spencer these same questions again. As to the surgeon, I was sure you would wish to speak with him yourself and I have asked him to come at five. I can say that Spencer survived the night and seems in relatively good spirits."

"Forgive me, my lord. I confess I am in considerable anxiety about him, and therefore undoubtedly too impatient. Thank you for your consideration in asking the surgeon to see me." She lapsed into silence, looking out the carriage window, although she could feel Rayfield's scrutiny. She felt awkward and prickly in his presence.

And no wonder. How should she feel in company of someone so deeply involved in an illegal enterprise? One, moreover, who believed he had some claim upon her person. She could not forget that humiliating night when Papa had wagered her away to Rayfield. Undoubtedly it rankled with him that the bet had not truly been paid.

Charlotte had to admit that from his standpoint he had good cause. Not only had her father made the bet, she had agreed, implying that she would have no scruples about offering herself if he won. She blushed, thinking of her bold words to him. She would never have said them had she not believed her father planned to rescue her. But she had realized when her father bolted that her rescue was never in his plans at all.

She glanced up to see Rayfield's knowing gaze on her. "We are here," he said, and she looked out the window to see his townhouse again, one of the largest in an elegant row of houses meant for the *ton* when they stayed in town.

Inside, as she started up the stairs to Spencer's chamber, she turned to Lady Adair's maid, who trod right behind her, and said, "I don't need a chaperone to see my servant. Go occupy yourself elsewhere while I visit him."

"But where am I to go, miss?"

Rayfield nodded at a servant standing by, who stepped forward and said, "I'll take you to the housekeeper."

Spencer looked much improved from the previous day. Seeing him washed, shaved, rested, his spirits restored, Charlotte was optimistic for the first time since she had received his letter.

She met with an instant check, however, when she suggested he leave Rayfield's townhouse and stay with her in some more modest place. "No, Miss Charlotte, I won't leave." His mouth set mulishly.

"You cannot like to be beholden to Lord Rayfield." Charlotte stood next to Spencer's bed.

He looked at his surroundings and then stared at her. The room was not large or luxurious, most likely a chamber for a less important guest, a companion or poor relation. But it was clean and bright, with white gauzy curtains at the window and soft carpets covering the floor; the bed was comfortable-looking, with a white linen counterpane and extra pillows supporting his broken ankle.

"I know I cannot afford lodgings such as this. But I would take good care of you, Spencer." Charlotte was almost crying with frustration and the need to get away from Rayfield and Lady Adair.

"It isn't fit that you should do so, Miss Charlotte."

"Of course it is. You cared for me for many years."

"That's the way it's supposed to be. I regret writing you that letter. You shouldn't disturb your life for me."

"But you did write the letter." Charlotte stamped, wanting to shake some sense into Spencer. "I shall have to pay Rayfield for your care if you stay here. And I do not see how I can do so. If I am not to care for you, I shall have to find a new position. I may have to leave London again, and I shall not be able to visit you in that case."

His eyes reflected panic, and his voice trembled as he said, "Miss Charlotte, it would mean much to see you as often as I may." He could not know what he asked, for it almost seemed he wished to throw her in the earl's path.

Spencer couldn't see, wouldn't cooperate, and how could she ask it of him? He was visibly tiring. Giving up, she sat in the chair set close to his bed and just talked with him until one of Rayfield's maids came to tell her the surgeon was here. "I'll come back tomorrow," she said, rising and kissing his forehead. He blushed.

The surgeon presented her with another setback. "It's a serious break," the man said. "You must understand, he is elderly, and their bones do not heal as quickly or as well. It's likely that Mr. Spencer will never be able to put his weight on the ankle for very long and thus will find it impossible to carry out his duties as a butler."

CHAPTER EIGHT

From the case notebook of Hugh Broderick Brooks, the Earl of Rayfield:

Entry dated the 19ᵗʰ of March, 1812:
Although inclined to believe Miss Treadwell innocent based on her recent behavior, I placed an agent of Wescott's at Adair House as soon as Miss Treadwell agreed to stay and participate in the Season. The agent, a woman named Condon, is an accomplished lady's maid. She is to serve as Miss Treadwell's maid and chaperone wherever she goes in the daytime to discover if Miss Treadwell has any contact among the Luddite organizers. Between Condon and my attendance upon her social events, her activities will be covered.

I continue to investigate my other suspects.

(Decoded by Alphonsius McMasters, PhD, LLC, AKC, OBE, BMW, historian and author of The Secret Wars of Napoleon, *2005.)*

Hugh waited in an adjoining room until the surgeon left, and then walked in.

Miss Treadwell sat in an upholstered chair, alone in his formal drawing room. Her posture, bowed over and with her hands over her face, must have been drilled out of her in every possible circumstance by her nursery maids and governesses, if her childhood attendants were like any of which he had ever heard. This situation clearly defeated all her training, and a stab of pity ran through him.

On his entrance, she glanced up and he saw moisture in her eyes, before she pulled herself erect and crisply collected. "Where is the maid Lady Adair sent to chaperone us?"

"She is still with my housekeeper. I will call for her soon. I wished to speak to you without her present first."

Miss Treadwell frowned and stiffened even more, but he hurried to say, "I believed you would prefer not to have an audience for the conversation we need to have now."

"I have nothing to say to you that anyone may not hear."

"That may be true, but I have a request to make of you, which I would prefer the maid not hear. Please do not speak of how we met to my sister, or anyone else."

"You expect me to lie?"

"You shouldn't need to lie. I told Sylvia we met through your father, which is the truth—just not the entire truth."

"I do not like to practice such a deception." She still frowned, her manner not having softened one bit.

"It is necessary." He paced about the room to still some of his frustration at Miss Treadwell's lack of cooperation.

"I don't see why."

He stopped and stared at her. "My God, Miss Treadwell! I know you've lived somewhat separate from society, but I would think you've at least been taught . . . ?" She stared at him blankly, and he finished, "If word got out about the wager and the details of that night, we would be forced to marry. I presume from your actions, that evening and since, that you are no more inclined for that result than I am."

"That is ridiculous. I would refuse. I cannot be forced into marriage against my will."

"Your situation if you refused would be far worse than it is now—hopelessly so." He stopped in front of her, studied the face that still appeared uncomprehending. "Miss Treadwell,

I dislike having to state facts so bluntly, but if you did not marry me, it would be presumed that I was the one who refused and that I did so because of certain knowledge of your character and, er, experience."

He stopped to gauge whether she understood, and the high color on her cheeks indicated she did. "Every door would be closed to you, no man would marry you, and you would find it impossible to find a respectable position so as to earn a living. I assume from your having gone out as a governess that you have no income—no inheritance from your mother?"

She shook her head, not explaining, and Hugh thought the situation needed no explanation. Her father had run through everything. He wasted a moment wishing he had Treadwell at hand once more and could punish him as he deserved for his notion of what constituted planning his daughter's future. What a mess!

"Listen, Miss Treadwell, Sylvia will soon offer to sponsor you for the Season, if she has not yet done so."

"How do you know this? She was not at all happy at having to take me to her house."

"I spoke with her this morning and brought her to see the advisability of doing so." Once he had pointed out the necessity of marrying Miss Treadwell himself if Sylvia did not agree with his plan. She obviously had her own plans for his future that did not accord with such an outcome.

He continued, "And, Sylvia's character has a quality of enthusiasm. Once decided upon the aptness of a course, she throws herself into it unreservedly. You need not fear she will be reluctant. As for you, I beg you will consider the advantages. If you can find a husband, you will be comfortable and you can see that Spencer is made so also."

"What you wish for me seems a cold-blooded arrangement."

"Not cold-blooded. Practical. That is the case with most marriages, I believe. Will you consider it?"

"I must, if I cannot find another way to care for Spencer."

"Good. I will call for your maid now. You may return at any time, with a chaperone, to visit Spencer." He was satisfied that his words had planted the seed. She would come around to see the necessity. If not the traitor, she was an unneeded complication in his investigation, and Sylvia would see her settled. To still the small doubt he yet harbored, he intended to place an agent within the household to keep an eye on her.

Lady Adair held two cards of invitation in her hand. "Should we attend Lady Duchesne's rout party tomorrow night, or the Throckmortons' musicale?" It was early in the Season—too early for the number of events Lady Adair assured Charlotte every evening offered once the Season was in full swing. Still, other invitations were spread out on the desk before her, sorted out by date and the desirability of each.

"Oh, the Duchesnes', without a doubt," said the Duchess of Moorewood. "They have two eligible sons. Lord Gilbert is especially popular and gathers most of the young men about him."

The duchess, a friend of Lady Adair, had called with her younger sister, Miss Astraea Vernon. Both were fair beauties. The duchess was of an age with Lady Adair, while Miss Vernon was no more than eighteen and making her debut.

Amongst so much beauty, Charlotte felt out of place and wished she could sink into the background. Ever since she had been virtually bullied into accepting Lady Adair's sponsorship for the Season, she had been too much the subject of attention.

She must have a wardrobe to carry through the multitude of events the Season was expected to produce, and her protests against such expenditure on her behalf were ruthlessly brushed aside. After the gowns were ordered, Lady Adair rushed her about shopping for hats, shoes, gloves, and other necessities to accompany the gowns that Madame Charicot was creating for her.

Then she must be introduced to a never-ending succession of Lady Adair's friends and acquaintances as they arrived in Town.

Now she was the focus of strategic plans between Lady Adair and her friend the duchess to place Charlotte in the path of a man who would overlook her lack of fortune and offer marriage.

"The Throckmortons will be most likely to have an older crowd, and very few unattached men. Goodness, all this tactical planning is exhausting. It reminds me of Harriet this past Season. That all turned out well, but it was an anxious time." The Duchess of Moorewood rolled her eyes in illustration of her difficulties. "We expect a very different outcome for Astraea. She has always been accounted the beauty of the family."

"Tell me," she continued, "are we to expect an announcement concerning Miss Treadwell and Rayfield?"

"Nothing of the kind!" Lady Adair replied. "Of course, we are all very fond of Miss Treadwell, but Hugh shows no sign of wanting to give up his present life. I quite despair of him."

Charlotte gained an impression that the information no match was contemplated between herself and Rayfield came as a relief to the duchess. Did she have hopes of attaching him for her younger sister? The two older women finished deciding which invitations to accept in the coming days.

"I will have several parties this Season. There will be Astraea's coming-out ball. I thought as well a picnic excursion to Richmond, after the weather improves. Perhaps a breakfast, a few supper parties after the opera or a play. And you must hold a ball for Miss Treadwell." The duchess beamed at Charlotte.

"Yes, I plan to give a ball. I wished to consult you as to the best date. You are always informed about other hostesses' intentions." Lady Adair stood up and stretched. "Now I think it time we all had some tea. It has been a busy morning."

Charlotte's misgivings about a London Season only grew with time, but she could not withdraw from her commitment. She had no recourse but to cooperate fully in the scheme to attach a husband who could afford to repay Rayfield and Lady Adair for their expenses on her behalf and to pension Spencer.

Over tea, Lady Adair and the duchess drew apart. Miss

Vernon and Charlotte sat in a cushioned enclosure in the bow window of Lady Adair's sitting room.

Charlotte's small store of confidence was undermined by Miss Vernon's radiant beauty. The younger girl seemed to suffer from no diffidence, opening the conversation as though she had known Charlotte for years.

"Pallas talks of our sister Harriet as though she were someone to be ashamed of," said Miss Vernon. "It is no such thing. Indeed, I envy her—she is the only one of us who has made a love match. But even Harriet and her Beldon were not in love when they became betrothed. He took her to India for their honeymoon, did you know? They have been there more than six months. So romantic! I shall marry for love, or not at all."

"That is an admirable goal," Charlotte agreed. From the conversation so far, she gathered Astraea Vernon was the youngest of several sisters, all of whom were accredited beauties, with the possible exception of Harriet, about whom the two sisters seemed to disagree.

"Station and fortune are all my family seems to consider of any worth. Now that Pallas has presented her husband with two sons, they go their separate ways. Yet everyone considers she made the best match, because her husband's a duke." Miss Vernon curled her feet under her in a pose that should have looked graceless but only added to her unstudied charm.

"Iphigenia is the only one who did not marry a lord, although Clytie's is just an honorary one, since Lord Robert is a younger son. My family seems to regard that as an advantage, though, because he is an MP and Clytie is a noted political hostess. Genie's husband is as rich as Croesus, which makes up for not having a title. But he's old. He spent years making his fortune before he went looking for a wife. I can't imagine marrying a man who is so much older than oneself, can you?" Miss Vernon looked at Charlotte beseechingly.

A stray sunbeam meandered through the window and struck a halo of light off the younger girl's golden hair, dazzling Charlotte. "I don't think age is as important as other qualities," she hedged.

If the Duchess of Moorewood entertained hopes for a match between Miss Vernon and Rayfield, as she suspected, there was some disparity in their age. Charlotte did not know his exact age, but assumed he was nearly thirty, hardly so much of a difference to prove an impediment.

The thought upset her more than she would have foreseen, since she knew neither of the parties enough to hazard a guess as to their compatibility. "I believe love is the most important reason for two people to marry. You have a perfect right to refuse to marry for any other purpose," she advised. "I think you will know when you meet the right man."

"I hope so," said Miss Vernon wistfully. "Harriet took two Seasons to find a husband. I plan to enjoy my first and not even think about making a match."

Charlotte felt a momentary pang of envy. She had no such luxury. If she did not find a husband in the next few weeks, she must take another position as a governess or companion and give up all hope of marrying, and all hope of squaring her accounts with Rayfield and Lady Adair as well.

Lady Adair had thrust fifty guineas upon Charlotte for "pin money," to buy any little frivolities she must have. Charlotte was embarrassed to take the money, but the older woman insisted in her usual overwhelming fashion that made it impossible for Charlotte to refuse. Certain she could never spend more than a tenth of the money, Charlotte only awaited a time she could meet with Spencer. Lady Adair had kept her too busy for the past week to have time to see him.

She would ask him to arrange for his nephew, Jehiel, to come to London for a visit, so she could give most of the fifty guineas to him for the impoverished families at Queen's Treat and Goddings' Mill. He had carried out such commissions for her before, although traveling north to Garwich would be a new charge upon him. She was determined not to forget those families, perhaps even more needy than the ones at her old home.

She resolved not to feel guilty for the money and effort Lady Adair was expending, or to worry that some of the money came from Rayfield. Whatever his motives for convincing her to undergo this Season, he seemed to have fulfilled his part. He had not called upon her or Lady Adair since she agreed to his scheme. When she made her visits to Spencer in the first days before Lady Adair had filled her schedule, Rayfield was never at home, making unnecessary the chaperonage of the maid, Condon, who had been assigned to tend to her needs.

Charlotte tried to subdue her disappointment over his absence. She reminded herself that he was a criminal and a man who lived for the same sort of risks that had proved her brother's and father's undoing. A man she could never consider as a possible match for her, even did he give evidence of any partiality for her. A man who made her feel all too alive and sensitized to his presence.

She could not entirely overcome her disagreeable sense of being in his debt. In contrast she regarded her obligation to Lady Adair as a more mutual sharing.

Lady Adair clearly enjoyed the challenge of sponsoring Charlotte in society. She marshaled her forces and planned her campaign with all the strategy of a seasoned general, and would not admit any possibility of defeat in attaining her objective.

Charlotte admired how Lady Adair's enthusiasms swept the lady, along with anyone in her compass. She still could not figure out how the baron's wife converted everyone to her plans. She never ordered or badgered, but gave the impression of good-natured indolence, and of not stirring herself to anything beyond her own enjoyment. Yet somehow she left in her wake hordes of people feverishly rushing to do her bidding.

Charlotte herself felt rather as if she had been rolled over by a juggernaut and left stunned and gasping. With Lady Adair, it seemed, one could only follow along. Not so different, after all, from the lady's brother.

For so early in the Season, the Duchesnes' party was a most satisfying crush. Charlotte tried not to allow panic to paralyze her as she stood waiting to be announced, with Lord and Lady Adair and the Earl of Rayfield.

That he had not after all washed his hands of her came as a surprise. He appeared at the Adairs' as they were leaving for the rout party, and Lady Adair looked somewhat taken aback. "Why, Hugh, I had no idea you would be joining us," she said.

"You did write a note letting me know of your plans, didn't you?" Rayfield's quiet air of command was enhanced by the impeccably fitting black jacket, the neckcloth tied in a neat but not ostentatious knot.

"But you did not reply, so I assumed you were not coming."

"I was not sure I would be able to get away until the last moment. Naturally I intend to do what I can to assist you."

He turned to Charlotte, dressed in white silk embroidered in gold with a laurel leaf design, a white hat, and a stole of pale gold embroidered in black. She waited nervously while he inspected her, and felt ridiculously happy at the approving smile he bestowed as he bowed over her hand.

His presence now added to Charlotte's apprehensions. She reminded herself that he only felt responsible toward her. And of course, her only feelings toward him were gratitude and the wish to free him from obligation. That flutter of excitement his proximity brought meant nothing.

Some time later she paused in the shadow of a potted plant, in need of a moment's solitude. The Adairs and Rayfield, as well as the Duchess of Moorewood, and her sister and brother, the Hon. Arthur Vernon, served as industrious miners prospecting the male guests on Charlotte's behalf. Her hand was solicited for every dance, and an endless parade of scarlet army coats or black evening dresses led her out. She had been nervous of dancing at first, afraid her long-ago lessons with Jamie would be forgotten; that she would turn the wrong way and mix up the set. However, she soon mastered her worry and her few missteps were smilingly corrected by her various partners.

Among those partners, though, not one face stood out, nor could she remember a single name. She fancied the candidates presented to her found her as unremarkable. She felt tongue-tied and awkward, forced to dance and converse with strangers.

She glanced to where Miss Vernon waited with a young officer for the next set of country dances to begin. Her partner looked dazed, and Miss Vernon luminous and merry.

"Hiding away, Miss Treadwell?" Rayfield ferreted her out. He handed her a glass of punch, and she discovered a thirst she had not previously noticed.

She took the glass and sipped slowly, not wishing to seem too greedy. "Thank you. No, not hiding, merely resting."

He looked at her in concern. "You are not allowing my sister to wear you out, are you?"

"No, Lord Rayfield, the schedule your sister keeps seems almost relaxing in comparison with my former life. It is all these people who tire me. Most of my life I have lived retired from society, and I find I prefer a measure of solitude."

He chuckled. "You and my mother have much in common. She clings to our country home and never comes to Town any more."

"There you are. No fair monopolizing Miss Treadwell." Arthur Vernon, accompanied by Lord Gilbert Duchesne, joined Charlotte and Rayfield. She quelled the flash of annoyance at having her *tête à tête* with Rayfield interrupted.

Mr. Vernon was a counterpart to his sisters, blond and handsome and with a lively disposition. Charlotte estimated he was close to her own twenty-two years but seemed far younger.

Lord Gilbert kept glancing to the floor where Miss Vernon stood with her partner awaiting the next country dance. Lord Gilbert's face carried a wistful expression. He was also in his early twenties, not tall but with an air of elegance that added an impression of greater stature.

"Will you dance with me, Miss Treadwell?" asked Mr. Vernon.

"I intended to ask first," said Lord Gilbert. He grabbed Charlotte's hand, not waiting for her accord. Startled, she handed her punch glass to Rayfield as Lord Gilbert hauled her to Miss Vernon's set just as the musicians began to play.

With amusement, Charlotte realized Lord Gilbert's purpose. Since they were an inactive couple for the first part of the dance, she had time to talk to him. "This was a ruse to get close to Miss Vernon," she said.

He flushed. "I'm sorry. It's unfair to you, I know. But she won't give me more than one dance—well, she won't give anyone more than one dance. She says if she did it would mean someone else wouldn't get to dance with her, and she's all the crack, you know. I can never be alone with her for a minute."

"I don't mind," Charlotte assured Lord Gilbert.

"You don't?"

"No, I'm happy to serve in the cause of young love."

He frowned. "I don't know if she loves me. She acts as if she likes me well enough, but I can never tell if there's someone else she likes better."

"I don't think Miss Vernon loves anyone yet. She wants to enjoy her first Season and is in no hurry to tie herself to one person. You're rather young yourself, you know."

"I suppose you'll say it's just a case of calf love the way everyone does," he said stiffly, the picture of injured dignity. "It isn't. I have thought myself in love before, you know. This is entirely different. And it isn't because she's so beautiful—although have you ever seen anyone as lovely?" he went on, not responding to the shake of Charlotte's head. "She is kind and gentle, and she has a voice like an angel."

"A paragon indeed," murmured Charlotte. They began to move through the figures, and their conversation was restricted to moments when they met.

"I suppose you're jealous," he said on their next pass. "All the young ladies are as green-eyed as cats over her."

"No, not jealous. Envious, perhaps. But I admire Miss Vernon too, and like her."

Charlotte danced the next set with Mr. Vernon.

"I should apologize for my friend. I can see he never even made a pretense of gallantry toward you," Mr. Vernon said. The movements took them apart.

When next they had a chance to speak, Charlotte said, "You must not suppose I took offense with Lord Gilbert. He has a *tendre* for your sister, and I could hardly compete with her beauty."

"That is a matter of opinion, Miss Treadwell. You will no doubt say I am prejudiced since I have seen Astraea nearly daily since we were both in the nursery, but I would much rather look at you."

Charlotte stiffened, more from Mr. Vernon's supposing she would be taken in by his flattery than by the impertinent direction of his conversation. "You need not play the gallant, Mr. Vernon. I'm well aware my looks are no more than passable."

"Miss Treadwell, please acquit me of any offense. It's true your looks are not in the common way, and it is quite possible many men would fail to appreciate them. But you really are most arresting. I doubt anyone who has met you has ever forgotten you afterward. I am an artist, you know, and from the moment I saw you I yearned to paint you."

She looked at him uncertainly, read sincerity in his eyes and relaxed. They again became the active couple, and their chance to further the discussion was gone. Charlotte resolved to ask Lady Adair or Miss Vernon about this strange young man.

CHAPTER NINE

The morning following the Duchesnes' rout party, Charlotte sat at breakfast with Lady Adair. Lady Adair had a pile of mail before her, mostly invitations. Charlotte had one of her own, and she looked up and asked, "Do you have any need of me today?"

Lady Adair glanced over at Charlotte. "I cannot think of anything. Have you received an invitation?"

"Yes, from Rayfield, to go driving this afternoon."

"Oh?" Sylvia's eyebrows rose at this intelligence. "How singular! He always appears so busy with his own concerns."

"Undoubtedly he merely wishes to make sure I am introduced to as many eligible men as possible. You have mentioned that Hyde Park attracts many of the *ton*."

Sylvia's brow cleared. "Yes, you are probably right. How obliging of him, to be sure. Of course, you must write to tell him you will be available."

The exchange strengthened Charlotte's belief that Sylvia and the Duchess of Moorewood held hopes of a match between Rayfield and Miss Vernon. Why that should cause a depression of spirits that followed upon the uplift she received when she read the invitation, she could not imagine.

Rayfield arrived promptly at four, wearing a brown coat, white waistcoat and fawn breeches. Charlotte was unfashionably ready for him, waiting in the salon. Sylvia had gone out upon some errands of her own, leaving Charlotte alone to greet Rayfield.

He gazed approvingly at her ensemble, ivory muslin with blue embroidery at the hem, a blue spencer with frogged closing, and a matching silk hat and plume. The look that warmed his eyes ignited an answering glow in Charlotte. He said, "Shall we go for our drive?" and took her arm. They went out the door, held open for their passage by a footman.

The sun shone, but the day carried a hint of winter. In the street before Adair House stood a curricle with two glossy bays in harness, watched over by a liveried groom. The dark green curricle made an eye-catching sight contrasted with the deep brown of the horses' coats. As Charlotte paused to admire the picture, the near horse tossed its head impatiently.

"Florizel doesn't like being kept waiting," Rayfield remarked. He handed Charlotte up into the seat, and, taking the ribbons from the groom, leaped up beside her.

"Florizel," murmured Charlotte. "Is that not a perilous name? You risk offending the Regent should he hear of it."

"It's intended in the most flattering way, Miss Treadwell. Isn't he a fine fellow? And thinks well of himself." Florizel punctuated these words by tossing his head and snorting.

Charlotte laughed. "And what is the name of the other?"

"What else could it be, but Prince?" He grinned at her and signaled the horses to move forward. The groom stepped aside.

Once they were underway, their pace necessarily slowed by the city traffic, he said, "You appear to have survived your first *ton* event in fine form."

"I admit that it was not as daunting as I had feared." And, if she but admitted it to herself, his presence had made it enjoyable. Oh, but she did not wish to admit such a thing, her pleasure in the company of a rogue such as Lord Rayfield.

They entered the park, and soon encountered acquaintances of Rayfield, to whom he had to present Charlotte. Everywhere other parties drew up to converse with friends, and she marveled how anyone could progress through the crush of carriages and riders.

The Duchess of Moorewood and her sister came their way in an elegant landau, with their brother and Lord Gilbert riding alongside. The two parties stopped to exchange greetings. "We are going to the Summerfields' ball tonight," Miss Vernon said sunnily. "Will we see you there?"

"Yes, we will be there," said Rayfield, at the same time as Charlotte replied, "I don't know what Lady Adair's plans are." They looked at each other, and Charlotte said, "It seems you are more *au fait* with the calendar than I."

"You must save a dance for me," said Mr. Arthur Vernon. "And for me," echoed Lord Gilbert.

Charlotte nodded agreement, and the groups parted company. Shortly thereafter, they were hailed by two men on horseback. "Da—dash it!" Rayfield muttered as he pulled up his team again.

"Introduce your lovely companion, Rayfield," one said.

"Charlotte, may I present Lord Leyland," he indicated the man who had spoken, "and Sir Percival Bagham. Miss Treadwell." His voice was curt.

Leyland, a thin man with dark hair going gray at the temples, rode a striking gray hunter. Sir Percival, astride a rawboned roan, was near Rayfield in age, a handsome man, but with something cool in his manner.

The two men seemed inclined to linger, but Rayfield said, "We are impeding the parade," and they rode on.

"You seemed unhappy to present me," Charlotte observed.

He took his attention from his horses to look at her, and his grim expression lightened. "It is the other way around. Although in truth, I know of nothing against Sir Percival. He has a tidy estate in Leicestershire and a good income."

"But you do not like Lord Leyland?"

"He is accepted everywhere, but I distrust him. He lives grandly with no known source of income to support it."

Charlotte's pleasure in Rayfield's company evaporated with this evidence she had guessed correctly about his purpose. "So you are not weighing their characters in a general way, only their eligibility as suitors for me."

"What else could I mean?"

She looked at his face, but his expression was closed, giving her no clue to his feelings. She reminded herself that she owed it to him and Lady Adair to cooperate with their efforts to find her a husband and remove from them the responsibility for her and Spencer. She could not say why, despite their unfortunate beginning and her certainty of his criminal endeavors, she found Rayfield fascinating.

As they progressed through the park, she exerted herself to be pleasant to everyone they met. When they left the park and drove along the streets back to Adair House, she asked him, "Would it be possible for me to see Flea?"

"Good Gad! Why should you wish to?" She could not tell whether he was merely surprised or displeased.

"I would like to thank the boy for his help on both occasions that I saw him." Charlotte deemed it ill-advised to tell Rayfield she wished to help Flea, as he no doubt believed he himself helped the boy all that was needed.

Her plan to send money to the needy families of Queen's Treat and Garwich waited for Spencer's nephew to get away from his duties as servant to the vicar in Rockcliffe. In the interim, she needed to feel that, among all the pointless activities with which Lady Adair kept her busy, she was accomplishing some good. "Do you object to my seeing him?"

"No, why should I?" His expression remained troubled, and Charlotte thought he feared she would try to question Flea about Rayfield's trade. If he knew her intent to wrest the boy away from such illegal activities, he would never indulge her whim.

"I would not try to meddle in your business with him. It is no concern of mine." Not entirely an untruth. She did not wish to know the details, merely to persuade Flea to give it up.

His blue eyes raked her face, arousing her misgivings for having raised the matter. She could not find Flea on her own, however, and she gazed back at him steadily.

"I'll send him to you at Adair House," he replied.

"Thank you."

The curricle pulled up at the house, and Rayfield helped her descend. "I will see you tonight," he said. "Oh, and save one of your dances for me!"

His words formed more of a command than a request. "If you wish," she agreed. As she went into the house, a dispirited mood possessed her. The easier association they enjoyed when their drive began had deteriorated into tension by the end.

The Summerfields' townhouse was small but lavishly appointed. The modern jewel box was filled to the rafters with guests. The crush prevented anyone from moving about between groups of people. To Charlotte's amazement, gentlemen who had bespoken dances with her managed to find her.

Going through the figures of the sprightly country dances proved a challenge; Charlotte seemed constantly to bump into another of the dancers or a bystander attempting to negotiate the crowd. The rooms became heated with the press of bodies.

Luckily lightweight gowns were the fashion. Her white sprigged muslin with a transparent stole kept her as cool as possible under the circumstances.

Lord Gilbert danced with her after he took his turn with Miss Vernon, and rhapsodized further about that lady's perfections, to Charlotte's amusement. She discerned no preference on Miss Vernon's part for the love-struck young man.

Following her dance with Lord Gilbert, Mr. Vernon solicited her hand for the next set. As they moved through the figures, he abruptly asked, "When will you sit for me?"

"Why, I have no plans to do so. I am a most unsuitable subject for painting. You should do a portrait of your sister."

"Oh, I've sketched Astraea and my other sisters any number of times. I've no desire to paint a formal portrait of her. She hasn't lived long enough to be interesting."

"Oh, it is *older* ladies you admire," she said, smiling.

"You are roasting me," he said, hurt reflected in his green

eyes. "I was not suggesting you are old. But you have lived a more interesting life than my sister has."

"You can have little notion of the life of a governess if you think such a life interesting." Charlotte rejoined. "Indeed, if working for one's keep makes a person interesting, then you should ask your servants to pose for you."

"I seem to offend you no matter what I say." Mr. Vernon's face assumed the stiff lines of affront. "I will not press you any further, but hope you will reconsider. You would be adequately chaperoned, if that is what concerns you."

Charlotte hastened to make amends. "I will consider it sometime. There is never any free time in my calendar at present. Lady Adair keeps me very busy." She concluded with gladness that Mr. Vernon only wished to paint her and did not have any romantic interest in her. He was a nice young man, but did not arouse in her any wish for a closer association.

He returned her to Lady Adair and Charlotte was relieved she had made no commitment to anyone for the next dance, giving her the chance to cool herself. Lady Adair lamented her own ineptitude as a matchmaker, failing to glean a partner for every dance, and was little appeased by Charlotte's assurances.

Shortly, however, she saw Sir Percival Bagham approaching. He bowed to her and Lady Adair, and begged permission to take Charlotte out on the floor. Sylvia's studied gaze approved him as her words did. Charlotte's spirits sank at being forced to do the polite with Sir Percival.

"A sad crush," said Sir Percival, as they awaited their turn to participate in the dance.

"Indeed," said Charlotte. She did not understand why she had qualms about being with him. He had regular features, with a chin a little weak, dark brown eyes and hair. His hairline receded slightly. A pale complexion and thin, slight figure. Nothing about him should put her off, and yet something did.

"I much prefer a gathering where one knows everyone who attends," Sir Percival asserted.

"I understand the Summerfields are a very popular couple," Charlotte offered.

"Too much so," he opined. "Cora is unexceptional, the granddaughter of a duke, but Summerfield got his money from trade. I don't know why her father allowed the match. Of course, for some people money erases the taint of the common."

They had no chance for further conversation until later in the dance, when Sir Percival talked of inconsequential matters. As he took her back to Lady Adair, he said, "I would like to call on you, Miss Treadwell."

"Of course you may," she said, concealing her dismay. No doubt Rayfield's words about Sir Percival and his friend Leyland unduly influenced her. He apparently thought both men would look for a fortune she did not offer. She should rejoice he was proved wrong, in Sir Percival's case at least.

Rayfield came to claim his dance with her, and all thoughts of anyone else fled. However, instead of leading her to one of the sets, he said, "You looked flushed, Miss Treadwell. Would you like to get some air? The Summerfields have a pleasant garden. I believe a number of others are strolling through it at the moment, so it would not be improper for us to join them."

Charlotte assented gladly, and they went out through open French doors into a shrubbery with graveled paths winding through. The area was lit by torches set into posts at intervals, and by the light of a gibbous moon. Charlotte saw several other couples strolling, although none were close by.

A light breeze cooled her heated cheeks. It was too early for flowers, but the scent of fresh green growth came to her, and gravel crunched underfoot. Her skin tingled with awareness of Rayfield beside her, and her arm was almost on fire where it rested on his. Even the brush of her skirt against his leg stirred her senses, sending electric impulses through her body.

"I talked to Flea today," he said abruptly into the silence between them as they walked. "He will call on you tomorrow."

"Oh, that's wonderful." Charlotte clasped her hands together. "Thank you."

"It was nothing." His voice was gruff.

He was displeased. She could read the emotion in his voice, although she did not know his reason. But her pleasure in his company dissolved. "Let us go in now," she said.

CHAPTER TEN

The next afternoon, Lady Adair's butler, Hastings, came to the small salon where Charlotte sat reading and Sylvia was engaged in writing some correspondence.

"Pardon me, miss," Hastings addressed Charlotte, "I hardly know what to do. A personage insists on seeing you."

"A 'personage'?" Lady Adair asked. "What kind of personage, Hastings?"

"It's a small boy—a street arab, milady. A most inappropriate caller." Hastings sniffed, giving rein to his annoyance at the indignity of belonging to a household where such an inferior person dared to call.

"Oh, please show him in at once," Charlotte said. Flea!

"I will do no such thing! The child is exceedingly dirty."

"Oh. In that case, I will come to him. Is he waiting in the hall?" asked Charlotte.

"Certainly not! He is at the back door. Mrs. Parsons would not have such in her kitchen!"

Charlotte sighed, aware of having fallen in the butler's estimation. "I will come to him, then, Hastings. Have him wait until I get my shawl."

"Miss Treadwell, you do not mean to see this guttersnipe?"

Charlotte halted in the act of walking out of the room. "Yes, of course. He is a . . . a friend."

Lady Adair rolled her eyes. "This can all be laid at Hugh's door, no doubt."

"That is true. Flea is a friend of Rayfield's as well as mine." Charlotte ran upstairs, grabbed a shawl from her clothes press, and dashed down to the kitchen, half afraid the servants would have run Flea off, or that he took fright at their inhospitable treatment of him. Or more likely, took offense, she thought, knowing that with his cheeky attitude he would not be easily frightened away.

The boy still lounged against the doorframe in spite of suspicious looks directed at him from the boot boy, who was apparently given the task of making sure Flea did not contaminate the kitchen with his presence.

"Hello, Flea," said Charlotte breathlessly. Aware of curious looks of the entire kitchen staff from the cook to the scullery maid, she added, "Let's go for a walk."

Charlotte was glad she had taken the time to get a shawl, for although the day was fine with a bright sun shining, a stiff breeze made the air nippy.

Flea had not yet spoken as they set out on the path to a small green nearby. Charlotte glanced at the slight figure. He looked anything but happy at this duty laid upon him by Rayfield. "How have you been, Flea?" she asked.

"I always be fine," he replied.

His terseness gave Charlotte no conversational gambits. She did not know how to speak to Flea, but she worried over his uncertain life and lack of prospects, and resolved that she would find some way to help him. "I am sorry that you were not made more welcome at Lady Adair's house," she said.

He chuckled and gave her a look that said, *Are you touched in the upper story?* He said, "What kind o' greeting did y'think I'd get?" and stopped as though staggered at her naiveté.

"I did not think about it," Charlotte admitted. "When you came with me to my house, Mrs. Whislehurst did not welcome you either. If I should have charge of a household again, I will make sure that whoever comes to the door is treated politely."

At this, Flea hooted uproariously and said, "You'd be took

advantage of, did you do that. Every beggar and thief in Lun-non'd be 'anging about."

Charlotte smiled and said, "Doubtless you are right." Her smile faded as she added, "And anyway, it is not likely to happen. I'll probably end up as a governess again, with no power to make rules in a household." She went on, "Flea, whatever happens, I'd like us to be friends."

"That can't be," he said flatly. "You're a lady and I'm a street boy." He walked on quickly, as though to lose her.

She quickened her pace to keep up with him. "Oh, but you are very special, Flea. You could be so much more than you are now. That's why I wanted to ask . . . you said Lord . . . Broddie told you he would see you were looked after. What . . . what has he said he would do for you?"

Flea scowled fiercely. "Dunno. Pro'ly set me up wi' an inn or some kind o' bizness. Nothing to do wi' you, any road."

"But it matters what he has planned!" Charlotte cried. "You told me you were all done with school. Did you ever go to school at all? Do you know how to read and cipher? You can't run any kind of business without knowing those."

Flea's face closed up. "Maybe Broddie'll take me in service in one o' 'is 'ouses. Don't you worry none. " 'E'll do whut 'e promised!"

Charlotte bit her lip, frustrated at her inability to get Flea to listen. Since she was not making any progress on that tack, she began another. "What about where you live? You said you had some friends you stayed with?"

The look he gave her was so full of suspicion that she quailed and nearly gave in to the temptation to desist. "I'd like to see your place of residence, Flea."

"Ain't proper, bein' a 'bachelor 'stablishment' an' all." This time his eyes shone with unmistakable mischief.

"Where have you heard such a phrase?"

"It's what Broddie'd say if you wanted to go callin' on 'im, i'n't it?"

"Yes, but it hardly applies in this case, Flea. You are just a boy."

"Mebbe I'll let you see my ken sometime," he conceded.

Charlotte rejoiced in this evidence he might be willing to continue their acquaintance. "Couldn't you take me there now?"

"Why 'ud you want to do that?" He frowned at her.

"I'd like to meet your friends."

"They'ms not likely to be there, this time o' day."

"In any case I need to know how to find you."

"Broddie can allus get word to me."

"I don't want to depend on that. I don't think he wanted to set up this meeting in the first place."

As Flea's expression took on that cast he always got when he defended Rayfield, Charlotte hurried to say, "I'm not criticizing him. He has been very kind to me. But he seems to think it unsuitable for me to associate with you—indeed, it seems no one believes I should. I prefer to choose my own friends, however, and not be dictated to by anyone, no matter whether they think they have my best interests in mind."

She chanced her reading of Flea's character and added, "Would you give up a friend because R—Broddie told you to?"

He gave her his cheeky grin, and said, "Mebbe. It depends on how much I wanted to see 'em."

"Please show me your home."

"Orright." He cast her a doubtful look and added, "It's a long walk."

"I have money. We can take a hackney."

They walked to Oxford Street and hailed a hackney. The driver scrutinized them, but apparently Charlotte's respectable manner of dress convinced him she could pay the fare, and he agreed to take them. Even riding, the distance seemed far. They passed the Tower and proceeded into a seamy neighborhood.

"This is far enough," Flea said.

Charlotte signaled the jarvey to stop. "You sure you want to get out here?" he asked. " 'Tisn't a safe place."

"I'll be fine," Charlotte assured him as she handed him the requisite number of coins.

Flea set a rapid pace, and quickly took them deeper into a very disreputable-looking area. He led Charlotte down a litter-filled, short stairway at the side of a tumbledown construction with boards over what must once have been windows. The building showed no signs of occupancy, and Charlotte would have said from the condition of the stairs that no one had come this way in a long time. At the bottom, she could barely distinguish a door in the murk. When Flea pushed it open, it protested with a squeak and then gave slowly.

Charlotte followed him into the building, and he pushed the door shut behind them, dimming most of the light, although thin streaks showed through gaps in the boards over the two windows. The floor was dirt, covered with detritus. As they walked a pathway only Flea could see through the debris, Charlotte heard the rustlings and squeaks of rodents. She tried not to think of the creatures running over her feet as she trod in Flea's footsteps. Across the room, another staircase led up, and a door at the top gave out into a tiny, gloomy courtyard. The only light reaching the confined space came from a small square of sky visible through the gap left by the surrounding roofs.

Behind them lay the building they just came through; to the right and in front, the windowless and doorless brick wall of a tall, L-shaped structure; to the left, three smaller houses leaned precariously against each other. Again, their few windows were boarded up, except for those of the most dilapidated pile of the row, in the middle.

Charlotte smelled the river nearby and heard sounds of traffic on the streets behind them and voices and activity in the large edifice that formed two sides of the square.

"That's a ware'ouse. Connected to the dock, it is. You can only get into it from the street on t'other side. Goods is stored there after they unload 'em from the ships." Flea took out a key from a pocket in his disreputable jacket and let them in

the door of the middle house, although from the looks of the
key and the door, Charlotte thought anyone could gain ingress
without the aid of the key.

The lock snicked open, and Flea pushed hard on the door.
"Frame's off-kilter," he explained. Once more, the room they
entered was dim, the only light coming from the windows
looking out on the courtyard they just traversed.

The walls were bare boards. A small brazier sitting on the
dirt floor in the center appeared to offer both cooking and heat-
ing, and four pallets took up floor space around the perimeter
of the room. Small piles at the foot of each pallet seemed all
each boy had in the way of personal belongings. Tattered blankets hung in two doorways leading to other rooms in the house,
probably either for privacy or hold in the warmth of the brazier.
She didn't know what to say to Flea. The barrenness of his life
almost brought tears to her eyes.

"We thinks this were Black Jack Biggins' ken," Flea said
into the silence.

"Oh," Charlotte offered. "Er, who is Black Jack Biggins?"

"'E were King o' the Thieves. 'E were hanged a couple of
years back—'im and 'is whole gang. We thinks the 'ouse in
front were kept as a blind. 'E prolly had working-folk in them
and pros—er, ladies who weren't, living in the big 'ouse we
came through. But 'lessen you 'appen to find the door in the
basement, there ain't no other way to reach this courtyard.
The 'ouse next door, the biggest one, was prolly 'is, and
mebbe 'is lieutenants 'ad the others. Ever'thing was all shut
up wif boards when we found this place. We figgered this
'ouse were about the right size fer us."

"It's very, uh, ingenious."

"Yep. Back o' these, there's some other 'ouses that front on
the street. They don't 'ave winders in the back, leastways not
the ones we've looked into. But we thinks that prolly Black
Jack 'ad a bolt-'ole in the big 'ouse, 'cause otherwise 'e'd be
like a rat in a trap if'n someone found the basement door.
Mebbe there's a tunnel that leads to one o' the 'ouses be'ind
these. We 'aven't looked, though. Ain't no reason to s'pose

we'd be 'unted down." He cast her a look as if he expected her to raise again the likelihood of Broddie's work being illegal.

Charlotte refrained. Instead, she walked to the back of the room and lifted aside the blankets to see the other rooms. They were smaller than the main room, and bare.

"Guess we could 'ave more privacy-like if'n we was to sleep in them rooms, but in winter it gets too cold. And none of us needs to be private, anyhow. We's just like fambly."

She forced herself to say something complimentary. "It's very nice, Flea. You've done very well for yourselves finding such a cozy place."

He beamed, wiping away the look that was on his face—an expression of anxiety, she realized. Apparently he wished for her approval more than he would admit.

A key turning in the front door drew their attention. Flea wrenched the door open. " 'Tain't locked," he said to the small boy in the doorway. "What be you doin' 'ome this time o' day?"

The boy wiped at a dripping nose with a filthy sleeve. "Didn't feel good." He coughed, not covering his mouth, then noticed Charlotte and his eyes got round.

"This 'ere's a friend o' mine, Miss Treadwell. She's a lady, so's you treat her polite, now." Flea looked at Charlotte. "This is Ned Tuttle, one o' my mates."

"How do you do, Master Tuttle," Charlotte greeted. She could not bring herself to offer her hand to the grubby, and no doubt diseased, one of Flea's friend. He was younger than Flea, seven or eight, she surmised, with a tangled mop of what looked like blond curls if they were washed free of the lifetime's accumulation of dirt. His rags were even more disreputable than Flea's. Looking at him broke Charlotte's heart.

"I could bring you some medicine for that cough," she offered. She would like to have offered more—a bath, a new suit of clothes, a home, especially two arms to cuddle him—but didn't dare breach that fierce independence she knew the boys developed in order to survive their appalling circumstances.

"Nah, I be orright," Ned said. "Jes' wants to rest."

She determined to talk to Flea about providing some

medicine and decent food for Ned until he recovered from his cold. "I must go home. They'll be wondering about me by now."

"I'll 'company yer," Flea said.

"That's not necessary. I can take a hackney."

"Wouldn't be polite fer me to let a lady go un'companied," he insisted.

Charlotte did not protest further. In truth, she was grateful for his escort, and glad to have a chance to talk to him about Ned. Surely she could bring Flea to see the sense in allowing her to help Ned. In such surroundings, a cold left untreated could quickly turn deadly.

To her relief, once they were seated in the hackney and she began her campaign to persuade him, she had already won the battle. "You really have sump'n as will help 'im?" Flea's hopeful expression showed his own worries about the small lad.

"It's not ready. I have a recipe I am sure will help him. If you'll wait, I will make up a batch." Flea's balky face made her add, "Or you could come by tomorrow and I'll give it to you then. He needs help, Flea. How old is he, anyway?"

"I dunno. We reckoned he were five or six when 'e came to us, and that was close on to two year ago. 'Is fambly sent 'im out to beg ev'ry day. 'E 'ad a drunken father an' a sick mother an' a younger 'un in the fambly. One day 'e come 'ome from beggin' and they was gone."

"Oh, no! You mean he never found out what happened?" Charlotte felt almost ill thinking of it.

"Lots of things c'd 'ave 'appened. Mebbe 'is mother died and 'is father was took up. Ned never did know 'ow is father made enough money to keep 'em fed. Ned din't make enough beggin' for all o' them. Mebbe they just run orf to Ameriky." Flea shrugged. "Me an' my other mates found 'im jes' walkin' the streets and cryin' 'cause he ain't 'ad nothin' to eat in days. We took 'im in and 'e bin with us since. If you means it about the medicine, I'll come back tomorrow an' get it."

Charlotte promised she would, and promised herself

she would persuade Lady Adair to provide some food and clothing—and some soap—for the boys as well.

"I think we've tracked one of Monsoor Mansson's agents." The Heaper tilted back his chair in Flash Annie's kitchen, resting one ankle upon his other knee. He drained his ale and waved the mug at Pearl.

Annie's maid refilled the mug, pressing against the Heaper as she handed it back.

Hugh stilled his face, not showing the hope that leaped inside him. He leaned forward. "Where is he? And who?"

"Don't know, to either question. Lost 'im on the way south. 'E had good horses. We couldn't keep up. But Craven 'ere," with a shoulder shrug toward the man sitting at the table with them, "saw 'im in mid-March at a tavern in Leeds, meeting wi' men who attacked several dressing shops in Huddersfield near the end of the month. Another of 'is mates was seen by Craven's man, Symms, attacking the shearing mill of William Thompson & Bros. at Rawdon on March twenty-third and twenty-fourth."

"You followed him south to London?"

Craven, small, with a rat-like, chinless face and protruding teeth, set his mug on the table and belched. "Lost him well before we got here. But I've no doubt that's where he was headed. Went to report to his master, I'm sure of it."

"What does this agent look like?" Hugh asked.

"Tallish man of middle years," Craven said. "Graying hair, has a bit of a paunch. A great scar right through the middle of his face, from brow to cheek. Makes him easy to spot."

"That will help. Heaper, give our men that description. If he calls on any of our suspects, I want to know about it. Maybe we'll finally collect evidence to discover our traitor."

"Saw Miss Treadwell with Flea yesterday in Oxford Street, buying 'im a pie from a vendor," Heaper said.

"You mean the day before yesterday. She asked to see him and I arranged it."

"No, 'twas yesterday. I don't mix up my days."

Had they met again the day following the meeting he had set up? Why would she meet him again, if thanking him was her only aim? He must question Flea before he met the opera party, and ask Miss Treadwell also.

Hugh stood. "If that's all, I attend the opera tonight with my sister and Miss Treadwell."

CHAPTER ELEVEN

From the case notebook of Hugh Broderick Brooks, the Earl of Rayfield:

Entry dated 7th of April, 1812:
Miss Treadwell continues to puzzle me. I can think of no logical reason why she should pursue an acquaintance with Flea, a child so beneath the notice of a young lady of her class. The fact that she assured me she would not probe into my business with him is a clear indication that she suspects me of conducting an investigation into the plot behind the Luddites. I made an attempt to prime Flea to draw her out and learn what he can, but I can no longer trust him where she is concerned. She has won him over, apparently by so simple a device as dosing a young friend of his with some nostrum.

Keeping all the suspects in view has stretched my available agents very thin.

(Decoded by Alphonsius McMasters, PhD, LLC, AKC, OBE, BMW, historian and author of The Secret Wars of Napoleon, *2005.)*

"How did your meeting go with Miss Treadwell the other day?" Hugh asked Flea.

"Orright." The boy shrugged and didn't meet Hugh's eyes.

"Did she question you about your activities for me?"

"Naw. Ast me whut you said you'd do for me when I got older." He paused a beat and added, "Ast me could I read 'n write 'n figger."

Hugh frowned. An education for Flea had not been in his mind. He shook off the faintly shamed feelings that came with this thought. He could not be diverted from his task by such irrelevancies. He would see to Flea's future once the threat of revolution had been defeated. "Have you seen her since?"

Flea looked down at the toes poking out from his worn-out boots. "Ye-es. She had some medicine for one o' my mates and I fetched it from 'er."

The boy was holding something back. Hugh was sure of the boy's loyalty to him, and to England. But could some bond of affection tie him to a woman who might be a spy? How far could he trust Flea's good sense?

"Did you make any arrangements to see her again?"

"I might've," the boy said, looking anywhere but into Hugh's eyes.

"Remember that she could be the spy for whom we are looking," Hugh cautioned.

"I 'member," Flea said. His lips turned downward and his posture was stiff.

No, he couldn't trust the boy any longer where Miss Treadwell was concerned. He made one more try. "Don't tell her anything about my investigation."

"She won't learn nothin' from me!"

"And you'll let me know if she lets fall anything incriminating?"

"'Course I would. She hasn't said anythin' in . . . incrim'nalating. But I'll pay real good 'tention in case she does."

"Good." He parted from Flea. He would have to prevent their meeting again. Flea could easily forget himself and say something to give Miss Treadwell an advantage.

* * *

Hugh sat next to Miss Treadwell in the Adairs' box at Covent Garden. Miss Vernon, Arthur Vernon, and the Duchess of Moorewood had accompanied the Adairs to the opera.

Miss Treadwell looked particularly fine in an opera dress of violet velvet over a white underdress, the overdress caught up to above knee with a flower. His awareness of her beside him was acute, and not only because of the questions he needed to ask. Everything about her, from the rose scent of her mahogany hair, to the aristocratic profile as she fixed her attention upon the performance below them, teased his senses. Would he have found her so fascinating if she were not a suspect?

When the first interval came, he asked, "Would you take a stroll in the corridor with me, Miss Treadwell?"

She assented, and he led her out, against the horde attempting to enter to pay their respects to Miss Vernon.

He took her arm as they maneuvered along the corridor through the press of people on their way to visit in others' boxes or to find refreshment. He drew her close to him to protect her from being jostled, and cursed silently to himself as contact with her sent a jolt of arousal to his body.

Hugh found a niche out of the pathway, and slipped into it with Miss Treadwell. "How was your meeting with Flea the other day?"

"It was fine." She looked down, not meeting his eyes.

"What did you find to talk about?" he probed.

"I wanted to thank him, especially for bringing me home from Flash Annie's. I had the impression you were angry with him for helping me, and I wanted him to know that I at least appreciated his actions."

Hugh frowned. Was that really all there was to it? "Have you seen him again?"

"What concern of yours is it if I have?" She glanced up at his face, her eyes sparking.

"The boy is my concern."

"If so, why don't you see that he has decent clothes and learns to read and write so he can make something of himself?"

"My question was a simple one. Can you not answer?" He leaned closer to her and saw the pulse beating at her temple.

She pressed back against the wall. "Very well. I saw him again yesterday. A young friend of Flea's was sick, and I told Flea I would make up a cough elixir for him."

"I see." He could not quarrel with such charitable intentions. If she told the truth. Flea gave the same story. But why did both behave as though they were hiding something? A band of pain tightened around his forehead.

"Miss Treadwell, it is good of you to wish to help, but you can have no real notion of what you do. Interfering in Flea's life, encouraging him in unrealistic wishes, cannot serve his best interests. I must ask you not to see him again."

"You are mistaken. I do not induce unrealistic desires in Flea, and if you had intentions other than to use him for your own schemes, you would not begrudge him an education and the opportunity to better himself." Her voice rose, and people passing by looked at them curiously.

"Moderate your tone. We are attracting notice." She flushed, but didn't reply, and he went on, "It is almost time for the opera to resume. Let us return to our seats."

The crowd was making its way back to the boxes and he negotiated the renewed crowd, frustrated at his lack of success. What did she mean by his "schemes"? She must have information about his investigation. If he weren't so caught up in her, he would have concluded long ago that she was the traitor.

Performers pranced about on the stage, but their actions made no sense. They opened their mouths to sing, but only noise issued forth, as far as Charlotte could tell. With the buzzing in her ears, she scarcely could hear even that.

The only thing to which her senses seemed to be fully alive was Rayfield's presence beside her. Every breath he took, the slightest stir of his muscles, vibrated all her nerve endings like a bow upon the strings of a violin. She wanted to slap him, to shout and rage at him . . . and at the same time felt this thing, this attraction; this foolish, wasted yearning.

He had as much as ordered her to stop seeing Flea. And he assumed she would fall in with his demands and brought her back to her seat. She had not given him her promise, and she would not stop seeing Flea. The man obviously prepared no plans for the boy beyond his own use of him, and Charlotte would help Flea to a better life—one with no Rayfield in it.

He might also tell Flea not to see her. She did not know if the boy would defy the earl and continue to meet. Flea possessed an independent streak, but he also obviously worshipped this . . . this boor. Flea had agreed to meet her in the park near Lady Adair's home next week. Would he show up? She could only wait upon the appointed time and the outcome.

She tried to banish these thoughts and concentrate on the opera, but Rayfield would not go away. He watched the stage, oblivious to the turmoil into which he plunged her, apparently enjoying the performance.

She stared at the stage, a fixed smile plastered on her face. No one should suspect she did not take in one morsel of what occurred below her.

An "at home" at Lady Adair's contained much the character of an afternoon at Astley's Amphitheatre. No horses, thought Charlotte, but it seemed like every type of person was packed into Lady Adair's drawing room.

The Duchess of Moorewood and her youngest sister had called. The duchess and Lady Adair enjoyed a soft-voiced conversation in another corner of the room.

Miss Vernon's presence doubtless brought most of the young men who cluttered up the space. She fulfilled her early promise of being the belle of the Season. A young man with pretensions to fashion simply must spend much of his time hanging about Miss Vernon with a suitably love-struck expression.

That did not altogether explain Mr. Arthur Vernon and

Lord Leyland, who, rather than making up part of Miss Vernon's court, sat close to Charlotte.

"I have not been in London for the Season in some years," Leyland said. "At first my wife was ailing, and then she died a little over a year ago. I have just come out of mourning."

"My sympathies for your loss, Lord Leyland."

He smiled, a tight unhumorous bending of the lips while his eyes stayed somber. "I am becoming more accustomed now."

"Did you and your wife have children?"

"I have a six-year-old son."

"That must console you somewhat for your loss."

"Yes, he is a great joy and consolation to me."

Charlotte turned to Mr. Vernon, who was eyeing the cluster of men around his sister.

"I collect, Mr. Vernon, that you are here to lend aid to Miss Vernon?"

"What? Oh, no, Pallas is more than able to watch out for Astraea."

Hastings announced Sir Percival Bagham's entrance. He crossed the room to make his bow to Lady Adair, then came to Charlotte's side. "Miss Treadwell. How do you do today?"

As they made small talk, Charlotte became aware of a general movement for the callers to leave. The duchess gathered up Miss Vernon. They took their leave of Charlotte, with most of the rest of the room's occupants following in their train. As Lady Adair's drawing room emptied, a swoosh of air swept in. Mr. Vernon, Lord Leyland, and Sir Percival remained behind. Mr. Vernon gave Charlotte a smiling look, as if to say, see, it was not on Astraea's account I am here.

Lady Adair joined them, calling for fresh tea. "Miss Vernon's come-out ball will be enchanting. Wait until you see the decorations the duchess has planned."

Hastings brought in a fresh pot of tea and more biscuits. She observed, "Sir Percival, you haven't been served yet." She poured him a cup and offered fresh tea to the others. They all declined, so she filled her own cup and resumed, "The ball is less than a fortnight from now."

Sir Percival sipped his tea and laid aside the cup. "I wished to ask if you would go riding with me tomorrow," he said to Charlotte.

"I most sincerely regret that I cannot, Sir Percival," Charlotte replied, somewhat untruthfully.

Lady Adair jumped in to say, "But Miss Treadwell, I have offered you the use of one of my horses."

Charlotte merely smiled and shook her head. For all her candor, she could not bring herself to admit her fear of horses.

"Then, would you go driving with me?" persisted Sir Percival.

"I should be pleased to."

They set a time for two days hence and Sir Percival took his leave, followed by the others.

"I must say, I thought Hugh would come today," Lady Adair observed.

"He is undoubtedly busy." Charlotte did not admit to their quarrel the previous evening. Perhaps not exactly a quarrel, but they did seem to disagree frequently. She also did not admit to her own hopes that she would see him that day. Would he attend Mrs. Brewster-Smythe's musical evening that night?

Lord Wescott swirled brandy in his glass, a thoughtful expression on his face. "I've received a report from a magistrate in Bolton, Lancashire, that there are plans to fire the Westhoughton Mill there."

"The disturbances are intensifying," Hugh said. "It appears efforts are building toward a general revolt. My agents are reporting rumors from Lancashire that May first is the day set for the start. That is just over three weeks away." He stood, too restless to sit, on the other side of Wescott's desk.

"I need a number of your men to handle the threat in the counties. I beg pardon for leaving you short-handed. Can you manage to tie things up soon?"

"I believe I am only days away from catching the traitor," he assured his superior.

"This is an ugly business. We must wrap it up as soon as possible." Wescott rose.

Hugh stood also. "Matters shall resolve soon." With these optimistic words, he took his leave. Miss Treadwell must be the one. He should be glad that he could concentrate his investigation on Miss Treadwell. Why had he not told Wescott of his deduction about her guilt? It must be that he was waiting for conclusive proof.

That evening, Hugh leaned against the far wall of the music room at the Brewster-Smythes' townhouse while the string quartet hired for the evening performed. Too many guests jammed the room, and its long, narrow shape did not promote auditory quality. The quartet seemed accomplished musicians, but the sound was distorted and muffled when it reached him.

Rows of hard chairs filled the room, each containing one of Mrs. Brewster-Smythe's guests, and several men besides Hugh ranged along the wall, lacking a place to sit. He would not have suffered this torture but for the importance of keeping Miss Treadwell under his eye in case she made contact with someone suspicious.

She sat several rows back from the musicians, with Mr. and Miss Vernon on either side of her, the duchess next to Miss Vernon. She seemed entirely attentive to the performance and had not turned her head more than necessary to indicate she listened to some comment by one of the Vernons.

Watching Charlotte Treadwell gave him an unexpected yearning to be sitting close to her. Mentally he kicked himself, remembering she was his chief suspect and he must not allow his attraction to her to cloud his judgment.

At last an intermission was declared, and the guests arose to stretch cramped muscles and partake of conversation and the refreshments in the next room. Miss Treadwell stood but remained near her seat. She looked lovely, wearing a blue gown with a low neckline and short puffed sleeves, with a frivolous little feathered headdress that seemed completely at odds with her practical manner. It gave her a charm he had not associated with her previously. She vigorously plied the little fan made of blue feathers that matched the dress.

Her companions had moved apart, Miss Vernon as usual surrounded by admirers. The duchess had been approached by a couple of other matrons and conversed with them. Mr. Vernon had joined the crowd attempting to exit the room. The others had probably given him a commission to obtain refreshments for them. Hugh knew Mrs. Brewster-Smythe's reputation as a frugal hostess and decided not to brave the crowd for little reward. He made his way to Miss Treadwell's side.

She looked anything but happy at his approach, reminding him of their awkward meeting at the opera the previous night.

"Sylvia is not with you tonight?" he asked.

"No, Lord and Lady Adair had an engagement to attend a dinner party given by one of his political allies. I came with the duchess and Mr. and Miss Vernon."

"Undoubtedly the Adairs are more comfortable and better cared for than Mrs. Brewster-Smythe's guests. Warm in here, isn't it?"

"I think I am about to expire," she admitted with a slight smile. She appeared to relax with the small talk.

"Would you care to take a turn about the room?"

"That would be most pleasant."

He took her arm and led her in the opposite direction from the guests still massed at the door. Few people remained in the room, giving them some privacy. As they circled the room, Miss Treadwell plied her fan again and he noticed her flushed cheeks. Were they due solely to the stifling air in the room, or did she respond to the palpable awareness between them?

She was unattainable, a woman one could only possess by marrying, and marriage was out of the question for him at present. Since he had no intention of pursuing a courtship, he should have no trouble controlling his attraction to her.

Perversely, since she had become his primary suspect, his desire for her had become like a serpent coiling inside him, refusing to rest. He could not stop the pictures that ran through his head—kissing her full, sensuous lips, seeing the passionate fire in those green eyes, touching her in intimate places. No matter what had ignited those pictures, they were a damned inconvenience.

They began a second circuit of the room. "Have you heard from your father lately?"

"Why, I've never heard from him at all since he left. He would not have known how to reach me, in any case. He could not have known I left you."

Hugh looked intently at Charlotte's face. "He never wrote to you through me, either. Do you not find that strange?"

She turned her face away. "You have a misconception about my father's concern for me. He almost never communicated when I was at Queen's Treat and he resided in Town."

"So, you have no idea where your father is?" Hugh's step hesitated, his stomach knotting with tension.

"No, why? Does he still owe you money? I should have thought—doubtless when he wagered me he had already pledged more than he had left. I am sorry; I wish had the resources to pay you back." Charlotte laid her hand over her bosom.

"Actually, now I consider, he does owe me money. The wager was all the vowels I had collected from him plus five thousand pounds against you. In truth, I believe I was so nonplused when I won that I never considered he still owed me the value of the vowels. And I didn't even get you," he added, half-seriously.

She stiffened, and came to a standstill. "You insisted you were not interested in that part of the bargain."

"That is not what I said." He turned about to face her, standing close, her warmth touching him, affecting his senses more than he would like. The notice of a lover gave him the best excuse to keep company with Miss Treadwell.

She trembled and looked pale. "Mr. Vernon must be looking for me. I'd better go back to my seat."

"Wait a moment. We have never spoken of this, and I think we must. Excepting that one kiss, I have never forced any unwanted attentions upon you, nor will I. That doesn't mean a lack of interest in you." For the foreseeable future, Hugh would be taking an enormous interest in Charlotte Treadwell.

She looked up, shock in her eyes. "You've never said you had any interest in me."

"It was too soon. It still is. I merely wish to improve our acquaintance. Isn't that fair?" He waited, more avid for her answer than she could know.

She pulled back, lowering her gaze. "Yes, I suppose so."

He brought her back to her chair. Mr. Vernon had not returned, but the duchess and Miss Vernon had resumed their seats, with a cluster of Miss Vernon's usual admirers flocking around. Charlotte wished for solitude to contemplate the strange conversation she and Rayfield had just concluded. Mr. Vernon finally came bearing a glass of punch, and she gratefu   ped the cool liquid.

Was Rayfield truly interested in her? Or was he playing some heartless rake's game? She could not avoid the feeling he had some purpose in his questions of her. She could not truly want him to be interested—he was a criminal. She must keep reminding herself of that fact. Her thoughts of him were in a tangle, and she did not know how to sort them out.

The musicians returned and warmed up again, and Mrs. Brewster-Smythe's guests began filing back into the room. Hugh returned to his place against the wall, well pleased with the work he had done. Or he would be pleased, if he didn't have this gnawing unease in his belly. He tried to dismiss it, but it would not go away until he identified it.

It was Miss Treadwell—Charlotte—herself. He practiced a

deception upon her, pretending an attraction he did not feel . . . no, that was not it, either. The attraction was all too real, but he could not yield to it. And he could not afford any disquietude about deceiving her.

She had spoken the truth about her father, he was almost certain. There was no communication between them, and she was puzzled about his flight. Perhaps it was she all along and not Treadwell who directed the Luddites. She might have inherited the role from her brother instead of being her father's delegate. She had been a mere girl when her brother died, however. And how she began was not the question he must answer.

CHAPTER TWELVE

An impartial observer might have said England teetered on the brink of revolution, with France standing ready to capitalize on its weakness. War, restrictions on trade, three successive years of crop failures, rising prices and enclosures all contributed to conditions of utmost misery throughout the country.

(From The Secret Wars of Napoleon, *by Alphonsius McMasters, PhD, LLC, AKC, OBE, BMW, 2005.)*

Once Spencer had proceeded well in his recovery, and with the demands Lady Adair placed on her time, Charlotte's visits to him had dwindled to once a week. At her call the morning following the musicale at Mrs. Brewster-Smythe's, Spencer's familiar face gave Charlotte an overwhelming sense of comfort.

He sat fully dressed in an anteroom outside his chamber. His ankle was healing too slowly, and his color unhealthy. She insisted he return to his room to rest and called the manservant who had been assigned to look after him. For all her unease over Spencer's being a charge on the earl, she conceded that he received far better care than she could have provided. Once he was back in bed, she went to his chamber.

"I fear you are pushing your recovery too hard, Spencer,"

she chastised him. "Please take care of yourself. I don't know what I'd do if I didn't have you."

He looked gratified but troubled. "No, Miss Charlotte, I must become able to get about and go back to work."

"You must not worry. I will look after you if you can't work again." At his frown, she added, "You should be happy that I am trying to bring someone to the point of a declaration. I shall find myself a husband by the end of the Season."

His eyes filled with tears. "I don't want you to marry to support me. You should take your time, find a man you love."

"Life doesn't always work out that way. I shall be fine, I assure you. Now, what news do you have for me?"

"Jehiel will be here next week."

"Excellent, Spencer! I will call on you on the usual day, and will have the meeting time and place for him."

"I still think you should give me the money and I'll pass it to him."

"I need to see him for myself, give him the money. I think Condon reports my actions to Lady Adair, and I don't want her to find out I have given away her money. I am planning to elude Condon's vigilance when I go out to meet Jehiel."

Of the fifty guineas Lady Adair had given her, Charlotte had decided that she could send fifty pounds to be split between the two communities in need. She would still have fifty shillings, or two-and-a-half pounds, left over—more money than she foresaw needing while she stayed at Adair House.

The next morning, the weather was blustery, and several violent rain showers passed through. In the afternoon, however, the rain discontinued and the skies lightened to a mere overcast. Still, the day looked uninviting.

Sir Percival arrived early for his driving engagement with Charlotte. She had rather hoped inclement weather would force a cancellation and was not ready.

Hastings showed him into the drawing room. That he still wore his caped driving coat told Charlotte he did not intend to forego the excursion. "Oh, dear. I presumed our appointment would be postponed on such an inclement day."

"It is not at all unpleasant out there. I brought along a rug to cover your, er, limbs, and a hot brick. I am sure if you dress warmly, you will be perfectly comfortable."

With Lady Adair's matchmaking eyes upon her, Charlotte could not excuse herself. "If you have no objection to waiting while I dress . . ."

"Certainly not! I shall wait right here for you."

Charlotte went upstairs. Knowing Sir Percival was standing in his coat, she tried to hurry. Charlotte selected an old blue wool dress she had worn for years. Condon said, "You cannot mean to wear this old gown."

"I've no intention of freezing in an open carriage. It's the warmest dress I have. If Sir Percival is put off by my attire, then he should not have insisted I go driving with him on such a disagreeable day."

Grumb'   the maid gave in. Charlotte descended with a warm pel   ver her arm. Sir Percival awaited her at the foot of the stairs and led her outside.

A bright yellow curricle stood in front of Lady Adair's townhouse. A tiger in black and yellow livery held two glossy black horses steady in their traces. Although the horses were well kept and showy, something looked a little lacking about them. Jamie would have said they were peacocky.

Still, the prospect of a drive in such a splendid equipage gave a lift to Charlotte's spirits as Sir Percival handed her up, fussily drew the rug over her legs and positioned the hot brick at her feet. She was a little chagrined at this evidence of consideration for her, given her lack of affinity for him.

Sir Percival seated himself next to her and the tiger jumped up behind. The horses sprang forward at Sir Percival's signal.

Silence reigned as they rode the short distance to Hyde Park and entered the grounds. There were few people about, the weather apparently having discouraged them from taking the a'

Once they were trotting along the carriage path, however,

Sir Percival turned to look at her and said, "I should tell you, I knew your brother at school."

"Jamie? Do you mean at Oxford?" A leap of puzzlement and joy rose in Charlotte—and a considerable wariness also. She seldom heard anything favorable about her brother.

"No, at Eton. Er, that is, I didn't know him well. I was a couple of years younger, and therefore out of his circle, don't you know. I always admired him greatly. What happened was a terrible tragedy."

An overwhelming wave of warmth flooded her chest. "Thank you." Her voice sounded strange to her, vibrating with the powerful emotions his praise engendered and with the threat of tears.

"I'm sorry," Sir Percival said quickly. "I shouldn't have mentioned him at all. I'm sure such thoughts must be exceedingly painful."

"Oh, no! You can't know how grateful I am to hear you say what you did. I would very much like to know everything you can tell me about him."

"I should be glad to, but it's little enough, as I said. I was an orphan, you see. I went to live with my uncle and he left me alone a great deal. By the time I went to Eton, I had become unaccustomed to the company of other young people. Boys at school can be very unkind, especially to one such as I, whom they perceive as lacking in confidence. I was subjected to considerable harassment. James defended me, kept the worst of the bullies from me. He was my hero."

Charlotte could not help the tears that came by this time, although she kept her face turned so other passersby would not see. "Thank you so much for telling me," she whispered. "You can't know how much what you have said means to me."

"I am glad, though very sorry to have overset you so. I should have chosen a more private place to tell you. I did not expect . . . It was foolish of me not to anticipate hearing this would be distressing for you. Are you all right? Perhaps I should take you home."

"No, I am fine. I have regained control of myself now.

Please, let us continue." She brushed at her cheeks with the back of her glove, ashamed that she had misjudged Sir Percival.

After a little pause, he said, "I do hope it is not too cool for you. Perhaps I was overly eager to see more of you and should not have insisted on our drive today."

"Oh, no, I am perfectly comfortable. I must thank you for your consideration in taking such pains for me."

"My pleasure," he said gruffly. "Miss Treadwell, I came to Town this Season specifically to look for a wife. I have two young children in my care—my niece and nephew. They need a mother. As I already explained, I was not used to the company of boys before I was sent to school, and I have no experience at all of young girls. I really don't know how to manage."

"Oh, I see." Her heart sinking, she awaited his next words. Surely he wouldn't propose so early in their acquaintance, would he? She would have to refuse if he did.

He went on, "I won't say any more." Charlotte relaxed at these words.

Sir Percival said, "We scarcely know each other. However, I felt I needed to speak honestly about my situation. With you being a little more mature than the usual debutante, and having some experience of children, you seem to be exactly the sort of helpmeet I need. Of course, I would expect you would wish to get to know the children before you were ready to even consider my suit. Could I bring them to meet you some time?"

"Er, certainly," she managed.

"Good, good," he said heartily.

Charlotte felt more easy at Lady Adair's soirée. Whether from the circumstance of being in the familiar surroundings of Adair House, or because she was coming to know a great many of the guests, she was glad that she could relax and enjoy herself.

"Oh! I'm so excited!" Miss Vernon rushed up to Charlotte as soon as the Vernons arrived. "You will never believe how beautiful my ball is going to be. Pallas has installed trellises against the walls of the ballroom and has already set ivy and roses—oh, and some other flowers too—climbing up them. It looks just like a garden!"

"That sounds lovely indeed," Charlotte said, smiling at the younger woman.

"And my sister Genie and her husband will be in Town to attend as well! I haven't seen her since the birth of her baby—oh, months ago now. She has decided to come for the Season."

"We will hear of nothing but balls until this affair is over." Arthur Vernon came up to join them.

Miss Vernon stuck out her tongue at her brother and said, "I have been waiting for my come-out ever since Pallas made her debut ages ago. I knew I would have a wonderful time, and it is everything I hoped it would be!"

Charlotte envied Miss Vernon her pleasurable excitement.

Mr. Vernon turned to Charlotte. "I do hope Lady Adair intends to have dancing this evening?"

"Yes, that is in her plans. I believe the musicians will arrive shortly."

"Good. Will you save me a dance?"

"Certainly you may have one."

"I shall await my fate, then." He bore his sister off, and Charlotte turned to greet more arriving guests. She promised dances to several, including Sir Percival and Lord Leyland. Charlotte had not yet danced with Rayfield, and she hoped she would finally have the chance tonight. He had almost indicated he had entered the lists to court her, so she thought it likely he would ask. The idea created fluttery feelings inside, rather uncomfortable really. He could have not have truly meant anything by his casual words anyway.

The musicians were warming up their instruments, and dancers began to form sets. Sir Percival, who had insisted upon being allowed the first dance, came to claim her.

Since her drive with him three days before, and his admission of admiration for Jamie, her opinion of Sir Percival had undergone a change, so she was pleased to stand up with him.

His intentions were more likely to be serious than Rayfield's, with the two young relatives he must rear. She knew he looked upon her as a possible mother for them.

As they stood in place, waiting for the music to begin, Sir Percival said, "Miss Treadwell, I shall leave soon for my country home to bring my niece and nephew back to Town. I hope that you will wish to meet them."

"I quite look forward to it, Sir Percival."

The dance began and their role as the active couple gave them no further chance for conversation for awhile. When they stood out at the bottom of the set, they spoke of generalities.

Charlotte kept watching for Rayfield to arrive, but he had not yet made an appearance. She danced with several of the young men who had bespoken dances with her.

When he came in, Charlotte missed his entrance. She only became aware of his presence as he was bowing before her just as she told Mr. Vernon he could have a second dance with her—the final number of the evening.

"Sorry, old boy, you are about to steal the dance she promised to me." Giving Charlotte no time to protest this lie, Rayfield grabbed her hand and pulled her into the bottom of the nearest set. Charlotte caught just a glimpse of Mr. Vernon's amused expression, no doubt in response to the outrage in her own, as she was whisked away.

"This is infamous! I did not promise you a dance, and if I had, you would have forfeited your right to claim it by arriving so late." Their position as an extra couple in the set gave them time to talk—to quarrel, actually, since Charlotte was disposed to take exception to his high-handed method of ensuring her agreement.

"You didn't want to dance with that popinjay, did you?"

"He is not a popinjay! He is a very nice young man."

"I thought so!" Rayfield said smugly.

"You thought what?"

"That you didn't care particularly for Mr. Vernon."

"I certainly do care for him!"

He looked at her with a thoughtful expression. "You don't think he is seriously courting you, do you?"

"Of course not! He is amusing himself, and me!"

"You shouldn't allow your time to be taken up with men who aren't candidates for your hand."

"As if you are! I should not allow my time to be taken up with you." She made as if to stalk away from the set, hurt by his thoughtless words. He caught her hand and stopped her. At that moment the couple above them turned to include them in the dance, and she was trapped.

They had no further opportunity to talk for some time. Charlotte simmered, and wondered why he had the power to overset her so. She didn't like him above half. Oh, she was only fooling herself. She liked him far better than she wished to. She must remember he represented everything she abhorred.

Hugh watched the play of emotions across Charlotte's face as they went through the motions of the dance. She smiled at the other dancers in the proper places, but when she faced him, a mulish expression set in. He needed to pacify her if he had any chance of getting close.

The problem was he'd lost his cool sense of detachment when he saw Mr. Vernon hanging 'round her again. It could only be because he feared the young man's becoming entangled in the web of a dangerous spy. Logic told him that Vernon was too young and immature to fall seriously in love, but men of that age were often vulnerable to the intrigues of a wicked woman.

He frowned at the absurdity of imagining Miss Treadwell as a practiced seducer of young men. He'd swear she would have no notion of how to set about a seduction—her manners with the opposite sex were unusually straightforward for a woman.

At that point they reached the top of the set and stood out a turn. Miss Treadwell lowered her gaze. He must speak first, as he could see by her pout that she would not.

"I apologize for coming in so late, and for compounding my sin by rudeness."

Her head whipped up, eyes wide with surprise.

"I have a very good excuse, however."

"And what might that be?" Her voice was cool.

"I had an important meeting." The skepticism in her eyes did not abate, and he said, more firmly, "I do take my duties in the House of Lords seriously." Miss Treadwell looked immediately to the side of the dance floor, where Lord Adair stood talking with some of his political colleagues. "No, Parliament was not sitting this evening. I still had a meeting, however."

He had waited hours for Norris, who in turn had waited for the last of his men to report in. It took longer to collect the reports with his men being so scattered.

The surveillance on his various suspects had been abandoned when Wescott had pulled several of his men to deal with the explosive situation in the midlands and north. However, during the time he had maintained it there had been no signs any of the other suspects had any connection with the Luddites.

If only Miss Treadwell knew what his meeting had been about. However, the suspicious look in her eyes faded. They rejoined the dance, and Hugh gave himself over to the enjoyment of the music, the touch of Miss Treadwell's gloved hand on his arm, the sensation of her nearness. If he could not understand her appeal for a handsome, well-to-do young man like Arthur Vernon, it was equally puzzling why he himself found her so fascinating. Doubtless it was merely the puzzle of whether she could be guilty of the heinous crimes of which he suspected her.

During the next three days, he stayed as close to Miss Treadwell as propriety allowed. He called at Sylvia's during her at-home hours and stayed by Miss Treadwell's side, attempting to persuade her to ride with him, and he attended whatever evening events the Adairs and Miss Treadwell graced.

He met daily with Condon, who had nothing of interest to report. Miss Treadwell's activities were wholly those of a young lady enjoying the Season. She never met with anyone the least suspicious, either during Condon's watch or his own.

Hugh's frustration mounted at this lack of progress. To occupy himself, and to make sure he had overlooked nothing, he pored over his copy of Debrett's to make sure he did not overlook any peer who was hiding motives or opportunities to become a spy and should have been on his list.

It was fruitless. He had to face the fact that the spy must be Miss Treadwell.

CHAPTER THIRTEEN

From the case notebook of Hugh Broderick Brooks, the Earl of Rayfield:

Entry dated 18th of April, 1812:
The hunt is coming to a close. I await reports from some of my agents in the field and expect to make an arrest within a few days.

Author's note: A section follows that was in a different code. I still intend to break this code as well, and will include the decoded message in the next edition of the book. (A. McM.)

(Decoded by Alphonsius McMasters, PhD, LLC, AKC, OBE, BMW, historian and author of The Secret Wars of Napoleon, *2005.)*

On Tuesday, Hugh was at Sylvia's again. Most of the morning callers had left, but he was taking advantage of his position as Sylvia's brother to linger.

He sat beside Miss Treadwell on the settee, one arm resting along the back, the fingers close enough to touch a lock of her hair if he gave in to the temptation. The spring sunlight poured in the windows of Sylvia's drawing room and touched Charlotte's dark waves, making them gleam. Increasingly, it was difficult to restrain his impulses around her. He should visit one of the accommodating women of his acquaintance, but the pressures of his investigation did not allow time for such indulgence. He didn't want anyone besides Charlotte, anyway.

He smiled gently at her. "Miss Treadwell, please tell me why you are so adamantly against borrowing a horse from Sylvia to go riding? As you lived in the country most of your life, I am sure it would bring back pleasant memories to ride again."

"Since you insist, I am the most abysmal rider. Jamie—my brother—attempted for years to teach me to ride. I was afraid of horses and not at all proficient upon the sidesaddle. After he died, Father sold the horses, and I have not been able, nor wished, to ride in many years now." She smiled sadly.

He made one last attempt to press her. "If it has been many years, you owe it to yourself to try again. You may find it wholly different. I am sure Sylvia has a quiet, docile horse in her stable that you will not find too taxing. We won't go out in the afternoon when the paths are crowded, but early in the morning when no one is about. Just go with me one time, and if you still find it disagreeable, I will never ask again."

"Oh, why are you so persistent?" Charlotte shook her head. "Very well, to end this discussion, I will go with you once."

"Excellent! I will consult Sylvia to make sure we choose the gentlest horse in her stable. Tomorrow morning?"

"Not so soon!"

"When, then?"

"Next Saturday."

"Very well."

"She sent me out on an errand. I left to comply, but some intuition told me she had some secret and I returned in time to see her go. I must be more alert, your lordship. It isn't easy to handle my duties as lady's maid and be able to follow her." Miss Condon stared down at the cup of coffee before her.

"Yes, I know that. Were you able to determine where she

went?" Hugh sipped from his own cup and looked about the coffeehouse. Everything seemed normal. The few customers paid no attention to a middle-aged maid and a male servant, a groom perhaps, who sat drinking coffee on their afternoon off.

"Oh, yes. It was easy enough to follow her. She never seemed to suspect a thing."

"Where did she go?"

"First to a bank, then to a coffeehouse, where she met a young man. I dared not follow her into either place, since she would have recognized me."

"I shall follow up on the bank. What about the young man?"

"I have not seen him before. He looked like a servant, and I should say Miss Treadwell looked much like a servant herself in those clothes she refuses to discard from her governessing."

"What did he look like?"

"Tall, blond, perhaps twenty-five or so, looked like someone who'd never think of committing a crime. One of those round, sweet faces."

"Did you attempt to follow the man when they parted?"

"I could not, your lordship. I had already been out longer than the time my errand would have taken. I needed to carry it out and return so she did not suspect."

It needed more men than he had available to keep a watch on Miss Treadwell. Who was the man she met? Her subterfuge in sending Condon away not only argued for her guilt, but her awareness of being under surveillance.

He went to the bank Condon reported Charlotte had visited.

"Oh, sir, I knew I should never have given her the money!" The clerk nearly had an apoplexy, so agitated was he at Hugh's inquiry.

"What money did you give her?"

"She had money—fifty pounds. I merely changed them into notes. I feared they were stolen. I refused at first, but she asked to speak to the owner. I didn't know what to do!"

"No need to fret. The money was hers. I am afraid she is

being taken advantage of by a suitor. I merely wish to protect her. She said nothing about what she wanted the money for?"

"Oh, dear! She dressed so poorly, I thought her a servant or . . . I don't know. You mean she actually has money?"

"She won't have if she keeps giving it away," said Hugh grimly. He half-feared his act with the clerk was true. If so, to whom was she giving it? She had the fifty guineas he had given her through Sylvia; fifty pounds was the greater part of that. Was that the money she had changed? If so, what had happened to the money the French had sent to carry out their directives? What was this woman about?

Later that afternoon, when Hugh met Norris, he finally had the break he had been hoping for.

Norris could hardly conceal his glee when he sat down with him. "I think we've found our link, Broddie. Spencer had a caller today, his nephew. Lives in some little village in Sussex. Sent a man to follow him back to his lair, and I'll send more men there to follow those he meets with back at home."

"Did you say a little village?" Hugh's heart pounded fast.

"Yes."

"Could it be Rockcliffe?"

"I think that's the one."

"Eureka! Miss Treadwell's old home, and where her brother was killed ferrying French spies. What did he look like?"

"A younger version of old Spencer. Tall, gangly, blond."

"Blond?" It could be the man Miss Treadwell had met. "I think we've got her now!"

"I'll send some of my best men so there's no slip-ups."

"No, wait. Those little villages—they know everybody around. If several strangers show up and start to follow a resident around, they'll be noticed. I'll go myself—no, I can't do that, I have obligations here. Damnation!"

He was shorthanded. He could not risk some fumbler throwing away all their work. "I'll ask Scott," using the code name Wescott went by, "to put a more expert man on it. Your man will follow the nevvy until he's relieved?"

"Young Spencer took the public stage back home. I sent onc of my best after him. He got a seat on the stage, but of course after that, Spencer will recognize him if he spots him following him around the village. I'm sure he'll do the best he can."

"I'll go to Scott and get it set up. Meet me tonight." Hugh could not conceal the triumph he felt. He would shortly have Miss Treadwell caught in the pincers of a trap. On the heels of that thought came a picture of Charlotte in prison and pain stabbed him. Would they execute a woman? How could he be responsible for her ending in such a way? No! For betraying her country, she deserved whatever penalty was meted out.

"You're quite sure she won't go fast and run away with me?" Charlotte looked dubiously at the pretty gray mare that stood quietly in front of Adair House, alongside a tall bay.

"She has been very well trained. She will not take any action you do not signal her to do."

"All right, then." She tried to keep the fear out of her voice, tried to block out the numerous memories of falls from the too-spirited horses Jamie always put her up on.

She had tried so desperately to keep up with Jamie, to follow him on his wild rides. He taught her to ride with as much patience as he possessed, but going slow was beyond his ability, even to help a fearful younger sister. Her very fears had frozen her muscles, made the falls inevitable.

The groom who brought the horse from the mews helped her into the sidesaddle. "Are you ready?" Rayfield asked.

At her tense nod, he mounted his own horse and led the way. The mare stepped daintily after, her stride smooth and quiet. Gradually Charlotte's heart moved back into place as she settled into the rhythm. They entered the park, and as Rayfield had predicted, it was deserted at this early hour.

He glanced her way from time to time, as if to make sure

she had not fallen off. When he finally spoke, however, he surprised her with, "You have a good seat."

"Thank you. My brother taught me to ride. He was an excellent teacher of the basics."

"You miss him."

Unbidden tears came to her eyes. "Yes."

"He must have been some years older than you."

"Six. He never treated me as a child, but as a friend. When I was four, we stole out of the nursery at midnight on Midsummer's Eve to look for faerie rings. When I was eight, he brought me an orphaned fox cub and helped me raise it. When it grew up, he made me let it go. 'Wild things must be free,' he said."

Charlotte looked at Rayfield, struck by his quiet listening and the warmth in his eyes. He smiled at her, and her heart performed an intense thump. This early morning ride she had dreaded became a delight. Her observations extended to the newly leafing branches of the trees and fresh blades of grass, the feel of the breeze on her cheeks, cool and fresh.

"You are doing so well," he broke into her thoughts, "why don't we have a little gallop?"

Instantly, she froze. "No!" Her voice came out as an inaudible squeak.

He obviously did not hear because his horse leapt into a ground-eating lope.

She felt the mare quiver beneath her as the animal responded, breaking into a stride to match. Charlotte tried to hold her back, but all her earlier competence disappeared in her panic, and the horse ignored her hands pulling on the reins.

It was the old nightmare from her rides with Jamie. She felt herself slipping from the saddle, saw the ground rushing to meet her, and closed her eyes against the pain.

Hugh heard nothing. Perhaps that was his clue—the lack of the sound of hoofbeats behind him. He turned to look and saw the riderless horse standing, perhaps a hundred yards back. Instantly he whirled Gerbold around and raced back to where Charlotte lay unmoving on the ground, almost beneath her horse. The well-trained mare had stopped instantly when her rider fell.

Cursing himself for his neglect, he jumped down and ran to her. She already stirred, trying to sit up. "Don't move!" he called. "Are you hurt?" he asked as he knelt beside her.

She didn't answer him but looked around her dazedly, her face dead-white and her eyes blank with shock. He pressed her to the ground against her efforts to sit.

"Let me make sure you are not hurt." He felt her limbs for broken bones, and then helped her to a sitting position. "Oh, God, Charlotte, I'm so sorry. Do you hurt anywhere?"

Slowly her focus came back. "I think I'm just shaken up." Her voice came in whispery gasps.

Hardly knowing what he did, he wrapped her in his arms, pulling her against his chest. She clung to him, shaking. Still shaken, himself, with fear, and lost in the warmth of her body, he kissed her. He felt her intake of breath against his mouth and then her lips softened and molded to his. He lost control, wanting more, wanted to go on kissing her until time stopped. He laid her down on the grass, his tongue seeking entry to her mouth. Then he remembered. She was most likely his traitor. He let go, staring into her eyes. Their green depths were dreamy at first, changing to confusion.

Finally, he asked brusquely, "Do you think you would be able to ride back to my sister's if we take it slowly?"

She shuddered but nodded, and he helped her stand and then lifted her into the saddle.

He mounted his own horse and they started back the way they had come. His whole body felt as though he suffered an ague. He could swear she even tasted like roses. How could he go on with this investigation? The faceless monster he had imagined at first now had a face, a personality.

He knew so much about her—her passionate caring for her

faithful servants, for even a Cockney boy of no importance; her fierce independence—and yet he didn't know enough.

What would lead her to betray her country? Clearly, the answer lay in her brother's effect on her life. But that was not his concern; he must only defeat the attempt to start a revolution and turn its instigator over to the authorities. He would do his duty, as he'd been so thoroughly trained to do by his father. But all his pleasure in the hunt was gone.

After Hugh returned Charlotte to his sister's house, he called on Wescott. He did not yet expect a report from Norris's man in Rockcliffe, or from the others Wescott had sent there.

Their plan was to send an official from the Home Office to gather information from the local riding officer about the village and its inhabitants. They also sent an agent disguised as a tinker and one to impersonate a reckless young aristocrat who suffered a curricle accident just outside the village and had to shelter there while the vehicle was repaired.

The three men had no doubt separately reached the village by now. But they would not have had time to report to Norris's man, or for him to carry information back to London.

Still, Hugh needed to confirm all the men had been dispatched according to plan. Although he only went through the motions, his heart no longer in his search, he must give it his best. He could not let England be ripped apart, blood spilled, the terror and chaos France had undergone coming to its shores.

Wescott met him anxiously. "Matters are coming to a head. On the eleventh, one-hundred-and-fifty men, who gathered from several different areas, attacked William Cartwright's mill. Luckily, the mill was well defended and the attackers were forced to retreat. Two of them were killed and others wounded.

"The attacks are becoming more general and widespread. Just yesterday there were riots in Stockport and the houses of several owners of steam-looms attacked. Food riots in Sheffield and Rotherham. We need to wrap this up quickly. It's less than a fortnight until the first of May, and it looks like 'M. Mansson's' plans are coming to pass just as he envisioned."

"I know, sir. This matter will be settled within a few days now. We must not move on Miss Treadwell without evidence."

Chapter Fourteen

"I am fine." Lady Adair's worried look chafed Charlotte. She could use her shaking up that morning to evade still another social event. After Rayfield's kiss, however, she decided to encourage an offer from one of her somewhat laggardly suitors.

How could she have allowed herself to do what she had promised she never would: love a man who trod the same path as the other men in her life? Even if his strange, sporadic courtship were real, he would only bring her heartbreak.

Papa's neglect had contributed greatly to her mother's decline and early death. As a young girl, Charlotte had seen her mother's anxious waiting for Papa's return from his frequent jaunts to London. She had slowly despaired that he would ever change, become resigned and listless, finally an invalid. Papa had gone through Mother's money, as through the remnants of his own inheritance after generations of gamesters and wastrels.

Papa had loved his wife, Charlotte had no doubt. His sincere grief when she died proved that. But his love was not enough to keep him home, to keep him from his ruinous course.

No, she could never allow herself to be ensnared in such a marriage. Far better to place herself beyond temptation.

When she arrived with the Adairs at Lady Templeton's rout party, though, she realized she had erred. The guests were the usual people one saw throughout the Season. Arthur Vernon still hovered, but even if she believed his interest was sincere, she was sure those feelings would not last. He had some quality, something still unformed in his character. He would be a good man once he was mature, but she could not wait that long.

Lord Leyland certainly looked for a mother for his son, but so far he had shown no sign that he saw Charlotte in the position. Would she wish to be married to him? He was so sober and conventional. Just the sort of man she always thought she wanted, but somehow, after Rayfield, he seemed tedious.

Sir Percival did not attend, and she remembered he had gone to his country home to bring his young wards to meet her. This implied the earnestness of his intentions. And since their drive a few days before, when he proved so amiable and pleasant, she favored him. However, he was not in Town, so she could not further her acquaintance with him at Lady Templeton's rout.

Rayfield, however, did attend. That made Charlotte regret her insistence she felt well enough to attend. While he greeted his hostess and gradually made his way toward her, she had to force herself to stand her ground. When he spoke to her, she would probably blush and make a cake of herself. Indeed, her cheeks felt very warm already. What could she say to him?

And then he was before her. "Good evening, Charlotte," he said softly. "Are you recovered from your mishap?"

"I am fine, sir."

"Charlotte, I deeply regret what happened. I wouldn't have wanted you hurt for the world."

Now she indeed felt herself blushing, noting his use of her name. "It was not your fault," she blurted. "It happens every time I ride. I should have refused to go with you."

"Every time? As good a rider as you are?"

"I haven't ridden for several years." Since Jamie died. "Perhaps I am simply out of practice." She looked away, but his gaze resting on her was still tangible. She turned back to him with a change of subject, and the moment passed.

Somehow, she survived the evening. As she stepped out of the Adairs' carriage upon the return home, a small form detached itself from a shadow and intercepted her. "Miss Treadwell?"

"Flea? What are you doing here at this hour?"

"I needs you. Could you come, and bring your medicines?"

"Of course. You're not ill?" In the lamplight, Flea looked just as usual. "Is it one of your friends? Ned?" Fear sharpened her voice. Ned had not had time to recover from his illness, and a boy his size, with his hard start in life . . .

"Not Ned." Flea hesitated. "A friend, I think."

Not Rayfield. She had just parted from him. "All right. Let me go in and get my medical supplies."

"You can't go with that ragamuffin!" Lady Adair gasped.

"I must. I'll be all right."

"I forbid it. Hugh will kill me if I let you go. If he doesn't kill you himself!"

"I apologize, Lady Adair." Whoever was so important to Flea that he asked for her help, she would not fail the boy.

Sylvia looked angrily at Charlotte for a moment, and then sighed. "Take the carriage at least. Hixon will provide you some protection. In fact, Hixon, get a couple of the grooms up to accompany you and arm them with stout cudgels."

Lady Adair silenced the coachman's grumbles with a glance.

Charlotte hurried to gather her supplies. Flea had said nothing about the injuries or illness his friend suffered from, so she could only guess what she might need.

Flea sat on the edge of the carriage seat, his small body vibrating so severely with tension that it conveyed itself to Charlotte also. What would she be faced with when they arrived?

The carriage ride seemed to take forever. Flea led at a rapid pace through the dark passage. She tried to keep up, but stumbled a few times. "Sorry, Miss Treadwell." Flea lent her his arm and they made their way to the courtyard to his rooms. By lit coals in the brazier, she dimly made out boys bending over someone, but her view was blocked by their small bodies.

"'Ow is she?" Flea asked.

"The same," said one of the boys.

She? What was going on?

"I brung Miss Treadwell. Move so's she can see."

With a shuffle and murmuring, the bodies moved aside and Charlotte got her first glimpse of her patient. *A dog?*

She looked sternly at Flea.

"I'm sorry, miss. I couldn't tell ya. I be afraid ya wouldn't come if'n you knew it were just a dog."

Sighing, Charlotte approached the animal lying on one of the pallets she had seen on her previous visit. She could see little in the dimness. All she could make out was mud, blood—mostly dried, it seemed—and bones thinly covered by hide. "I need more light. Do you have a torch or any candles in here?"

Flea and the others quickly produced some stubs of candles, lit them in the coals and stuck them into the dirt on the floor around the dog. As Charlotte knelt to examine her, she lifted her head, curled her upper lip to expose her teeth and rumbled low in her throat. Charlotte jumped back. "Good heavens!"

"'Er don't mean nothin'. She's just 'fraid o' bein' 'urt."

"I know that. But how did you ever get her in here?"

"'Er knows we were trying to 'elp 'er."

"She doesn't seem to have confidence in me!" Charlotte looked into the wary golden brown eyes. She read a world of distrust, but also of appeal. She sighed. "Flea, could you come around and hold her head, maybe talk to her?"

Flea scrambled around to stroke the creature's head tenderly and leaned over to croon in her ear. "It's orright, lovey, 'er's goin' to make you all right 'n' tight."

The dog relaxed and allowed Charlotte to run her hands lightly over her. "She has at least one broken rib, perhaps more. I can do nothing for that. If it were a person, I'd wrap her chest, but she would only tear bandages off, and such effort wouldn't be good for her. Otherwise, she seems all right. I can't tell if she has any internal injuries. If a broken end of a rib punctured a lung or other vital organ, she will die."

Not the heart. The dog would not have survived as long as it took Flea to travel across town to get Charlotte and bring her back if her heart had been pierced. "I can make her more comfortable for now. You'll need to keep her as quiet as possible. Time will tell about any complications. The ribs will heal on their own."

Charlotte took a closer look at the dog. Her first impression that she was mostly skin stretched over a skeleton was correct, but the dog appeared to be pure foxhound, if Charlotte could guess correctly at her conformation under the blood and mud that marked her piebald coat.

"Whatever brought you to London?" she asked the dog. "You should be living in the country somewhere, well cared for along with the rest of your pack."

"Don't know 'ow she come to be 'ere," said Flea. "She were wandering the streets and then a carriage run her over."

"You poor thing," Charlotte said. Then, getting to her feet, she looked for her bag and took out the bottle of laudanum. She had no idea of the dosage to give a dog.

With the boys' help, she dosed the dog with a small amount of the laudanum and cleaned some of the dirt and blood off her coat. "That's all I can do tonight. I'll return tomorrow to check on her—later today, I should say."

She looked at the four boys. Flea spoke up. "Oh. You ain't met Blackie 'n' Tom. They's my other mates."

Blackie was easy to identify, at least if the dirt that packed every crevice of his face and hands was the reason behind the name. Tom was the largest of the four boys, although Charlotte surmised that he was no older than Flea.

With one last look at the dog, already relaxing into sleep, Charlotte said, "I must go now." Flea led her back to the alley. Charlotte noticed for the first time that Hixon had armed himself with a blunderbuss. The two grooms looked around suspiciously, tapping their cudgels against their hands.

"Goodnight, Flea," Charlotte said, as one of the grooms helped her into the carriage. "I'll come back tomorrow."

"I'll come get you again," Flea promised. "You don't want to find yer way 'ere alone."

* * *

"Your Lordship! Wake up! There's one of your assistants to see you—says it's an emergency!"

Hugh reluctantly pulled his awareness from the depths of sleep and looked up at his valet. "Who is it, Bracegirdle?"

"Some female—says her name is Condon."

No! Something's happened to Charlotte! All traces of sleepiness vanished as he jumped out of bed and reached for the breeches his valet handed him. Pulling on a shirt, he went downstairs and into his study. Condon stood, a remarkably still figure. Away from Sylvia's she resembled little her lady's maid pose and much the efficient secret agent she was for Wescott.

"What is it, Miss Condon?"

"Miss Treadwell got away from me tonight."

"'Got away' from you? How did that happen?"

"She returned home with the Adairs and met with a street urchin who requested her help with a medical matter."

Flea. Condon apparently saw his fractional relaxation and hastened to add, "Miss Treadwell called the boy Flea. Lady Adair only reported what Charlotte said. It occurred to me that Lady Adair has not seen the boy; Miss Treadwell could have taken advantage of that fact and arranged matters accordingly."

"Yes, that's possible. I can't imagine why Flea should go looking for Miss Treadwell in the middle of the night. Did you say he claimed a medical emergency?"

"Yes, but the boy himself seemed to be healthy. Miss Treadwell did put together a medical kit before she left, whether in genuine need or only as a pretense I can't say."

"And Miss Treadwell's taking time to gather medical supplies did not give you time to arrange to follow her?" Anger at her incompetence overcame him.

"No, my lord, unfortunately Lady Adair gave her the use of her carriage, so nothing delayed her, whereas I could not find a hackney to follow at that time of night until it was too late to catch her up. If you think it likely such incidents may recur, we shall need to have a vehicle handy for the future. Sadly, I did not think to be prepared for this emergency."

"No, you are right, I do not see how we could have foreseen her taking such impulsive action. If it was Flea, I can find out from him why he called for her, but if not, we must take steps to prevent a recurrence. However, it would have been better had you waited until our normal meeting time to report to me, Miss Condon. You may have been observed coming here, which would do neither our cause nor your reputation any good."

"I thought the circumstances justified the risk, my lord."

For the first time, Hugh regretted not knowing where Flea lived. He could always get hands on him within a few minutes through Pearl or one of the street boys, and the boy had been remarkably protective of the secret of his "ken." Still, if the story was true, he had shared it with Charlotte this night.

And if the boy Charlotte Treadwell went off with was not Flea . . . Hugh shuddered at the possibilities. The carriage had not yet returned when Condon sought him, and making a carriage disappear was a more difficult matter than doing the same for a woman. He would have to wait until morning to investigate further, although sleep was beyond him now.

Later that morning Hugh easily found Flea, who admitted he had come for Miss Treadwell in the middle of the night.

"It were a dog, Broddie."

"A dog?"

"Ye-ah, it were in pain. Run over by a carriage, it were. I were scared for it."

"You brought Miss Treadwell back into the slums in the middle of the night for nothing more than a dog!"

"Saved Ned's life, it did! 'E were 'bout to get runned over by the carriage and the dog knocked 'im outer the way. Took the wheels instead, poor thing. Couldn't leave it to suffer after that!"

"And you explained that to Miss Treadwell?"

"No." The boy looked down, clasped his hands behind his back and scraped a toe in the dirt. "Was afraid she wouldn't come if'n I told 'er. She thought it were a person I'd come to find 'elp for. She treated the dog right fine, though, when she saw 'er. She ain't no spy."

Hugh ignored this last and went to call on Charlotte and Sylvia. When he arrived, his sister grabbed him by the arm the moment he walked in, and dragged him off to the library.

"You must do something, Hugh! That ragamuffin boy you have befriended came for Miss Treadwell the moment we arrived home and she insisted on going off with him. I have never been so alarmed. He said someone was ill and she never had a thought of refusing to accompany him! I was sure she would be robbed."

"If I'm not mistaken, I saw Miss Treadwell in your drawing room before you dragged me away. She looked none the worse for the experience."

"No, she came home about dawn. She would only say that her patient was a lady who had fallen upon hard times. I scarcely know what to think, Hugh. Please talk to her and make her tell you more about this . . . this folly. Let her know that she must not traipse off in the middle of the night."

"I'll talk to her, but don't expect results, Sylvia. If she didn't listen to you, I doubt she will put much stock in what I have to say."

Hugh strolled to Charlotte. She glanced at him cautiously as he approached. "I understand you have been giving succor to a lady who has fallen upon hard times." Despite the gravity of the matter, he could not restrain the humor in his tone.

"Why, yes. Poor, dear lady."

"And what have these hard times reduced her to doing?"

Would Charlotte even understand the question? But she blushed as she replied. "Oh, she has been reduced to begging for such scraps as she can persuade anyone to part with. She is in even worse case now after an unfortunate carriage accident."

"I talked with Flea this morning, Miss Treadwell."

"Oh." She frowned in reproach. "So you set a trap for me just now. You know the 'lady' is a dog. She is a lady, all the same. I would swear she is pure foxhound of very fine breeding. How she came to be lost and in the city I do not know."

"I suppose it would be a waste of breath to suggest that where Flea lives is an exceedingly dangerous area for a young woman alone in the middle of the night?"

"Did Lady Adair not tell you I could not have been safer? I was attended by three strong, able men armed with cudgels and a blunderbuss. And Flea. I do not imagine such a need will arise again, but if it should, I would help a friend."

He sighed. "That's what I was afraid of. And if I pointed out that my sister was exceedingly worried about you?"

"I am sorry about that. She has been very kind and I would not give her pain for the world."

It was no kind of promise, but he would have to accept it. Matters were rushing to a conclusion in any case, and it was unlikely Charlotte would be living with Sylvia much longer.

At his meeting with Condon, he informed her of what he had learned of Miss Treadwell's late-night excursion and approved the outlay of a hackney upon call for Condon's possible need.

With mixed feelings, Hugh awaited Wescott's arrival in Lady Bristow's private salon. There should be a report from Norris. Despite his wish to have matters wrapped up, he hoped young Spencer's activities since returning home were innocent.

Wescott bustled in. "Interesting developments, Rayfield. Young Spencer works for the vicar in Rockcliffe. Vicar's a good man, no connection to smuggling or any other illegal business. Bachelor but has a sister with a large family that he helps support, so he's too poor to pay Spencer. Gives him room and board, and a deal of freedom to earn some money on the side. It's an unusual arrangement."

"Any word on how Spencer makes his side money?"

"Yes, he's a musician. Fiddler. Takes jobs playing at dances and weddings. Not much work in the village so he often goes farther afield."

"Is there any proof that he actually does take such jobs?"

"From all we've been able to learn. We've not uncovered any evidence that he has been involved in criminal activity. Before this, at any rate."

"And now?"

"Since he arrived back in Rockcliffe, he has called on the families of the men arrested smuggling with young Treadwell the night he was killed. Those still in the area, that is. They've fallen on hard times, and a couple have left to find work."

"Hard times, eh? How have they been surviving?"

"No proof any are still involved in smuggling. Lashford, the riding officer, keeps an eye on them for caution's sake."

"That's all the agents have to report?"

"So far."

"It isn't evidence. It's possible Miss Treadwell asked young Spencer to learn how the families were faring, or brought them some message of concern on her part." Hugh stood and paced, ruffling his hair with a hand. "Have you enough men to watch those families—at least able-bodied men in them?"

"Not for long. Small village, strangers are noticed. I've an agent posing as a wealthy Cit looking to buy country property. But his story limits him. He can't skulk around in the dark. We'll continue to send men with an excuse for passing through. We're doing what we can; asked Lashford to step up his vigilance. You must do more at this end. Keep up your watch on Miss Treadwell; try to get anything useful from her."

"I'm playing the devoted swain. It's the best excuse to be near her, but it has its limitations." The worst of which was his desire to make the pose a reality. "Condon keeps an eye on her whenever I cannot. She has examined Miss Treadwell's belongings and found nothing incriminating. I'm meeting with Condon later to learn if she has anything new to report."

CHAPTER FIFTEEN

Charlotte did not know whether the matter of her trip to treat the dog was laid to rest. Rayfield had seemed almost amused, although he tried to hide the emotion.

Flea came for her again in the afternoon, reporting the patient was better. Charlotte checked her, told Flea she judged the dog had suffered no internal injuries and was healing well. Flea named her "Lady" after the tale Charlotte told Lady Adair.

That evening she accompanied the Adairs to another of the everlasting balls. She hoped Rayfield would attend. No, she hoped he would stay miles away and not offer the temptation his unattainable presence would give her.

He was there and came to solicit a dance. She felt trembly and fevered each time the dance brought him close. Everything about him—his masculine, spicy scent, the underlying quality of danger, of leashed power—brought her senses alive. She no longer thought his looks ordinary. Those regular features hid depths she could only guess at but which fascinated her.

Her self promptings that his hints at courtship were flippant, and he was not the sort of man she wished to marry, couldn't stop her heart from beating faster when he gave her that serious, slow look.

She could not fall in love with a man who carried so many secrets, one who lived for the risks and adventure that had led

Jamie to his death. The trouble was, she very much feared it was already too late.

At the end of their dance, he brought her back to Lady Adair, and stood exchanging pleasantries with his sister, before bowing to Charlotte and saying, "Perhaps you will favor me with another dance later?"

She faltered, "I am not sure if I have any available."

"Try your best." He smiled and moved on. She was aware, however, as she danced with other partners and the night wore on, that he stayed nearby, his attention never straying from her. She became increasingly flustered with this marked notice.

Sir Percival arrived at the ball late. He came promptly to her side, saying, "I arrived just this evening. I am glad I discovered where you were. I brought my nephew and niece to Town with me and hope you will go for a drive with us tomorrow."

Charlotte agreed, glad for the distraction from Rayfield. Though she could not take seriously Rayfield's courtship, she knew Sir Percival had sincere intentions. He was a good man, taking in two young relatives, earnest in his plans for his estate. He was not romantic, but he was exactly the sort of man she had wished to marry, in her dreams before her father's ruin destroyed her hopes and in her plans since coming to Lady Adair.

"Jehiel Spencer has set off for the north." Wescott met Hugh with the news the following day.

"Have you had him followed?"

"Yes, by chance our agent impersonating a tinker had come back to Rockcliffe. Norris got word to him, and he travels just behind Spencer. He has the direction of someone in each area of Luddite activity so he can report Spencer's actions."

"He's making for Leeds, for Garwich."

"Why do you say that? He could intend to visit Stockport, Macclesfield, or Manchester. Or even all of them."

"He comes from an area connected with Miss Treadwell. I'll stake my life he's headed for another one."

"So, what do you think it means?"

"I don't know. That's been the trouble since the start. I believe the link is there, but I don't know what. Dash it! If I could count on her to tell the truth, I'd ask straight out."

"That would be a disaster."

"I know it, sir. I have proof that she isn't above lying when it suits her needs."

"What do you mean?"

Hugh told him of the dog and her tale to Lady Adair about the "lady" in distress.

"I don't like it," said Wescott. "I can't see rescuing a dog as the act of someone spying for the French."

"If she's the spy, I'd take an oath money isn't driving her. She's sympathetic, and the Luddites have cause for anger."

"They may have cause for anger, but that doesn't justify such destruction, or betrayal of their country."

"I know that, sir. But Miss Treadwell may not believe it." In fact, given the woman's rash disregard for rules or concern for her own safety, it was a sure bet that she believed the end justified the means. If the destruction were not so serious, he would probably admire the boldness of her vision.

Rayfield called on Charlotte just after Sir Percival arrived for their drive. She excused herself to the earl and could not help the puff of delight at his unhappy expression.

The afternoon was chilly although only a few high wisps of cloud floated in the sky. Instead of his curricle, which would not have contained all the party, Sir Percival had brought a barouche. The children were already ensconced in one of the seats, well bundled up and looking healthy and well cared for.

"Miss Treadwell, may I present Master Mercutio Queech and Miss Bianca Queech. This is Miss Treadwell, children, an especial friend of mine."

"How do you do, Master Mercutio and Miss Bianca. My, what unusual names!"

Sir Percival, handing a blanket to Charlotte to tuck about herself and placing a hot brick at her feet, said, "Their father was a Shakespearean actor. I believe, however, their given names were a folly more of my sister's than the children's father." He climbed up into the seat beside her.

The tiger jumped up beside the coachman and they started off. Sir Percival said, "I thought we might go to a nearby inn and have tea. It would not be proper to bring you to my bachelor apartments, and I do not know of any other place. If it were a warmer day, I would have suggested a picnic."

"That would be fine," Charlotte agreed.

As they drove off, she asked, "How old are the children?"

"Bianca is eight and Mercutio six."

The children had been silent so far. Charlotte thought they looked a little intimidated.

"How long have you had the care of them?"

"Only a few months. After their mother died about a year ago, they lived with my other sister for a time, but with several children of her own, she has neither the room nor the means to care for them. I try to help, but she is proud. Taking Bianca and Mercutio off her hands was all I could do."

The carriage pulled into the inn yard, and Sir Percival assisted her to dismount. The young tiger helped the children, although Mercutio hopped out of the carriage on his own. They went inside, and Sir Percival requested a private room.

While they waited, and the children stood some distance away, Sir Percival said to her in a low voice, "It is only fair to inform you that my sister ran away with their father and they were never married. He abandoned her. She endured much need before coming back to her family. I believe shame at her circumstances prevented her from asking for help until she was ill and feared what would become of the children if she died."

"How sad," said Charlotte. She lauded Sir Percival for taking in the children in such conditions. She liked him more and more.

When they were shown into the private room, Sir Percival busied himself removing Mercutio's outer clothing while Bianca struggled with the buttons on her coat. Charlotte approached the girl. "Would you like me to help you with that?"

Bianca smiled up shyly and nodded. Charlotte was struck by the girl's beauty; her violet eyes were accented by thick dark lashes, and a tumble of luxuriant black curls framed her face.

Charlotte unbuttoned Bianca's coat and took it off, then saw Sir Percival was still struggling with Mercutio's. "Here, Miss Treadwell, you seem to have a knack for small fastenings. Come help me with the boy's coat while I see to our order."

She complied, noting as she loosened the buttons that Mercutio resembled his sister, with ivory complexion, dusky curls, and eyes of dark gray rather than Bianca's violet ones.

Their tea arrived, chocolate for the children, with bread-and-butter and cakes. Sir Percival set cups of chocolate and a plate of bread-and-butter before the children. Charlotte poured tea for her and Sir Percival. Bianca and Mercutio looked wistfully at the cakes before taking up slices of bread.

"Can they not have one of these cakes, Sir Percival? I am sure there are too many for us to eat."

"Indeed, they may not!" Sir Percival looked sternly at the children, then turned toward Charlotte, his look softening. "Until recently they led a most irregular life, and it had a weakening effect on their health and character. It is most important for them to have a routine and a healthful diet."

"Indeed, you are right. How astute of you!" She too a slice of bread and bit into it. "Do you know, since the Season began, I am sure my own diet has been much too rich, as well."

The children watched with sober faces, but when she smiled at them, they returned it with cautious upturns of their lips.

"I shall be an actor when I grow up, like my father," Mercutio suddenly announced. Amused, Charlotte decided the statement was an act of small rebellion against the ban on cake.

Annoyance fleeted across Sir Percival's face, she saw. "You are very young to make up your mind," she replied to the boy. "Whatever you decide, you shall need a fine education. Actors must learn to read and study the works of great writers, as well as to figure. And those are the same subjects on which a person must take instruction for nearly any profession."

Sir Percival smiled gratefully at her calm turning aside Mercutio's provocation. She could help these children, she thought, and help Sir Percival with the challenge of rearing them. It would be rewarding to influence their young lives.

Even in the dimness of the theater, Charlotte looked alarmingly pale. Hugh could not count how many people had packed into the Adairs' theater box. Sylvia should have known better than to invite the Vernons to make up their party. The mass of young men trying to get near Miss Vernon during the interval seemed to suck away all the available air.

"Would you like to escape for a bit, Miss Treadwell?"

"Indeed, but we cannot reach the door."

"I'll get us through the crowd." He placed his hand under her elbow and assisted her to stand. Then, with his left arm around her, he put his right shoulder forward and pushed against the nearest body. "Let us through, please. Miss Treadwell is unwell." He repeated his words and shoved aside any who did not make way, and finally gained the corridor.

The air felt heavenly cool and fresh, although a crush of people milled about there also. He found a place away from the path of the mob, setting Charlotte against the wall where she would not be jostled. Looking down at her, he brushed a lock of hair that had come undone from its coiffeur. "How are you now?"

"Much better, thanks. I fear I am not intended for the rigors of the Season. Large crowds are most unpleasant for me. Miss Vernon seems to thrive upon it."

Her color was better. He had a mad impulse to carry her far away from any crowd and make love to her. He could not, but surely a few stolen kisses . . . he looked around and saw he could not risk even that without their being seen. He drew back a safe step to lessen temptation. "How does your 'lady' patient?"

"She is improving." At mention of the dog, animation came into her face. "Have you not yet seen her for yourself?"

"I have not the privilege of visiting Flea's domicile." He lost the battle to refrain from touching her and took her gloved hand in his, lifting it just short of his lips and caressing it.

"Not at all?" She tugged on her hand, but when he resisted letting loose of it, she left him in possession of it.

He smiled at this small triumph. "I do not even know where it is. He has been remarkably reticent about the place, and I have not forced the matter. I can always find Flea when I need him, through Pearl or his friends, and I know his usual haunts."

"I did not realize Flea had granted such a rare privilege." She made another effort to free her hand, but this time he not only hung on, he upped the level of his caresses, slowing the tempo and rubbing his gloved fingers over each of hers in turn.

God, this was incredibly erotic. He could stand like this all evening. Perhaps not, on second thought. He would lose control. "He was worried about that dog. You made an impression on him when you treated Ned's cold."

High color crept into her face, and she moistened her lips. "Yes, I suppose that's true."

"I think the play is about to resume. The box must have emptied by now. Shall we go back?"

Her eyes widened in relief. "Yes, that is a good idea."

The next evening Sylvia hosted another party. Her rout was well attended by an eclectic gathering of Adair's political cronies, Sylvia's cosmopolitan friends, and the young crowd that gathered around the Vernons.

In such a crush, it took Hugh a little while to spot Charlotte. She danced in a set of country dances, partnered by Sir Percival. As he watched, she laughed at something Sir Percival said and then glanced up at him from under her lashes in a flirtatious gesture that sent a jolt straight to his gut.

He could not be jealous of Sir Percival. He must simply be feeling anxiety over any man's becoming too entangled with her before he obtained the evidence needed to arrest her. This thought made him feel worse, sick to his stomach. How had Charlotte Treadwell crept into his blood and messed up his orderly life? This case was cursed.

Mr. Vernon came to stand beside him. He followed Hugh's stare at Charlotte and said, "I don't suppose you care to see her with a man such as Bagham."

"Why should you suppose that? I know nothing to Bagham's discredit."

"Neither do I, really. It's merely that it was known he was living on his expectations before his uncle stuck his spoon in the wall. Now that Bagham's come into his inheritance, he still hasn't settled most of his debts. If you were concerned to see Miss Treadwell established in comfort, I would worry that Sir Percival may not be as well off as he seems."

"Are you certain of your facts, Vernon? I knew nothing of this. I had heard Sir Percival's estate had sound prospects."

Vernon shrugged. "I don't know how closely you are involved with settling Miss Treadwell. If you care to see her happy, you might want to check on Bagham's affairs."

"I'll do that." Hugh felt a grim pleasure in the thought, even knowing his case against Charlotte might come to fruition before he learned anything to the point about Sir Percival.

At the time appointed for the picnic with Sir Percival and the children, unquestionably the occasion could not take place. It was chilly and raining. Sir Percival arrived alone. "I came here to tender my apologies that our picnic must be postponed."

"Nonsense," broke in Lady Adair. "Why don't you bring the children and picnic upstairs in the nursery? It will not be as delightful as an outdoor excursion, but at least the children will have an outing and the treats they have been promised."

"That's very kind of you, Lady Adair. Are you certain it will not be an imposition?"

"Not in the least."

"Does the idea also meet with your approval, Miss Treadwell?" Upon her smiling agreement, he said, "Then I will return with the children," and left. He brought them back within the hour, and he and Charlotte took them up to the second story, to the schoolroom and nursery area.

At first Bianca and Mercutio merely stood in the doorway, eyes wide with awe at the profusion of toys. Charlotte, who had not previously looked into the room, was nearly as awestruck as the children, although she hid it better. Shelves lined the spacious room, containing as many toys as could be neatly aligned. Dolls, soldiers, carved wooden animals sat or stood gazing out at the room's trespassers. Charlotte saw a carved chess set, books she itched to take down and page through.

"Oh," breathed Bianca. "May we play with them?"

"No, they don't belong to you," came from Sir Percival at the same time as Charlotte said, "I am sure you may."

She smiled at Sir Percival. "Truly, Lady Adair is a most generous person. She would not send the children to this room and then forbid them the treasures it contains."

"Very well, children, but handle the toys very carefully."

Bianca immediately began to examine the dolls, not touching any, and chose one with a china face and blonde horsehair curls, gingerly removing it from its shelf. Mercutio ran to the shelves where the toy soldiers stood and pulled several of them down, lining them in military ranks upon the floor.

Bianca cradled her doll in her arms, then placed it on the floor and returned to examine the shelves. She found a small blanket and brought it back to wrap the doll tightly, then sat, rocking her body and crooning a song Charlotte didn't know. She stopped singing and asked, "Are these yours, Miss Treadwell?"

"No, they belong to Lady Adair's children."

"Where are her children?"

"They are at their country home." Charlotte looked at Sir Percival. "I believe Lord and Lady Adair share your beliefs about the efficacy of a regular routine for their children. They only come to Town for a few weeks each year."

And, if they have this many toys for such a short period, what is the nursery in the country like? she wondered.

"Are Lady Adair's children the same age?" Bianca pursued.

"Not precisely. I believe they have a boy about twelve and two girls who are around nine and ten."

Mercutio, who had added to his armies, looked up from arranging two platoons of the metal figures to face off against each other in something that resembled battle formation. "I shall be a soldier when I grow up," he announced.

"That's a very noble ambition," Charlotte assured him, deciding it was wiser not to mention his previous aspiration.

"Do you need to have a fine education to be a soldier?"

"Indeed you do. You have to study strategy and tactics, and have knowledge of history and politics."

"I thought so. Is there any profession where you don't need an education?"

"I'm afraid not. Even if there were, you would want to know as much as possible about your world." Charlotte found a couple of blankets and spread them upon the floor.

The small boy crashed two of the soldiers together and dropped them forcefully on the floor.

Bianca said, "I don't have to have an education. I am going to be a wife."

Charlotte said, "Oh, but you do need an education. If you marry, you will have to run a household, so you will need to know how to keep accounts. You may need to help your husband with his business and certainly must supervise your children's education. And, should you choose not to marry, you will need to earn your living as a governess, teaching other children, or as a companion. For that, you will need to know how to read and carry on a knowledgeable conversation."

"As you can tell, the children and I have had a debate on the necessity of a governess. I am afraid I did not choose wisely when I engaged their first one. She was much too strict and frightened the children badly. I had to dismiss her."

Charlotte sat on one of the blankets and motioned Sir Percival to join her. "How unfortunate. I hope you will have better luck with the next governess. Then the children will undoubtedly change their minds about their schooling."

Rather stiffly, he complied, sitting a few feet away. "Yes, finding a governess for them is one of the matters I came to Town to arrange."

"Could you be our governess, Miss Treadwell?" Bianca asked.

"No, Miss Treadwell will not be your governess." Sir Percival's face turned red. "I have another role in mind for her," he added, too softly for the children to hear, gazing at her in a significant way as he spoke.

An awkward silence descended upon them. Charlotte, not knowing how to turn his hint aside, managed, "Lady Adair will send up a picnic basket very soon."

A footman came in shortly after Charlotte spoke, bearing a large basket covered with a cloth, which he set on the floor next to the blankets. "There's bread, cheese and some fruit in there. Oh, and a jug of lemonade. Do you want anything else?"

"No, this will be fine, Martin." The footman departed, and she opened the basket and laid out the food.

Sir Percival's gaze was on the children. "I confess I have never seen such a profusion of toys."

"I have not seen so many, either," Charlotte admitted.

"I must tell you, I grew up in impecunious circumstances. My father eloped with the daughter of one of his father's employees. My grandfather cast them off, so they lived in terrible poverty. My father suffered from a weakness of the lungs and could not even support his family. He died when I was five, and my mother moved back in with her father."

"Back to the lands of your grandfather?"

"Yes, but my paternal grandfather had died in the meantime, and my uncle had sold that property and moved to another estate he owned. So I had no contact with my father's family, until my uncle found me and brought me to his home. I think he had realized he would not have an heir of his own. Being unable to prevent my inheriting the baronetcy, he determined to see that I was brought up to fit the position. I was appallingly ignorant, so he sent me away to school for the next several years."

"You have had a difficult life, it seems." Charlotte looked at him in sympathy.

"Yes, but that has all changed now. And I must do what I can to alleviate the difficulties these two young scamps have suffered, in return for the good fortune that has come my way."

"An admirable goal, Sir Percival," she said. "Children, come and eat. We have a wonderful picnic here."

Sir Percival arose to help the children put away the toys they had played with and then led them back to sit on the blankets, where they dug into the food with relish.

CHAPTER SIXTEEN

After Sir Percival and the children left, Lady Adair came to Charlotte's boudoir. Charlotte sat in a chair by the window, reading a book she had found in the nursery: Pope's *Essay on Man*. The older woman waved her back into the chair and took another. "It appears Sir Percival is a most diligent suitor."

"He has expressed that he is looking for a mother for his wards. I believe he considers I would fill the role suitably."

"Is that what you want?" Lady Adair looked at Charlotte, her blue eyes, so like Rayfield's, unwontedly serious.

Squirming a little, Charlotte lay her book aside. "I believe it would be a useful and agreeable life."

"What about love?"

"Love was not part of the plan Rayfield and you plotted. I only must find a husband who can provide for Spencer and me."

"It was far easier to plan your future before I knew you."

"We have become better acquainted, but my circumstances are the same. I still must marry or else earn my living. I know many marriages are contracted without love, and the spouses rub along together well enough. I daresay Sir Percival and I shall do the same. Who is to say? I might come to love him in time."

"You miss your brother a great deal, do you not?"

"Constantly." She braced for some belittling of Jamie, but Lady Adair touched her upper arm in a gesture of sympathy.

"Has Hugh ever mentioned Martinville to you?"

Charlotte strained her memory to come up with any hint of the name—was it a place or a person? "I don't believe so."

"I was sure he had not. We lost an older brother too. Martinville died in a carriage accident when Hugh was ten and I thirteen. Our whole family was affected, Hugh most of all."

She smiled, her eyes dreamy, lost in the past. "Hugh was such a wild little boy. From the time he could walk, he constantly escaped from the nursery to play with the tenants' children. He got into such mischief—poaching game right under the gamekeeper's nose, stealing pies, climbing trees. He was Nanny's despair, coming home scraped and bruised, with torn and bloody clothing, and a few broken bones. Papa acted angry with him, but I think he was secretly pleased at his son's daring.

"Hugh suddenly became the heir. Papa always had a strong awareness of his duties, to the House of Lords and the people on his estates. Martinville had been brought up from birth to fill his eventual position as earl; Hugh must instantly comprehend all his duties. I think Papa's health was already failing.

"It is to Hugh's credit that he accepted the necessity, and adopted his father's code of responsibility. But that wild streak will show now and again. To restrain one's true nature must be difficult." She gave an embarrassed smile. "I suppose you wonder why I am telling you all of this?" At Charlotte's nod, she went on, "You and Hugh got off to a difficult start. I thought it might help if you understood a little better."

"Thank you, Lady Adair." The older woman stood, touched Charlotte's arm again, tentatively, then left the room.

Despite her glib explanation, Charlotte wondered why she had been the recipient of such confidences. If it were not improbable, she would have said Lady Adair promoted a match between her and Rayfield. But if so, what had happened to the plans she and the duchess had made concerning Miss Vernon?

The revelations certainly were enlightening, however, and gave Charlotte much to contemplate. However, this was no time to entertain doubts about the wisdom of her course of action. Rayfield was almost certainly not serious, and there was that wild streak his sister had mentioned. It would cause him to stray far from the hearthside and leave her in despair.

"Now we know Spencer's destination, Rayfield. He went to the Goddingses' mansion." Wescott's expression revealed his shock at the news.

Hugh whistled. "I never expected that. He called on the Goddingses?"

"No, went to the servants' entrance. Stayed no more than an hour and headed south again." After a pause, Wescott asked, "What do you suppose was the purpose for his journey?"

"I can think of no reason but that Miss Treadwell must have an ally in the house. May we discover whom he saw?" Hugh rubbed his face. Lately he had been unable to sleep.

"We cannot question the servants without alerting the Luddite sympathizer in the household. We are at a critical point. Riots have occurred in Stockport, Sheffield, Barnsley, Macclesfield, Rotherham, and Manchester. Assassination attempts, attacks on mills. We must wind up this case before it comes to the general uprising intended for the first of May." Wescott punctuated his words with a fist.

"I'm well aware of the deadline looming. Keep following Spencer to see if he makes any more calls on his way south and send someone to report to me when he gets back to Rockcliffe."

Hugh had sent Hamnet Williams to question the financial experts of the City about Sir Percival's state of affairs. Williams returned in the afternoon and said, "Young Vernon was right, sir. Sir Percival owes money to quite a few merchants. He has paid his gambling debts—those are the most likely to get noised abroad among the *ton*. The outstanding balance he owes is considerable. Would you like me to make inquiries about the inheritance he received from his uncle?"

"Yes, you had better. I'd be adding him to my list of suspects at this rate except he has no ties to the industrial area where they are, and no ties to France. In any case, it more and more appears that Miss Treadwell is the spy. In case she is innocent, I must know as much as possible about Bagham."

Williams cast a sympathetic glance his way, but said nothing further. Egad, was everyone aware of his growing partiality for Charlotte? He had not expected his investigation to become so personal, and the unraveling of the mystery to cause him so much guilt and pain. Still, whatever his feelings for Charlotte, he had to stop this threat to England.

That evening, at Lady Bristow's, Wescott took him aside. "I've just learned that Goddings' factory has been fired."

"My God! It can't be a coincidence that Spencer just was there!" Hugh felt ill.

"I think it's conclusive myself."

"Yes. You had better arrange to have Spencer arrested. Let me know when you have him. I'll go question him myself."

Miss Vernon's sister, Iphigenia Harborough, and her husband had finally arrived in London to participate in the Season. Mrs. Harborough had enjoyed a leisurely recovery from being delivered of a daughter the previous autumn, and the doting parents had brought their six-month-old with them.

The duchess had persuaded them to lend an estate Harborough owned just outside of London for a picnic outing. The setting was ideal, a classical house and gardens, right on the river. The day was sunny, the air even warm for April.

Mrs. Harborough was a fair-haired beauty like her sisters, with brown eyes instead of blue. Harborough was a hard-bitten man in his forties, some twenty years older than his wife. At first, Charlotte was dismayed to see the couple. Harborough's stern appearance and his age seemed to argue that Miss Vernon was correct in her assertion the marriage was based on his vast fortune. Shortly, however, she saw the tender looks that passed between the couple, and realized Arthur Vernon had been right—it was a love match. When they brought out their daughter, a round-cheeked, blonde, laughing cherub,

Harborough held her with an ease and expertise that impressed Charlotte.

The guests strolled the grounds, then ate a meal that qualified more as a feast than a picnic.

Mr. Vernon sat with Charlotte while they ate.

"He bought the house for Genie, so that they could come to London for the Season and not subject the baby to the unhealthful air of the city," said Mr. Vernon. "She would not leave their child behind at their country home."

"It was an extravagant gesture, but very loving," Charlotte said. "Not many husbands can afford to give such a gift."

"Yes, Harborough is one of the richest men in England. But money does not always protect against trouble. Genie miscarried several times before she was able to carry this child to term. If there had been anything money could do, I am sure Harborough would have paid any price to save her from such heartache."

Again, Charlotte was struck by the flashes of insight Mr. Vernon showed.

"Come walk with me. I know just the setting I would like to paint you in." He retrieved his sketchbook, and Charlotte, shaking her head at his persistence, went with him. At a little remove from the house, a small building resembling a Grecian temple stood in an artificially created valley. "Stand just there," indicating the columns at the front, "and look at the river. Yes, that's it." He opened his sketchbook and rapidly began making strokes with a charcoal.

Members of the party gathered to watch, and Charlotte was uncomfortable with the audience. "Please release me from posing for you any longer, Mr. Vernon," she begged.

"Very well, Miss Treadwell, but you must promise me you will pose again, for a real portrait this time."

"Very well, when I have the time."

Lord Gilbert, along with a couple of the other young men who made up Astraea's court, looked over Mr. Vernon's shoulder as Charlotte came toward him.

"Oh, this is very like, Vernon. You've captured her."

Mr. Vernon smiled at his drawing. "I should like to do better, but this is a beginning. 'Now no more, the hours beguiling, Former favourite haunts I see—'"

"Byron, isn't that? It's from 'Hours of Idleness,' I believe," said Miss Vernon.

He smiled at his sister, a look that spoke of their sharing the works of the poet.

Lord Leyland had joined the group in time to hear this last. "'Hours of Idleness.' What an appropriate title for the works of such a man."

Mr. Vernon's jaw jutted pugnaciously. "I wouldn't call him 'idle.' He made a fine maiden speech in Parliament in February."

Lord Leyland gave him a look of incredulity. "'A fine speech'? Promoting riot and the wanton destruction of property? More of such fine speeches and the whole populace will be engaged in plunder and murder."

Mr. Vernon kept his voice tightly controlled, but Charlotte could sense the vibrancy thrumming under his surface as he replied, "Byron never promoted rioting. He merely pointed out the desperation of men who have lost their means of sustenance for their families through no fault of their own. Poverty and starvation are powerful inducements to action, no matter how little such actions may gain them."

"Allowing such 'inducements to action' will result in another revolution such as happened in France." Leyland glanced at Miss Vernon, who stood watching their interplay with wide eyes, and added bitterly, "When you see your sister dragged from her bed and driven in a tumbril to the guillotine, perhaps you will see the folly of condoning such lawless behavior."

Miss Vernon flung her hands up to her mouth, the color draining from her face. Charlotte lost her composure and blurted, "I beg your pardon, my lord, but it was not 'condoning lawless behavior' that led to the revolution. It was the refusal of the aristocracy in France to recognize that the common man had any rights. By the time riot had erupted, the situation had gone beyond being saved by any means.

"I fear we may indeed be at risk of some such event. While I was in the north, I witnessed the hardships of the families of cloth workers who have lost their jobs. I saw also the insensitivity of the factory owners, who, worried about providing their families with the luxuries to which they have become accustomed, have installed machinery to increase their profits and take away jobs from the laboring class. When a man sees his family starving, the threat of hanging will never deter him from taking action to try to save them."

Leyland looked at Charlotte, a sneer curling his lip. "To think I had contemplated you as a suitable mother for my son. I am glad I discovered in time that you harbor these seditious poisons. I would never allow my son to hear such treason!"

Charlotte felt her face go pale, then flush. How had she allowed her desire to protect Miss Vernon—and defend the desperate families of the cloth workers—lead her into such indiscretion? As Leyland turned and stalked away, he passed Rayfield, who stood close enough to have heard her most unladylike diatribe.

"Miss Treadwell, may I speak to you a moment, please?"

Charlotte had shamed him, as her sponsor for the Season, and his sister also. She had no choice but to concede meekly to the lecture she was about to receive. She lifted her chin to conceal her quaking insides, said, "Very well, my lord," and stepped away from the support of her friends.

"I fear we may indeed be at risk of some such event."

Had the chit all but confessed to her treachery? How could she know of revolution plotted to occur in England? He had to question her now, when she was all in the fire of her passionate convictions. He waited until her speech wound down, until Leyland had stomped away, before he made his move.

As they walked apart from the others, he cast about in his mind for how to begin the conversation. He glanced at

Miss Treadwell, but her profile gave him few clues. Her rigid posture suggested a strong emotion repressed. The tack to take with her would be sympathetic listening. She could very well say more than she ever would when not in high dudgeon. He was heartsick over using her emotions against her, but he must.

However, as soon as they had passed out of hearing of the others, she spoke. "I must apologize for putting you to the blush over my behavior. I am fully aware of what I owe to you and your sister, and I never would have wished to shame you in front of others. But that . . . that odious man was making references to the guillotine and terrifying poor Miss Vernon, and I could not keep silent."

He examined her face and could discern no sign of awareness of anything but the social solecism she had committed. Could she be concealing a far more serious sin beneath her words? "I accept your apology, Miss Treadwell. Tell me, did you really witness the conditions of the cloth workers around Leeds?"

"Of the families living near Mr. Goddings' estate and mill, yes, I did. I cannot see how one could dwell for any time in that part of England without coming in contact with the extreme suffering of the people there."

"I would have thought, living in Mr. Goddings' comfortable mansion, you would have been insulated from the common people."

She frowned, but it appeared a frown of puzzlement rather than annoyance or fear. "I suppose you are right, at that. Certainly Mrs. Goddings could never have felt the least concern about the people in her husband's employ, or those who had been in his employ but were replaced by machines. I suppose I should have said that no one with a conscience could have lived in that area without awareness of the people's hardships."

Conscience. Could she commit the crimes of which he suspected her and still speak with such sincerity of conscience?

"I think, Lord Rayfield, that is one trait we share."

"I'm afraid I don't follow you, Miss Treadwell."

"I'm speaking of sympathy for the lower classes, certainly of an understanding that they feel and suffer just as we do."

"Good Gad, Miss Treadwell, what makes you say that?"

"It is something I presume from your association with Flea, and such types as Flash Annie and the Heaper. Whatever your motives in the first place, becoming acquainted with people who were not born to privilege must teach one that they have all the traits of humanity and be in no way different from us."

"I am surprised you have that opinion of me. It is very different than you have expressed before."

"I know. I had decided to find no good qualities in you to begin with. I have come to know you better. I do wish . . ."

"Wish what, Miss Treadwell?"

"I understand how a sense of adventure and need to do daring deeds drive you. I am also sure that you believe you are providing for needy people. However, if you only saw the results of such activity, you might reconsider what you are doing, as I'm sure my brother would have in time. For if you believe the families of the people you are hiring are now in need, you should see what happens to those families when their wage earner is taken away altogether. Their case is truly desperate then."

Whatever the truth about her spying, he could not doubt the sincerity that made her voice shake with passion. "Your brother?"

"He was the lucky one, although I didn't think so at the time. He is out of it, at least; his men were all transported or sentenced to prison. Two of them died of fever in the prison hulks. Of those who went to Botany Bay, communication is most difficult with their families. The men are illiterate. They have to find someone to write for them and send the message all that way. When I used to live there, I read the letters to their loved ones when they received them.

"The families have undergone the most terrible privation. I did what I could for them when I still lived at Rockcliffe, though that was little enough. Since Papa sold Queen's Treat

and brought me to Town, I have been able to do even less."
She turned away, but he saw the gleam of tears in her eyes.

The goal of trapping her fled from his mind. Impulsively,
he gathered her in his arms and held her close. Her place in
his arms had such a feeling of rightness that at this moment
he believed she could not possibly be the traitor, no matter the
evidence. She shivered and sobbed against his shoulder.

The need to comfort her blotted out every other thought.
Without quite knowing how it happened, he turned her face
up to him and kissed her. She returned his kisses passionately,
her arms tight around his shoulders. She tasted of salt and
roses and his one coherent thought before he was completely
lost was that he could never get enough of her.

Then another thought intruded. God, in a matter of days he
might be arresting this woman. He had abandoned every pre-
cept of decent behavior. He let her go abruptly. She stared at
him in shock. He felt a little shocked himself. What had he
done? His desire for her drove everything he was working for
from his consciousness.

"Let's walk a little to give you time to compose yourself,"
he suggested. "It is obvious you have been crying."

"Oh, dear, I completely forgot how I disgraced myself. I'm
so embarrassed. Must I go back and face them?"

"They will probably take me to task more than you. They
will assume I am a monster for making you cry. And yes, I
think it better for you to go back and face them now. It will
be easier now than later. After all, they are your friends;
they'll forgive you."

"No doubt you are right. I shall tell them you read me a
great lecture on the impropriety of a woman's expounding on
political matters."

A lecture on propriety. That was what he needed. No, perhaps he needed a leash to restrain him, for he had no self-re-
straint where this woman was concerned.

CHAPTER SEVENTEEN

From the case notebook of Hugh Broderick Brooks, the Earl of Rayfield:

Entry dated 23ʳᵈ of April, 1812:
Everything is in place. Spencer will be arrested when he returns to Rockcliffe. This is my last case. I no longer have the heart for hunting human beings. I shall settle down to doing my parliamentary duties and taking care of my properties. And I must—never mind, I shall not think of that now.

(Decoded by Alphonsius McMasters, PhD, LLC, AKC, OBE, BMW, historian and author of The Secret Wars of Napoleon, *2005.)*

At Adair House, Charlotte allowed herself another storm of crying. She had unleashed forbidden memories, the ones that caused unbearable pain. They came back with a vengeance.

She didn't know what had awakened her that night. Jamie had gone to France several days before; perhaps she expected him home. But urgency gripped her, and she hastily dressed and went out. She heard faint sounds from the beach and ran along the path. As she approached she heard gunfire and shouts. She thought she shouted herself, "No! Jamie!" and rushed down.

On the beach, all was confusion. Jamie's sleek boat, bodies milling, a flash of red coats. Excisemen! Everything stilled; men—Jamie's men—held by the soldiers. Then she saw the dark form on the shingle, and she knew. Forgetting all else, she rushed to his side, sobbing and calling his name.

Darkness kept her from seeing where he was wounded or attempting to treat him. She knew it was hopeless from the weakness of his voice and his grip when he clutched at her.

She tried to hush him to save his strength, but his words broke urgently from him. "Sis, don't . . . believe what they . . . say. I couldn't . . . refuse to bring the . . . the Frenchy with us— it would have . . . gone hard with my men. But I swear we . . . held him close, and . . . we planned . . . to turn him . . . over to . . . the authorities . . . when we . . . landed."

"Oh, Jamie, you don't have to tell me. I'd never believe anything bad of you, no matter what. Jamie, don't die!"

But he didn't hear. He had already gone.

They found the contraband on the boat and the damning papers on the Frenchman. No one believed Charlotte when she insisted that Jamie would never betray his country.

Jamie's men told her Jamie had feared the whole crew would be seized by the French unless they agreed to carry the man across the channel. They voted, agreed to bring over the spy and then turn him over to the authorities when they landed. At Charlotte's advice, none of his crew reported these facts to the officers. The only reason none were sentenced to hang was they were presumed merely to have taken orders from Jamie. But all six had been sentenced to transportation or long prison terms.

The case was hushed up. No one wished Society to know that one of their own betrayed England. Charlotte never went into Society, so she little cared what anyone thought. Her grief was too overwhelming to heed what others believed about her brother.

After her tears, she felt her heart lightening. Thoughts of Jamie had brought agonizing pain ever since his death, but the pain was lessening. Perhaps she was healing of that hurt.

* * *

At Lady Braithwaite's ball, Sir Percival approached Charlotte. "Would you dance with me, Miss Treadwell?"

Charlotte assented and they joined one of the sets forming.

"I have something about which I most particularly wish to speak to you," Sir Percival said, unsmiling, as the music started. "Would you come for a walk with me after this dance?"

Did he wish, like Lord Leyland, to say he would remove her evil influence on his wards? Charlotte studied him for clues, but could not tell what he had in mind. She assented, uneasy.

He took her arm and led her from the floor. "Lady Braithwaite has a conservatory, said to be most interesting," he said. "I thought we might be able to speak privately there."

"Very well." Despite a sinking feeling that the impending interview would be unpleasant, Charlotte's steps lightened as she walked along with Sir Percival. Another lecture on her unsuitability meant she would not need to make a decision if he proposed, would not have to tell him she could not marry him.

Her steps faltered as she realized where her thoughts had led her. She could not marry Sir Percival; she did not love him because she loved Rayfield. The feelings she fought so hard to deny could not be denied. No matter that she had no belief in Rayfield's intentions. If not Rayfield, she would marry no one.

The conservatory was a large, high-ceilinged room with a bank of windows on its outer wall. Tropical plants created an artificial jungle, and the air was warm and moist. Sconces placed at intervals around the walls cast dim shadows.

Sir Percival stopped behind a giant rubber tree and turned to look into Charlotte's eyes.

This time she had no trouble interpreting his expression and instantly realized her guess about his purpose was wrong. She was to hear a declaration after all. "Please, Sir Percival, I think I should not have come here with you. Let us go back."

"I have honorable intentions, Miss Treadwell. In these last weeks, I have become convinced that we share many things in common and would deal exceedingly well together. I wish to make you my wife." He pulled her into his arms.

Charlotte did not know how to answer him. She did not wish to hurt his feelings. "Oh, do not ask such a thing. I esteem you very much, but I cannot marry you," she faltered.

"I applaud your modesty about your adverse situation. It makes no difference to me. We will work side by side for the good of England. I have determined that you are the ideal consort for me." He leaned closer, his lips puckered, to seal the bargain he believed he was making with a kiss.

Charlotte bent back and turned her head, trying to twist out of his grasp. "Please, Sir Percival, I cannot. I do not feel for you those sentiments a wife should have for a husband."

"You will learn to care for me when we are married." Now he had a bruising grip on her face and pressed his lips to hers.

She struggled to get free from the damp lips and hard hands. For a moment she broke loose and, gasping for breath, begged, "Please let me go." He imprisoned her mouth again.

One hand held the back of her head while the other fumbled at her neckline. She protested, the sound muffled, her skin crawling with dread and disgust. With a ripping sound her gown gave way. My God, he was going to rape her in the Braithwaites' conservatory. She renewed her battle to free herself, knowing it was hopeless, that Sir Percival was far stronger than she.

All at once Charlotte was freed. Sir Percival had been lifted away and she opened her eyes to two men grappling in the dim light. As she sorted out what was occurring, Rayfield slammed his fist into Sir Percival's jaw. The other man flew back against the thick trunk of an orange tree, and both tree and man crashed onto the tiled floor.

"Get out of here," Rayfield ground out. "Don't come near Miss Treadwell again."

Sir Percival half-sat, shaking his head. Then he focused his stare at Rayfield and his face suffused. "I'll pay you back for this, sir!" Turning his attention to Charlotte, he snarled, "You have no idea what you have refused. You'll regret this."

Charlotte was shaking too badly to think of replying. She stood immobilized as Sir Percival pulled himself upright, and, with a last glare in their direction, limped out of the room.

Rayfield stepped quickly to Charlotte's side. "Are you all right?" His eyes searched hers.

"Yes." Her voice came out whispery, and she vainly tried to pull the torn edges of her gown together and, with equal lack of success, suppress the sobs that choked her throat.

He pulled her transparent stole around her in an effort to cover the exposed flesh of her bosom. She didn't know who first reached for the other, but she was in his arms and no longer trying to stop her tears or the shudders that wracked her body.

He held her closely, sounding meaningless words to soothe her. Then he brushed her eyes and cheeks with soft kisses until she turned her face to take his mouth fully with her own. Passion surged between them. She forgot Sir Percival as she gave herself over to the sensations that shot through her.

His lips possessed her, slicking over hers, and his tongue pressed her mouth open, sliding inside to caress the sensitive surfaces. A fiery bolt of power ran through her, and at the same time her legs felt too weak to hold her. She leaned closer against him and tentatively plied her own tongue against his.

With a groan, he pulled back. Momentarily lost in a fog, Charlotte was only gradually aware of another presence. She looked up to see their hostess standing not six feet away.

Rayfield moved in front of Charlotte. "Lady Braithwaite, you may congratulate us on our betrothal. We were just now sealing the bargain."

A broad smile crossed Lady Braithwaite's face. "What exciting news! The elusive Lord Rayfield finally to join the ranks of benedicts!"

"Please, if you wouldn't mind, don't breathe a word of this yet. I must, of course, let my mother and sister know, but also must write to Lord Treadwell. As you know, he is traveling on the continent, and a letter may take some time to reach him. I do not expect him to refuse his permission for us to marry, but it would be premature if word got out before he learned of it."

"Oh, er, certainly. I'll, er, leave you to work out the details, then, shall I?"

"If you could send someone to get Miss Treadwell's cloak, and let my sister know that I am taking her home, I would greatly appreciate it. We became a little, ah, overzealous, and I do not think she wishes to rejoin your other guests tonight. Oh, please see that my carriage is called for, also?"

Reminded of her torn gown and disordered state as their hostess agreed, Charlotte applauded Rayfield's quick thinking. For herself, she was so overcome with joy at his words claiming her as his bride-to-be that she had no rational thoughts.

When he turned to her after Lady Braithwaite departed, though, she plunged into despair. His face was devoid of expression, but she knew him—he didn't want to marry her.

What had he done?

He'd pledged himself to a woman who very likely was betraying England to its enemy. Even while the sick knowledge of this fact swept through him, he accepted he could not have done anything else. Their kiss was enough in itself, but Charlotte's disheveled state, her torn gown, topped it off. If he had said nothing, she would have been ruined after all.

A footman brought Charlotte's evening cloak. Hugh wrapped it around her to cover the visible signs of her near-ravishment by Sir Percival and took her outside to await his carriage.

They didn't speak until they were in the carriage.

Charlotte said, "Please, Lord Rayfield, it isn't necessary for you to marry me. It was just a kiss, and we both know that Sir Percival is responsible for the rest of my state, not you."

"Sir Percival was gone by the time Lady Braithwaite came upon us. In any case you could not marry him after that."

"No, I do not wish to marry him. It was because I refused him that he attacked me. That is, he acted as if he didn't hear me refuse, but what he said afterward made it clear he knew."

He almost wished Sir Percival were there so he could hit him again. The rage that had seized him when he saw Charlotte struggling against his attack overwhelmed him anew. "Then there is nothing more to say."

"Oh, but there is." He could tell she fought fresh tears. "We should not be forced into marriage because of a situation neither of us provoked. What kind of marriage should we have?"

"We will manage. We have more to begin with than many couples." They could not have a marriage if she were a spy. He had not foreseen the wreck he would make of this case.

If he were capable of thinking at this moment, he should be convincing Charlotte that he loved her, that this incident had only pushed forward the declaration he would have made anyway. But he was too exhausted, and his thoughts in too much disarray. Tomorrow, when he was fresher and could think, he would settle matters with her.

His carriage pulled up in front of Adair House. He helped her descend, gave her a light kiss on her brow, and said, "Get some rest. We'll talk tomorrow."

She nodded shortly and went inside.

"What did you do to Miss Treadwell? Did you two have a quarrel?" Condon looked almost belligerent.

"No." Not until she had protested his solution of offering marriage to her.

"She is bruised all over—her face and bosom, anyway."

"That was not my doing, I assure you." The savage desire to rip Sir Percival apart roughened his voice. "What have you to report, Miss Condon?"

"There isn't much. She has made no more middle-of-the-night excursions. I have seen nothing in her manner or dealings to give us any evidence. I found this." She pulled a folded sheet of paper from her reticule.

Hugh recognized Spencer's handwriting. He scanned the letter hurriedly. It was brief, one line, "Jehiel has written that he carried out your commission in Rockcliffe. He has gone to Leeds to finish. I'll let you know when he returns."

"There is no doubt young Spencer has been acting on Miss Treadwell's behest, at least. This doesn't give any information about what his 'commission' was, however."

"Is he not being arrested?" Miss Condon was fully in Wescott's confidence about the affair.

"Yes, as soon as those following him receive the orders Wescott sent to Rockcliffe. Probably later tonight. Miss Vernon's come-out ball is also tonight. I will be there and keeping an eye on Miss Treadwell. After I receive word of Spencer's arrest, I will journey to Rockcliffe to question him. I think this matter will be over soon."

He turned away and Miss Condon left.

Matters would never be over for him. During a sleepless night, he had come to few conclusions except that his urge to murder Sir Percival arose from loving Charlotte. It did not seem to matter that she might be behind a most evil plot; her motives in becoming involved were a genuine desire to help those less fortunate than she and loyalty to a brother and father who did not deserve her affection.

But would such motives be enough to keep her from being hanged? There was nothing he could do to save her—was there?

If he declared himself to her, begged her to give up the plot, promised Wescott to keep her out of future conspiracies?

And yet, how could he intervene against justice? It went against everything he believed. Damnation! Was there no way out of the trap he and Charlotte were in?

Charlotte stared at her image in the pier glass in the blue gown with short, puffed sleeves, ribbon trim and an embroidered hem that she would wear to Miss Vernon's come-out ball.

The bruises Sir Percival had inflicted upon her stood out clearly: The mark along her jawline, others on her neck and the expanse of bosom exposed by the gown's low neckline. Even if she changed, she had no evening gowns cut high enough to hide them all. Although she had no heart for attending a ball, she could not bow out, after the Vernons' kindness this Season.

"I have a cream that will cover the bruises. No one will notice them, I promise." Her maid, Condon, came up behind her.

"Thank you, Condon. I would appreciate that very much."

The maid had not asked the source of the bruises, and Charlotte had not offered any explanation.

She had avoided Lady Adair all day, pleading she wished to rest in her room before the ball. If Lady Adair wondered at Charlotte's sudden delicacy when she had never before needed such a retreat, at least she had not acted to disturb her.

Beyond her bruises, Charlotte did not know how to explain to Lady Adair her progression in one day from two suitors to none. Rayfield, she would not count. She would persuade him that such a sacrifice as he contemplated was unnecessary.

Condon finished applying the cream and Charlotte looked at herself again. Indeed, the bruises did not show. Condon had even managed to remove the dark circles under her eyes from lack of sleep. The shadows in the eyes themselves remained, however.

Condon placed the feathered headdress over Charlotte's coiffeur and gave her her wrap. Thanking her maid, Charlotte went downstairs, masking the dread she felt about this evening.

Not the least was the fear she would encounter Sir Percival at the ball. She shuddered. She wished she never had to see him again. Seeing Lord Leyland would be almost as awkward.

And how would she pretend to Miss and Mr. Vernon that she had nothing on her mind but enjoying the evening?

CHAPTER EIGHTEEN

From the case notebook of Hugh Broderick Brooks, the Earl of Rayfield:

Entry dated 25th of April, 1812:
Matters have become unbelievably complicated. I no longer have the impartiality that this investigation demands. I expect an arrest to be made momentarily of one of Miss Treadwell's major associates, and the case will be tied up within a few days.

Author's note: Again, a section follows in a different code. I hope to include the decoded message in the next edition of the book. (A. McM.)

(Decoded by Alphonsius McMasters, PhD, LLC, AKC, OBE, BMW, historian and author of The Secret Wars of Napoleon, *2005.)*

At Rayfield's look of admiration when he came to her at the ball, Charlotte's determination to refuse his offer faltered. Perhaps something could be made of a marriage between them. That he was attracted to her was clear. Her love for him would ensure she worked toward making a success of this match.

"We must talk," he murmured to her, and she assented.

She could not help remembering her private interview with

Sir Percival the previous day as the earl ushered her into a small sitting room, unoccupied at present. She needn't worry about a repeat. Rayfield was a very different sort of man.

He closed the door behind them, which was a solecism.

He came close to her. Charlotte's heart beat faster. "Miss Treadwell—Charlotte—we left things unsettled last night. I have to make sure you understand that marriage is indeed a necessity for us. I bought us a little time with my story about getting a message to your father. I should do so in any case. Do you have any idea where he can be reached?"

"No, I told you that before."

"If we cannot get a message to him, that doesn't change things. You are of age, so you don't need his permission. But, believe me, if she does not read of our betrothal within a matter of a few weeks, Lady Braithwaite will begin spreading the tale of what she saw, and you will be ruined."

"Does it not even matter that the worst of what she saw was the marks on my skin and tear in my gown that Sir Percival was responsible for?"

"No, how could it? He wasn't there when she found us. I thank God for that! If she had caught you with him, it would be him you would have to marry now."

"You are joking! Nothing would induce me to marry him!"

"It's not a joke, Charlotte. Do you think anyone would offer for you if this gets out?"

She brushed at her lower lashes, where moisture was gathering. "I believe you are gloating at my sorry condition."

"Not at all. I wish you still had free choice in all your decisions. But I'll do my best to make you happy."

And then he closed his arms around her and his lips were on hers. She met him in gladness. After a moment, he pulled back. "Listen to me, Charlotte. I have to know the truth. I only want to protect you, but I can't unless you tell me everything. Then, I swear, somehow we'll find a way."

She stared at him. His words were as meaningless as though he spoke a foreign language. "What are you talking about?"

But he was going on, caught in the flow of his words, as if he had not heard her question. "I understand so much, about your brother and your father. Undoubtedly you feel loyalty to them. And the Luddites, you have good reason to be sympathetic. I know the plight of the cloth workers is appalling."

"What do you mean, Rayfield? What do my father and brother have to do with Luddites?"

He took her hands. "Not Luddites. The French."

A terrible coldness was growing inside her, freezing her from the inside out. Her face stiffened. "Are you saying that my father, as well as my brother, sold out to the French?"

His eyes searched her, and he seemed to lose some of his assurance. "I don't know, Charlotte. Tell me what you know. He fled to the continent, but most of the countries across the channel are closed to British citizens. How did he manage it?"

"I don't know, but you are mistaken if you think my father would betray his country, any more than my brother did."

"You can't insist your brother was innocent! He was caught with the evidence—the French spy on his boat carrying papers with Napoleon's seal."

"I don't care what the evidence says. He died in my arms assuring me of his innocence. He wouldn't have lied. But then, you apparently believe I would lie to you also, so you won't accept my word. But I won't stay in this room and listen to these accusations." She matched her words with actions, dashing around him and opening the door. He moved to stop her, but she slipped by him and ran.

She could not go back to the ballroom in her present state. She was so agitated she would not be able to speak to anyone or hide her emotions—and right on the heels of her anger came a rush of pain and the need to burst into tears. She went to the retiring room set aside for ladies, but several women bustled at the mirrors, gossiping and adjusting clothing or coiffeurs.

She backed out and stood a moment, considering what to do. Adair House was only a square away. She went to the back stairs, worried now that Rayfield would find her. A footman asked if she were lost. Giving him a haughty stare, she replied she knew where she was going. He looked at her uncertainly, and she took the opportunity to pass him and continue downstairs.

When she reached the ground floor, though, she paused. She could not go through the kitchens, bustling with servants.

As she stood, indecisive, she realized she could not simply run away. Miss Vernon's ball had barely begun. Lady Adair would wonder what had become of her. She must go back and somehow avoid Rayfield for the rest of the evening. Mr. Vernon would help, she was certain, providing her with dance partners from among his friends. She had not even had time since arriving to determine if Sir Percival or Lord Leyland were in attendance. She giggled, almost hysterically, at the way she seemed to be turning suitors into enemies.

Rayfield had accused her of something, she suddenly understood. What was it? Something to do with Luddites? And somehow his misconceptions about her father and Jamie and the French were mixed up in it. She could not figure it out now, though. She had to pretend to enjoy Miss Vernon's ball.

Strolling back into the ballroom, she was accosted by the guest of honor. "Where have you been, Miss Treadwell? I saw you leave with Lord Rayfield. Do you have good news?"

"Good news? Oh, no, indeed. He wanted to show me something. I've been in the ladies' retiring room. I have a little headache and needed to rest. This is a lovely ball, Miss Vernon. Every bit as delightful as you said it would be."

"Yes, isn't it?" said Miss Vernon on a sigh of satisfaction. "Oh, here comes Lord Eccleston. I am pledged to him for the next dance."

Lord Eccleston bowed to her. She giggled and, placing her hand on his arm, went off with him into one of the sets.

Charlotte looked around, but did not see anyone likely to rescue her from wallflower status for this dance. She went to join a group of dowagers sitting along the wall.

A short time later, Rayfield found her there. "Charlotte, we still need to settle this between us."

"It has been settled and we have nothing to discuss."

"I only wish that were true. However, there is the matter of . . ."

"If you do not go away and cease this . . . this persecution of me, I shall make a scene that your sister will find exceedingly embarrassing."

He bowed to her. "We will talk about it tomorrow, then." He walked away.

Charlotte wished the next several hours were over and she could go home—home!—to Adair House, and drown her misfortunes in a sea of tears.

He had mishandled the situation. A public affair such as Miss Vernon's ball was a poor choice of locale for a serious discussion, but he had been too impatient to wait until they could be private. He should at least have secured Charlotte's promise to marry him before he began to question her.

But he expected to hear at any time that Jehiel Spencer was in custody, forcing his departure to question him. He had rushed his fences, and now he might have missed his chance to protect Charlotte from the results of her schemes.

It was what came of becoming personally involved in a case. If she had been some anonymous miss, instead of the woman with whom he had fallen in love, he would never have made such a mull of things. But then, he would never have wished to protect her.

A footman approached him with word that an urgent message had come for him. Spencer, he thought. He must leave immediately, and any further attempts to make peace with Charlotte would have to wait.

Finally in the relative peace of her room, Condon dismissed for the night, Charlotte paced.

We will talk about it tomorrow. Rayfield would not accept that she could not marry a man who did not love her, moreover suspected her of some unspecified but heinous crime.

Who alleged shocking crimes of her father and Jamie. Alone, with no need to put on a cheerful face, Charlotte let her anguish free.

He would not give up his idea that they must marry. He would insist until she agreed, and that must not happen.

He apparently thought that besides saving her from the improper situation they had been caught in, he could protect her from the crimes he believed she committed. Crimes that involved both the French and the Luddites.

Could he believe that the Luddites represented a threat to the government? That must be it. She had read of widespread instances of machine breaking throughout the industrial belt of England and food riots in several towns, but she did not believe the Luddites intended to overthrow their masters. They only wanted jobs and food for their families.

But was there a French plot to capitalize on the unrest? What a terrible thought! It fit with the facts he had revealed.

What knowledge did he have? If he knew things he was keeping from her, it was most unfair. And if he supposed, upon his knowledge, that Papa was somehow sending orders from the French to her, to do with the Luddites, that was absurd.

Papa would never do such a thing, and neither would she. She could not prove it, though. What if Rayfield used his belief to blackmail her into marriage?

She would have to leave Adair House, must go where he would not find her. Where could she go? She could not count on Lady Adair to help her, and to find a position through advertisements as she had before would take time Rayfield would not grant her.

Flea trusted her—at least far enough to show her his home, and to ask her to treat the dog he had rescued. His "ken" had extra rooms. And Rayfield did not know where Flea lived. With a rising excitement, she thought of how she could persuade Flea to let her live there. She would teach him and the rest of the boys in return for her board, and finally be able to do something concrete for them to improve their chances in life.

Her only difficulty would be persuading Flea that keeping

her presence secret did not betray Lord Broddie. No matter what Flea felt for her, his first loyalty was to him. She thought over this problem as she packed the few belongings with which she had arrived at Adair House.

Solutions did not seem so easy as she walked along the silent streets of Mayfair lugging her portmanteau a few minutes later. Hackneys, usually thick upon the streets when she was abroad, were nowhere to be found at this time of night. She could not walk all the way to Flea's; even if the distance were not impossibly far given the burden she carried, she would very likely be set upon before she reached his quarters.

She could not have waited until morning, however. She could never have left Adair House carrying all her property without being questioned and stopped.

Quickly she reviewed the contents of her portmanteau and concluded that none of it could have been left. She needed her books and writing materials to instruct the boys; she had taken none of the clothing the family had given her, only the sturdy "governess" clothes she had stubbornly kept in case no husband materialized during the Season, and only the minimum of those.

A short while later, she could not believe her good luck, for there around the corner from Lady Adair's a hackney stood waiting. Her elation was short-lived, however, for the driver refused to take any more fares that night.

"Why are you still sitting there, then, instead of home in your bed?" Disappointment made her sharper than her wont.

"I be awaiting someone. 'Tain't nothin' to do with you."

"What am I to do then?"

"Try nearer to St. James. There usually be a few 'ackneys still about this time o' night. 'Tis only a few streets away."

She had no choice but to try the area around St. James. Somewhat grumpily thanking the man, she trudged on. Luckily, she did find another hackney. She had another setback, however, when she told him where she wanted to go.

"Ain't going there. Be robbed, mos' likely. Young lady like you shouldn't be going to such a part o' town, neither."

She had to part with too much of her dwindling money to persuade him. As she rode in the musty-smelling hackney, she wondered if she should have sent quite so much money to the families in Rockcliffe and Garwich. She had not foreseen that she might be equally in need not so far in the future.

If Flea refused to take her in . . . in that case, surely he would at least find her some safe lodging, and give her advice on finding a position.

The hackney stopped by the building, and Charlotte paid him. Almost before she had pulled her baggage out of the carriage, the driver whipped up his horses and hurried away.

Charlotte entered the front house and faltered. She had never had to negotiate the dark, refuse-strewn room without Flea's escort. The resident rodents were more active at night; their scurrying noises nearly made Charlotte's resolution fail. She left the portmanteau by the door; she simply could not be burdened by its bulk as she crossed the room. She stumbled, seemingly finding every obstacle between the two doors by nearly falling over each one. Her skirts were frequently brushed by animals, once a large one running over her feet. She had nearly screamed at that. She lost her way and had to feel along the wall for the stairs, several feet from where she had fetched up.

At last she dashed up the stairs and out of the terrifying building. Flea's house was dark; the boys were all abed. She disliked awakening them, but a light mist was falling, bringing a distinct chill to the air. She could not wait until morning.

Lady began to bark, clearly hearing or smelling Charlotte's presence, shortly after the door opened. "'Oo's there?"

"Flea, it is I, Charlotte—Miss Treadwell."

The door swung wider. "Miss Treadwell? What be you doin' 'ere this time o' night?"

"It's a long story, Flea. May I come in?"

Lady rushed to her, baying her full-throated hound song, and Charlotte bent to pet her, saying, "Hush, Lady, you'll wake the boys." The dog had nearly recovered from her injuries and seemed in fine fettle, squirming and leaping about in pleasure.

While Charlotte was calming the dog, Flea lit a lamp and appeared in the doorway again, saying, "Come on in."

The boys were all wakened by the commotion. But as she stepped in, Ned turned over on his pallet and fell right back to sleep, while Tom and Blackie half-sat up and looked at her in an unfocused fashion that spoke of their not being fully awake.

"So, what is your long story, Miss Treadwell?" Flea stood with the lantern in one hand, and the other fisted on his hip. He did not look very welcoming.

"I've run away," Charlotte burst out. "That is, I've left Lady Adair's. I don't have any other place to go besides here."

Flea frowned, and Charlotte's heart sank. "'Tisn't a proper place for you. This is bachelor quarters."

"I can sleep in one of the extra rooms. I'm going to be your tutor, that's the same as a governess. No one would think it improper. A governess always has a room near her charges."

"A governess?" His frown had grown to fill his whole face.

"Yes, I am going to give all of you boys lessons in return for your letting me stay here. You'll have a better chance to make something of yourselves. We will all benefit."

"You still 'aven't explained your long story. Why'd you leave Broddie's sister?"

"Rayf—Broddie and I had a terrible quarrel. But Flea, you will agree with me. He insists that we must marry, and he doesn't want to marry me! It will ruin his life. I had to leave." Despite her resolve to state her case in a cool, logical fashion, it all came tumbling out most illogically, and she felt a very un-governesslike desire to break into tears.

"Don't think this is something we can settle tonight." Flea began rolling up his pallet.

"What are you doing?"

"Giving you my bed. Ned and I will tuck up together for tonight." He carried the roll under his arm, the lamp in his other hand, into one of the rooms. "This 'un be the cleanest."

Charlotte followed, protesting. Pointlessly, because she

truly didn't think she could sleep on the floor with just her cloak under and around her. She had not thought about one of the boys having to give up his bed to accommodate her.

Flea unrolled the bedding, shook the dust out and puffed it up. "I'll leave the lamp wi' you." He closed the door behind him. Charlotte noticed that Lady was in the room with her, and she felt grateful for the company. She lay down on the pallet, blowing out the lamp and staring up in the darkness.

Her rest was disturbed by more rustling sounds. Oh, no! Sleeping on the floor, or as good as, was not comfortable when sharing the quarters with what was probably a large, ugly rat.

With a low growl, Lady suddenly made a lunge. Charlotte could not see what was happening in the dark, but she could hear Lady's paws scrabbling, then a squeal and a noise that sounded like bones crunching. She shuddered, but could not help being grateful for Lady's hunting instincts.

CHAPTER NINETEEN

Letter from Kate McMasters, cryptographer and ex-wife of Alphonsius McMasters, London, to her sister, Vera Smith, New York, 7 April 2005:

I can't believe that I was so blind to Alphy's many deficiencies. He is a phony and a cheat. Nothing was real, except all the help I gave him. I found and decoded Rayfield's casebook. Does he give me any credit? Never mind, you know the answer to that! You warned me, but I didn't want to hear you. Alphy doesn't have one bit of original work in his book. And look at those initials he's so proud of after his name! AKC, for heaven's sake! The American Kennel Club. That's the only set he's entitled to—he's a dog!

And the sections in a different code? I decoded them. However, I wasn't about to let him know. They were personal and confidential, but he wouldn't have hesitated to use them. I'm tempted to write the real story. I'd have to disguise it as fiction, though. I could never violate the privacy of actual historical persons.

Hugh arrived in Rockcliffe at dawn, having ridden through most of the night. He went straight to the riding officer's quarters, where young Spencer was being held under guard.

The customs officer, a big, florid man in his forties, greeted Hugh with a hearty handshake. "Wouldn't have suspected young Spencer of any illegal doings."

"I know of no crime he has committed. However, I need to question him about the commission he performed for my suspect."

Spencer had a faint resemblance to his uncle; he was a tall man in his twenties with an open, innocent-looking face. He was very frightened at present, however. "What is this about?" he asked.

"On April fifteenth, you came to London, you called on your uncle, Lucius Spencer, and met Miss Treadwell at a coffeehouse. Afterward, you came back here and called upon all the families of the smugglers who were caught with James Treadwell in '06.

"You then took a coach to Leeds, you traveled on to Garwich and went only to the house of a Septimus Goddings. You were there less than an hour, whereupon you set off for home again. Some eleven hours after you left Garwich, Goddings' Mill was fired. What can you tell me about these events?"

"A mill was fired? What has that to do with me?" A perplexed expression appeared on Spencer's face.

"You deny any foreknowledge the mill was to be burned?"

"How would I know such a thing? I'd never been to Yorkshire in my life before. I don't know anyone there."

"What instructions did you receive from Miss Treadwell?"

"Why, it was just to take money to the families."

"Money? What money?"

"Fifty pounds. Miss Treadwell received the money from Lady Adair, and she wanted to help the families. Twenty-five pounds to them here in Rockcliffe, twenty-five to Mrs. Lawliss, cook at the Goddings'. Mrs. Lawliss would see it went to families of workers who lost their positions at the mill. A pound or two to every family was all, but it could help for a time."

Hugh stared. Damnation! Was that all it was? "She received

fifty guineas from Lady Adair." Hugh knew, because the money had actually come from him.

"I don't know about that. I reckon she kept a little back for herself. But she didn't tell me anything more about the money. Asked me to tell the families not to squander it, because she didn't know when she'd ever receive any more."

"You had better tell the truth, or it will go hard with you. I think you carried orders from Miss Treadwell to someone in the Goddings' household to burn down the mill. I don't know your purpose in calling on the smugglers' families here. You better come forth with exactly what your errand was with them."

"Miss Treadwell wouldn't do such a thing! Why, she worked her fingers to the bone, growing a garden and raising chickens at Queen's Treat to have vegetables and eggs for the families. She never had money to give, but she did what she could to help while she lived here. Mrs. Lawliss said she did the same up in Garwich—near wore herself out spending every minute she could visiting families, treating them and giving them a little food."

It was the truth. He'd witnessed her activities, but believed they only covered her true purpose. Honesty and admiration shone out of young Spencer's eyes as he defended Miss Treadwell. And why did everyone in this case defend another person and not protest his own innocence? Charlotte had done the same—defended her brother and father and ignored his accusations against her.

God, what a fool he'd been.

He asked Spencer more questions, but the answers only reinforced the truth—he'd been following the wrong trail with Miss Treadwell. He had to rush back to Town and make amends.

Not to mention, begin the investigation all over again, with no more idea now than when he began who the spy was.

* * *

The next morning, Flea brought in Charlotte's portmanteau. "We 'ave to talk more about this plan of yours."

"It will work, Flea, I know it will."

"What am I to say if Broddie asks if I know where you are?"

"Oh, dear. I hadn't thought of that. I can't ask you to lie to him, Flea. But I don't think he will consider my going to one of his own people. He will look among people I know."

"You know me."

"Yes. If he should ask you, you will have to tell him. And, I must tell you, he questioned me last night about being a Luddite and a French spy. I'm not, Flea, I give you my word."

"I tole him you wouldn't do no such thing."

"You did?" Charlotte felt absurdly pleased at his defense.

"Didn't do no good, did it? He didn't believe me."

"Yes, but I don't think he can find any evidence to support what isn't true. But if he should say to you that he has such evidence, you must tell him where I am. I may have to face charges and try to prove my innocence. Except for that, I know my staying here will work. I can help you and your friends."

"We'll see about that."

He would let her stay. Charlotte breathed a happy sigh.

"Gone! How could she be gone?" He was caught on a wheel, turning about to the same scene he had lived through before.

"She sneaked out in the middle of the night." Sylvia looked a little haggard, worried about Charlotte.

"Did she leave a note, give any hint of where she went?"

"A note, yes, thanking you and me for all we have done. There was nothing in it about where she was going."

"I have to find her. Ask Condon to come down here."

Sylvia's brows rose at his imperious tone and the fact he knew the name of Charlotte's maid. She rang for Hastings and asked him to have Condon come down if she could spare the time.

"I need to talk to her privately," Hugh said.

Sylvia's brows rose anew, but she shrugged and left the room.

Shortly after, Miss Condon came in. "I suppose this proves Miss Treadwell's guilt," she said.

"No, on the contrary, I am convinced she is innocent."

"Why would she have left in that case?"

"Because I accused her, and used her precious father and brother as justifications for my accusation. It was not guilt that made her flee, but fury, Miss Condon. But I am hoping that you have some idea where she has gone."

"No, how could I? She sent me to bed. She was in her nightgown and seemed set to go to bed herself. I had no idea what she had planned. The irony is that she approached the hackney that we have hired to be available for our needs, asking him to take her to her destination and he refused."

"He refused? But why?"

"He was following orders: turning down any fare but mine so as to be ready in case I needed him. He did not realize who she was. He sent her to find another hackney."

"Damnation! I'll have to see if I can trace her movements. You may as well leave Adair House and work openly with Wescott again. Get someone to visit the coaching inns and find out if anyone has seen her there. We'll have to keep an eye on Rockcliffe and Garwich—maybe she has a friend in either place she can go to."

"Sir, I protest. If she is indeed innocent, it is no part of Wescott's job, or mine, to trace her. We still have a spy to catch, which you must not forget. May first is approaching."

"I haven't forgotten, but Miss Treadwell is on her own, God knows where, due to my meddling and false allegation. It is my duty to find her and make sure she is safe."

"It is not part of my duty. I'll go and pack now." She walked out of the study.

Hugh was at a standstill. Charlotte could not have left the city unless some friend had given her transport. In the days since she had left Adair House, he had checked with every person of whose friendship with Charlotte he was aware.

Except Sir Percival. Surely the circumstances of their last meeting would have prevented Charlotte from thinking of him as someone to whom she could turn. If she had done so, she must consider her case desperate indeed.

Or could the baronet have happened upon her when she had left his sister's, and taken advantage of her being alone? That thought was even more chilling.

He sent for his secretary. When Williams appeared, he said, "Have you learned anything more about Bagham?"

"As a matter of fact, I have turned up some disturbing facts. I would have told you, but you were so taken up with Miss Treadwell that I hesitated to distract you. Bagham was indeed deeply in debt. He has paid a good portion of them, now, but not until several months after he came into his inheritance. As you said his principal estate is in Leicestershire, but some years ago his uncle owned property and a stocking mill near Nottingham. The older baronet closed the mill and sold the property while Bagham was still a boy.

"The shocking thing is that Bagham's mother was the daughter of one of the stockingers in the uncle's mill—actually his grandfather's mill at the time. It was a runaway marriage and a scandal at the time, although the grandfather hushed it up. He cast off his younger son after the elopement. The uncle may have closed the mill and sold the property in an attempt to disassociate from that scandal, after he inherited. There are still relatives of Bagham's mother living in the area."

"Dash it, I wish I'd known all of this. Bagham has to be considered a suspect. Did you uncover any ties to France?"

"No, my lord."

Still, that proved nothing. All his men were involved in the search for Charlotte, and he had no time to waste. If Bagham was his spy, and also had Charlotte in his power, he must find out. Could he find out the truth from Sir Percival? First he would observe his townhouse and find out what he could. He dressed in the tattered workman's clothing he wore when he worked covertly and left his house by the servants' entrance.

Several hours later, he had not learned all that much. He had watched the building Bagham lived in for a couple of hours without seeing anybody suspicious entering or leaving. He had walked all around the neighborhood familiarizing himself with it. He had stopped in the pub a few streets away, the only place where a footman or other male servant of Bagham's could have enjoyed a pint of wet and a relaxing evening off. Inquiries there had resulted in denial of ever seeing Sir Percival or anyone from his household.

He must confront Bagham. He returned home to change into his earl's clothing. It was late afternoon and he didn't know as he came back to Bagham's residence whether the man was home.

A shifty-looking servant answered the door. When Hugh presented his card and asked if his master was at home, the man wordlessly snatched the card and closed the door in Hugh's face.

Bemusedly, Hugh wondered if the servant's action meant he was taking the card to Bagham and inquiring whether he would receive Hugh, or if he had been given the gate.

In a short while, a glowering Bagham opened the door. "Have you come to offer amends for our last meeting?" he asked.

If any amends were due, it was by Bagham. But mentioning that fact would hardly be conducive to receiving the information he sought. "I came to inquire if you have seen Miss Treadwell."

"How should you suppose I have seen her? I am hardly likely to call on her given the way in which we parted."

"You say you have not seen her in the past three days?"

A gleam appeared in Bagham's eyes, making Hugh aware of his strategic error in letting the other man know Charlotte was missing. "Your question does not deserve an answer, but the last time I saw her was at Lady Braithwaite's rout. I am indifferent to the possibility of ever seeing her again."

He closed the door again.

He could not count on the truth of the answer. He had no more information than before, unless the momentary expression he had caught meant Bagham had not known Charlotte was gone. He shrugged and turned away. He must spare a couple of his men to watch Bagham's house for evidence that either he did know Charlotte's whereabouts or to identify him as the spy.

As he walked slowly away, his attention was caught by a man approaching Bagham's door. Something about him appeared familiar and yet Hugh was sure he had not seen him before.

As the two passed each other, Hugh caught a glimpse of a long scar cutting across the man's face. He kept walking, giving no sign of his interest in the other man, all the while trying to recall from where he might know him. And then he remembered a few weeks before when his man had described M. Mansson's deputy. At last, the break he had needed.

In case the other man was watching, he continued to the corner, only looking back when he was screened by some shrubbery. He could swear the man had entered Bagham's house. He crossed the street to the vantage place from which he had watched the house earlier in the day, a recessed doorway into a house that appeared vacant.

He waited more than an hour, then at last the man emerged again and strode rapidly away. Hugh followed, determined to see where the man went.

On St. James, his quarry suddenly flagged down a passing hackney. He was almost out of sight before Hugh could secure one to follow. The man was heading toward the river near the docks. Hugh was consumed by impatience to see his long investigation finally bear fruit. The traitor's underling left the hackney near a warehouse close to the docks. Hugh paid off his driver and watched as the man entered the dark warehouse.

He watched the building for some time but saw no activity, either within or in the immediate vicinity.

He crept up to the window closest to the entrance and peered in. The window was smeared with dust and he could not see anything. He moved along the building, looking in each window he came to, but saw no light or movement anywhere.

Suddenly a shadow moved behind him. Instantly pain exploded in his head and everything went black.

CHAPTER TWENTY

The days had been exceedingly busy. While the boys were gone about their profit-seeking activities in the day, Charlotte occupied herself with cleaning the quarters and making them more habitable. She could not do much with the limited resources, but she wanted to bring some comforts to the boys and herself.

She could do little about the front building that served as entrance, but also hid the fact anyone lived beyond. The trash that littered the room served to discourage strangers from entering. Nevertheless, her unnerving experience on the night she arrived made her determined to create a path, disguised to the casual eye, but one she could traverse without bruises.

In the evenings, she worked on lessons with the boys. They had fallen in with her plans, lacking enthusiasm but with good nature, except Tom, who proclaimed, "I had reading lessons at the orphanage and didn't like 'em. Didn't see no use, neither."

Charlotte had returned, "Ah, but I'll bet you didn't read *Gulliver's Travels*." She started a tradition of reading a chapter of the book every night before they retired, and the boys had been caught up in the adventures of Gulliver. They probably missed the satire but enjoyed the stories immensely. With this treat to look forward to, the lessons she made them learn in the evening after supper were accepted painlessly.

Her triumph in introducing them to the pleasures of reading

made up for the privations of living in the Spartan quarters. Wherever she had lived, the crumbling ruin of Queen's Treat, the drafty halls of Treadwell House, and the labor and frustration at Goddings', she had more in the way of amenities than here.

This evening, the boys were late returning. As May approached, the light lasted longer, and the boys never came home until after dark. The older boys took it in turn to cook supper. Cooking was one skill Charlotte had never acquired.

Flea came in, laden with some stale potatoes and carrots and a leg joint of beef. He tossed the joint in the pot of water. Tom arrived and washed the vegetables—a new routine, started since Charlotte joined them—and peeled and chopped them into the pot. Soon their stew was bubbling away. Ned showed up next. The food was nearly ready when Blackie came rushing in.

"Your Broddie is in trouble," he announced.

"What do you mean?" asked Flea.

"Saw a man cosh 'im and carry 'im into the warehouse t'other side o' our ken. 'E weren't awake arter that. Might'a even been kilt."

They all rushed for the door. Charlotte grabbed a shawl with a vague idea it might come in handy to bind up Rayfield's wound. Ned was the one with the presence of mind to set the pot aside, off the fire, and bank down the coals before they left.

They went through a narrow alley that ran to the street on which the warehouse faced. Stopping at the alley mouth, Charlotte looked down the street toward the warehouse door. Lady caught their excitement and ran back and forth sniffing alongside the building. When she opened her jaws to let forth a bay, Charlotte grabbed her, holding her mouth closed.

"Tom, take her back to the courtyard. She'll alert the villains with her baying."

When he returned, Charlotte said, "Flea, walk casually by and try to see what's going on in the warehouse."

As the others waited at the end of the alley, he stuffed his hands in his tattered pockets and strolled along the street in front of the warehouse, whistling. He came back and reported, "Can't see nothing in the windows, they're all grimy. But I can see light inside and I heard voices."

"Blackie, how many men did you see attack Broddie?" Charlotte asked.

"One man sneaked up on 'im, then 'e and another 'un carried 'im inside."

"You didn't see anyone else?"

"Nah. Doesn't mean there ain't any though."

"I know." Charlotte bit her lip, thinking. She could send one of the boys to Flash Annie's for help, but Rayfield could already be getting murdered inside the warehouse. And yet, how could she endanger the boys' lives trying to save him?

"Ned and Blackie, go back to our house and look for anything that might make a weapon. Stout sticks, rocks or any small heavy items that might be thrown. Get the knife we were using for cooking. Hurry."

They scrambled to follow her instructions. Charlotte and the other boys watched. As they kept vigil, a carriage pulled up to the door.

"Oh, no! They are going to take him somewhere. Flea, do you know where we can get a carriage quickly?"

"Not a carriage, but Ducky Jed lives just over on the next street. 'E's got a 'orse we can borrer."

As they watched, a man came out of the warehouse and talked to the driver of the carriage, then returned inside.

"Hurry!" she urged Flea and he took off running.

Two men came out again carrying the inert form of a man. Rayfield appeared to be unconscious or dead, and perhaps tied up as well. Charlotte couldn't tell for certain. If he was tied up, that argued for his still being alive, however. They had some difficulty stuffing him inside the carriage, but finally succeeded. One climbed up to join the driver, and the other stepped inside the carriage with Rayfield.

The carriage set off. Charlotte ordered, "Tom, run after

them and see which way it goes. I just hope we can catch up when Flea brings the horse back."

Impatiently she waited for the boys to return from their various assignments. Ned and Blackie returned first, carrying an assortment of sticks and missiles. Ned handed her the knife.

"Ned, go back and get Lady. Tie her up with a rope so she can't get loose. Then take her to Flash Annie's and try to find any of Broddie's men. Tell them what's happened. Lady is a hound. She might be able to track us and the men who have Broddie." Ned nodded and ran back through the alley.

Charlotte gave Blackie the shawl-wrapped "weapons."

Soon Flea came, leading an enormous gray horse, haltered. There was no saddle, and her back was out of reach of any of the group except Charlotte, and it was a stretch for her as well.

"'Er name's Snowdrop," Flea announced.

She looked more like a patch of snow that had lain on a city street for days, covered with soot and dirt.

"Cor, 'ow are we going to ride 'er?" asked Blackie.

"We'll manage. We don't have a choice," said Charlotte, quelling a shot of pure terror that ran through her at the thought. "You boys will have to help boost me up onto her back, and then I'll pull you up."

Flea and Blackie together made a step out of their hands. Charlotte set her foot in it and threw herself upward. Once on top, the ground looked a long way down. She settled her right leg on the other side. She was shaking inside—the horse had to feel the quivers that ran through her.

No sidesaddle meant she would have to ride astride. Maybe with two legs to grip with, she could stay on. The trouble was, Snowdrop's back was so wide her legs didn't extend very far down her sides. The skirts of her gown rode up, exposing an indecent amount of leg. Another problem that could not be helped.

She'd never fallen off a horse this large. She swallowed, took the lead rope from Flea. Her fingers curled around the rope and through the unkempt mane for good measure. "Flea, give Blackie a lift up high enough for me to grab him."

She pulled up Blackie behind her and said, "Wrap your arms around me."

Flea held back. "I'm skeered of 'orses."

"We don't have time, Flea. If it makes you feel any better, I'm scared, too. But we won't save Lord Broddie unless we catch up with the carriage."

"All right." He made a leap, and she and Blackie caught him and pushed him behind Blackie.

The gigantic carthorse had one benefit, Charlotte thought. They all fit on her back, with room for Tom if they caught up with him. She kicked the horse in the ribs, but Snowdrop didn't move. She had probably never been ridden and had no idea of the cues a rider gave a horse. Charlotte tried again, signalling her with the rope and a firmly spoken "hup." The beast lurched forward, rocking the riders precariously.

Her throat dry, Charlotte dug her legs into the horse's sides as they moved down the street. "Hang on, boys, we don't have time for falls. And don't look down."

Tom was already some distance away, and had lost the carriage. They pulled him up behind Flea and continued in the direction he had last seen it. They found it easily enough. It was the hour when the streets were packed with traffic, and their quarry had not been able to make much headway.

If their horse had been very spirited or much younger, they would have had difficulty keeping her back far enough to escape notice by the coachman and his outside passenger. She guided Snowdrop to stay back far enough that they might not be spotted, trying not to fall so far behind that they lost the carriage.

It started to rain, a penetrating drizzle. Charlotte was quickly soaked to the skin. She gave a brief thought of regret for the shawl sacrificed to hold their weapons. The shawl would not have kept the rain off for long, however. She chattered to the boys, whatever words came to her mind, to keep up their spirits. Whatever happened, they must keep going.

The ride seemed endless. Charlotte's shaking increased as they left Town and followed the carriage down the highway. She must not give in to fear. If she fell, she would probably pull the boys down with her, and the fall was high enough that someone could be seriously injured. Most ruinous, they would lose the chance to save Rayfield. She could not fail!

Once the carriage reached open road, it picked up speed and Charlotte had to keep urging the horse to a faster pace. Snowdrop was not built for speed. Charlotte's heart raced erratically from the region of her throat. Somehow, perhaps only through sheer desperation, despite her awkward position, the horse's damp and slippery back, the boys' pulling on her and the lack of a saddle, she managed to keep her seat.

They gradually fell farther behind. Charlotte could barely make out the lantern swinging at the carriage's side to assure her they had not lost it completely. They followed it onto another road, still less traveled, and continued for a long way.

Suddenly, though, it slowed. Perhaps it was at first looking for the side road branching off the main one, and then slowing even more to safely negotiate the sharp turn.

The new road was narrow, lined on both sides with a tall hedge. The carriage was far ahead, and then its light disappeared. The unbroken hedge gave no place the carriage could have turned off, so Charlotte and the boys continued along the lane, meandering through the countryside with several turns.

At last it opened up at an old abandoned farmstead. The carriage stopped before the house, but Charlotte could see no lights or signs of activity. They dismounted a safe distance from the house, behind a shed, Charlotte looping the lead rope around a tree. She whispered, "Parcel out the weapons among us, Flea. No more noise after this, not even a whisper."

Hugh woke to intense pain that made starbursts of light in his head and nauseated him. He tried to unfold his body and roll over, so he could reach under his bed for the bedpan to vomit into, and discovered he couldn't move. Instantly he was aware that it was fortunate he had given no outward sign of returning consciousness, because he was not alone.

He was being jolted, in a moving vehicle on a rough track. He gathered his throbbing senses to ascertain his situation. The unrelenting darkness—a cloth over his head. Not able to move—tied hand and foot. Good thing he'd not retched—another cloth stuffed in his mouth. He'd have choked on his own vomit.

He listened, trying to determine who was with him in the carriage, but there was no sound. Only a presence. Outwardly still, he worked to loosen his bonds. Nothing gave.

He had a knife in a pocket. What were the odds that they had not discovered it? He didn't dare try to find out in the close quarters of the carriage. The other man would feel his movements. Would he have an opportunity to try to free himself before they subjected him to whatever fate they had in mind?

The carriage stopped. He heard voices and the carriage door creaking open. Then rough hands hauled at him. His battered head protested anew at this jostling. He was dropped on the ground and for a moment blackness overcame him again. Another door nearby opened and he was lifted a second time.

"Put him on the floor. He'll keep until Percy gets here."

He was dropped again. Retreating footsteps and a door closing. Silence.

Slowly, ignoring the excruciating pain movement brought, he moved his hands to find his knife.

The men stood out in the yard, arguing. A familiar voice said, "Why didn't you just kill him at the warehouse? You could have dropped the body in the river, or even in the streets as long as you carried it away from the warehouse first. Everyone knows he is an habitué of the slums. People would assume his luck had finally run out and he was set upon by robbers. No one would have wondered at his death."

"We're not killers. And anyway, how would we know you'd want him dead? Maybe he had a good reason for nosing around the place and I shouldn't have hit him."

"Never mind. Just take care of it now."

"You want him dead, you kill him." The third man spoke.

"Come on," Charlotte whispered. "There should be a back door. Maybe we can get him away while they are arguing."

They made a wide arc around the house, so as not to be detected, moving quickly and quietly. When Charlotte tried the back door, she thought at first it was locked, but it finally yielded, though with a groaning noise that she feared would be heard in the yard. As she pushed the door open, a fourth person she had not known was with the kidnappers rushed her and slammed her back against the wall. A squeak escaped her; it would have been a full scream except that she didn't have enough breath.

"Charlotte? Is it you? What are you doing here?"

Rayfield! Her legs went boneless with relief. "You're all right! We didn't know if you were alive!" Then she almost leapt into his arms, needing the reassurance of his touch.

He held her briefly, then set her back on her feet. "We're not out of this yet. My God, you brought the nursery along!" He gave Flea a very hard look, and the boy lowered his head.

"Come on, let's get out of here," Rayfield said.

"I don't think you're going anywhere." A man came into the room through an inner door, carrying a lantern and a pistol. Charlotte recognized Sir Percival.

"Run!" she yelled at the boys, who still stood outside.

"There's men out there too, Miss T.," Flea said.

"That's right, Miss Treadwell. They will prevent anyone's going that way. Why don't you all come inside?" Sir Percival called to the others. "It will be a lot easier that way."

His men pushed the boys into the room, a large kitchen.

"Meet my brother, Billy Queech," he pointed at the youngest of the men, "my sister's husband, Jeremiah Applewhite," he indicated the large man with the scarred face, "and another associate, Lige Teaser." The third man held a musket. Sir Percival continued, "Do you want to introduce these boys of yours? My, you do have an affinity for children, don't you?"

"I don't understand. What's going on?" Charlotte asked.

"What is going on is that Lord Rayfield's curiosity interfered with my plans. I was just on the brink of leaving to set them in motion. Starting tomorrow, England will be in a state of revolution."

"Why would you want that?" Charlotte asked.

"Why? Because rich people like your friend there stay rich by keeping poor people from earning a decent living, letting them starve, throwing them out of their homes. I thought you understood, that you felt the same."

"I am very sorry about those problems, but revolution is not the answer," Charlotte said.

"You ain't gonna kill them all, are you?" Billy asked. His face was damp with sweat, and he looked scared enough to cry.

"No, the only one who will die tonight is Rayfield. I have another plan in mind for Miss Treadwell, and, as for the boys, well, ships are always looking for cabin boys."

The boys' expressions were afraid but defiant. Sir Percival seemed to notice their manner of arms for the first time. "Let's put down those sticks and rocks, shall we? What did you think you could do with those against guns, anyway?"

Flea looked at Rayfield. He gave a short nod, and the boys put down their pitiful weapons. Charlotte said nothing, but she clutched the knife she held in her pocket. She would wait to use it when there might be a chance to change the outcome.

Sir Percival turned to her. "Too bad you refused me. You could have been my consort after the revolution was over and I was emperor. I won't marry you now, but I think I will make you my mistress for a while. You might still be amusing."

"I won't be your mistress."

"You won't have any say in the matter, Miss Treadwell. Don't look to your lover to save you."

Teaser broke in. "What do you mean, when you become emperor?" He frowned at Sir Percival.

"Someone will have to run the country after all the bloody noblemen are destroyed. I shall be the best qualified to do so.

Look at the greatness France has achieved under Napoleon. England will see just such a flowering."

His fellow conspirators looked angrily at him. "You never said nothing about France, or being emperor," said Billy.

"Of course not. Such talk was premature. We needed to plan the revolution first. Everything in its time."

At that moment a huge dark shadow leapt through the outer door and launched itself at the nearest of the would-be revolutionaries, who happened to be Jeremiah. He crashed to the floor, yelling. Rayfield threw a knife at Sir Percival. It hit him in the hand, and he dropped his gun. Rayfield followed by launching himself at Sir Percival and they grappled, exchanging blows. Sir Percival took a hard hit to the chin and crashed to the floor. Rayfield reached to pick up his pistol.

At the same time, a huge explosion rent the air, and blood bloomed on Sir Percival's chest.

Charlotte whirled to see Teaser lowering the musket, tears running down his face. "He cheated us. He intended all along to use us for his own glory. Selling out to the French, setting hisself up as emperor of England. I won't be part of that."

Lady was sitting on Jeremiah's chest, her nose hovering threateningly over his throat. The boys picked up their makeshift weapons again and stood ready to defend themselves and Charlotte drew forth her knife to help them. The earl threw a punch at Billy, knocking him to the floor.

A lock of hair fell over Rayfield's brow. In the dim light, the color looked darker than its normal medium brown tones, and Charlotte said on a shocked intake of breath, "Sam!"

He knelt by Sir Percival, then said, "He's dead," and stood again with Sir Percival's gun in his hand.

The Heaper came in with two more of Rayfield's men. "Sorry we didn't get here in time to 'elp," the Heaper said. "Dog ran away from us, and it were 'ard to follow in the dark."

"See if you can find ropes to secure our prisoners."

They found enough to tie the three men's hands. Rayfield ordered the prisoners into the carriage in which he had traveled to the farm, and his men secured the doors so they could not be opened from the inside. "I'm going to deliver them to Lord Wescott, and let him question them as to the details of the planned revolution. I think the danger is over, though."

"Lady tracked us! You were right, Miss T.," Tom said.

"She is a heroine." Charlotte stroked the silky ears.

"How did you get involved in this?" asked Rayfield. "I thought I would have a heart attack when I saw you here. All of you," he added, looking sternly at the three boys.

"Blackie saw the men capture you. Naturally we would do what we could to help."

"And I see you lied to me," he continued, looking at Flea.

"Flea! I told you not to lie if he asked you about me."

"I did, din't I? I wasn't going to see 'im stuck wi' a wedding 'e din't want."

Now Rayfield bent that accusing stare on her. "Is that what you told him?"

"Yes, it is. And it was the truth. I saw the look in your eyes when you told Lady Braithwaite we were betrothed. If you told her you'd just received a sentence of hanging you wouldn't have looked more sick at heart."

"That wasn't because I didn't want to marry you, Charlotte." The look in his eyes this time was very different. Then he turned to the boys. "You stay here and guard the carriage. Keep the dog with you."

He walked Charlotte a little distance away, stopping under a tree with drooping branches that sheltered them. "I owe you an apology. I learned the next day after our quarrel that you could not have been the spy, but you were gone before I could try to make reparation for my suspicions. Charlotte, I love you. Surely you know that. Why else would I have offered to save you from the consequences even when I thought you might be the spy?" He put his hands on her shoulders, a gesture somehow more timid than his usual style.

"You've suspected me for a long time. You even disguised yourself and followed me to the Goddings'." She was still shocked by her realization that the groom Sam and Rayfield were the same person. "What has been real between us? Is anything you've ever said true?"

He tightened his hold. "Everything was true, except that I couldn't tell you what I was doing or that I suspected you."

"Because of my brother and my father, and whatever it is you think they've done." She stood rigid, hurt spreading through her. She couldn't love a man who believed such awful things. It would destroy everything, make distrust grow again between them.

"We'll have to talk about this some more, but if you believe they are innocent, then I will too."

"It can't be that easy." She pushed against him, trying to free herself.

"It is that easy. I love you. And you care about me too. Why else would you put your life at risk to rescue me when I was in danger?"

She gave him a tentative smile. "That might be true. That doesn't mean it's a good idea for us to marry."

Rayfield had pulled her closer, and she could not resist snuggling against him, but she protested still, "I think we are most incompatible. You love danger, and I don't think I could stand to see you go off putting yourself at risk all the time."

"Oh, my darling, it is a toss-up which of us gets into more danger. All you have to do is hear somebody is in need and you go dashing off with no thoughts at all for the consequences."

Her eyes widened. "That's true. But I never seek to risk myself. I merely must help people when they need me. Papa and Jamie loved risk for its own sake, and you are the same."

"I'm not like your father or brother, Charlotte. I was working for England. But I had already decided to resign from my post after this case. Since I met you, trying to guess what you will do is as much adventure as I can take."

"Are you really going to resign?"

"Yes, from now on I shall be a dutiful landlord, except to

go up to Town for Parliament. Can you not trust me? Besides, I have an irresistible wedding present to offer."

She looked at him inquiringly.

"It is Treadwell House. I bought it. We can have it refurbished. It occurred to me that it would make an excellent school for homeless boys."

"Boys and girls!" she insisted. He nodded, smiling.

She twined her arms around his neck and tugged his head down until his lips met hers. She gave herself up to a passionate kiss to seal the bargain.

He pressed her against the trunk of the tree. His tongue touched her lips, and on a soft sigh she gave him access to her mouth. He traced the sensitive surfaces, and waves of heat rushed through her and she clung to him, expressing all her desire and passion in her kisses.

He looked seriously down into her face. "Charlotte, you have a heart as big as this whole island we live on. I just want a little part of it."

"Oh, Hugh, you already have it! You have it all!" His lips quirked in a tentative smile, as if he didn't quite believe. She smiled back. They had their whole lives in which she could convince him.

EPILOGUE

London, Six months later

Rayfield lifted the knocker on the front door of Treadwell House. Charlotte stood beside him, smiling to hide her state of nerves. It was the first time she had returned to her old home since leaving on a stormy winter night nearly a year before.

The door opened wide and Spencer said, "Welcome, my lord and lady."

They stepped inside. Charlotte hugged Spencer and he turned bright red. Hugh shook his hand.

Mrs. Whislehurst bustled forward, saying, "Oh, Miss Charlotte, that is, Lady Rayfield, how good it is to see you!" Charlotte threw her arms around her housekeeper.

In the next moments, several of the even dozen students who lived at Treadwell House also gathered in the Great Hall. Some of them were new to Charlotte, although she knew that they had been carefully chosen among far too many candidates, as having the intelligence and ambition to take advantage of the program offered at the Charlotte Treadwell Brooks School for Orphans.

She greeted young Tom, who now went by the name of Hercules Tomlinson, and Blackie, now Delmore Blackwell. They had settled in admirably. Charlotte had received reports from the teacher she had hired for the instruction of the students. Miss Marrymire had a broad education in the classics and several other subjects.

The younger students joined in, and Charlotte hugged Sir Percival's niece and nephew. She had learned that his sister, whose husband was transported for his part in the Luddite revolt, had all she could manage to care for her own brood and was more than happy to see her deceased sister's children in such a felicitous situation.

Ned gave her a shy smile, and she ruffled his hair.

Flea walked in from the kitchen, with one of Lady's pups at his heels. They had discovered she was *enceinte* shortly after their adventures. A few weeks later she had given birth to five puppies. The five were such a hodgepodge of appearances that the identity, or even the breed, of the father could not be established. This one was short-legged, with a curly black coat and hound ears.

Lady and her other pups resided at Rayfield Hall. One of the puppies, the runt of the litter, would accompany Flea— Philip Knight as he now was styled—when he apprenticed as a law clerk after the first of the year. Charlotte had tutored him herself to prepare for this change in his circumstances.

He and the other three boys who had shared their lives for so long went off to catch up on recent events, and Charlotte and Rayfield accompanied Mrs. Whislehurst and Spencer to the small drawing room to have tea. Spencer walked with only a slight limp as reminder of his accident several months before.

A maid came to the door of the room. "There is a letter just arrived for Lady Rayfield," she said.

Puzzled, Charlotte took the letter, recognizing the writing. "It's from my father," she said as she unfolded it and scanned the lines quickly. As she read, a squeak of surprise escaped. "Oh, Hugh," she looked up from the page before her, "Papa is in Barbados. He is remarried to a wealthy widow!"

"What?" Rayfield took the letter from her and read aloud: "I shall be remaining here to help my wife manage her estates. I have refrained from gaming for the past several months, since I fled to avoid my creditors. I am a changed man, and I hope you may forgive me, dear daughter, for my past errors and sins.

"Charlotte, I beg pardon for the unconventional way I chose to settle your life. You must have been unhappy at first at the way I managed things, my dear, but I did the best I could for you in the limited time I had. I thoroughly looked over Rayfield and knew him to be an honorable man. I wish you every happiness in your life."

Charlotte laughed. "I always believed in his ability to turn his luck around. Shall I ever forgive him for trying to force you to marry me?"

Hugh gathered her into his arms, careful of her delicate condition. "But Charlotte, think of how much he cared for you. He did his best to see you well settled. I agree he chose a very subtle way of handling matters, but look at the results. We are amazingly well matched."

AUTHOR'S NOTE

There is no evidence that France was involved in the Luddite revolt.

When I first began to research the Luddites, several years ago, I came across the above remark in one of the library books I read. Unfortunately, I no longer remember which of the many books I checked out contained the statement.

Logically, this is not the same as stating there *is* evidence that France was *not* involved in the Luddites. Hmmmm. My writer's mind seized upon the implications. This book is the result.

Except for Godding's Mill, which is my invention, and its burning, the other mill attacks and food riots mentioned in *The Lady in Question* did occur, including the rumors that a general insurrection would take place on May 1.

A book I found most useful for my research was *Popular Disturbances and Public Order in Regency England: Being an Account of the Luddite and Other Disorders in England during the Years 1811–1817, and of the Attitudes and Activities of the Authorities*, by Frank O. Darvall.

There are other sources for Lord Byron's maiden speech to Parliament, but I found a copy in *From Luddism to the First Reform Bill: Reforms in England, 1810–1832 (Historical Association Studies)*, by J. R. Dinwiddy.

More Regency Romance
From Zebra